Books in This Series

The Kate Morgan Series

Simon Says… Hide, Book 1

Simon Says… Jump, Book 2

Simon Says… Ride, Book 3

Simon Says… Scream, Book 4

Simon Says… Run, Book 5

Simon Says… Walk, Book 6

Simon Says… Forgive, Book 7

Simon Says… Swim, Book 8

Simon Says… Die, Book 9

Simon Says… Think, Book 10

Simon Says… Fight, Book 11

Simon Says… Believe, Book 12

About This Book

Detective Kate Morgan is tasked with determining if a recently discovered body floating in the harbor is the result of a crime and, if not, to move on to one of the team's many other pending cases on their desks. However, nothing is ever simple in her world. So, when she finds several similar cases in the surrounding police districts, … the scope of her hunt expands proportionally.

However, getting to the bottom of this one crosses into Simon's penchant for revitalizing old buildings in downtown Vancouver—or, in some cases, just giving those structures a whole lot of love.

As Simon warns her several times, he sees both himself and Kate participating in the final fight. Yet it's so much uglier than either of them can imagine.

Sign up to be notified of all Dale's releases here!
https://geni.us/DaleNews

CHAPTER 1

First Week of the New Year ...

KATE WALKED BACK into the office.

Rodney looked up at her and smiled. "You look better. Nothing like taking a week away to help reset your system."

"Yeah, it was a pretty rough for a bit."

"Ken really shot up your apartment, *huh?*"

She nodded. "Yeah, he didn't care. He waited until I got close to opening the door and started blasting. Simon tackled me from behind. As I was headed for the door, he had some vision about my body being riddled with bullets, and, the next thing I know, I'm flat on the ground, and my apartment is being razed with gunfire."

"Jesus," Rodney muttered, his eyes wide in shock. "I guess your stepfather figured that, as long as he was going down, he might as well have something to go down over."

"Maybe," she conceded, staring at him. "It still makes no sense to me. Anyway, I very much want things to get back to normal, whatever normal is."

"Around here, *normal* can be all kinds of things, but it's never what we expect it to be," he said, with a smile. "I'm more than happy to have you and Lilliana back."

"Did she take off for the holidays too?"

"She was dragging by the time we got Peter's case dealt

with, so she took some days to regroup."

Kate nodded. "Hopefully it'll be calm for a bit."

Rodney smiled. "I could go for calm. Calm for more than a bit would be nice."

"I agree, although evidence to blow my brother's case wide open would be nice."

"Sorry. Everything on Timmy's case was a false trail, which we figured, coming from Ken," Rodney noted.

She nodded. "How about *calm* for a long time?"

"I could get behind that," Rodney agreed. "Yet we've got this case …"

Just then Kate's phone rang. "Morning, Simon. What's up?"

There was an odd tone to his voice as he asked, "Do you guys ever have cases … where fighting is going on?"

"Fighting?" she repeated. "What do you mean by *fighting*? As in husband and wife, domestic kind of violence stuff?"

"No, no, as in an arena for boxers only, … more like underground street fighting."

"I'm sure underground street fighting is going on all the time, especially with people betting on it, but it's rarely something that comes to us. Why?"

"Because I just had one of those really unpleasant visions, with me in the ring, and everybody around was screaming, *Fight, fight, fight.*"

"*Uh-oh,*" she muttered, "often your visions don't mean anything even close to what we think they mean."

"I know," he said, "but I still got the feeling that something really ugly was going on, and it has to do with some fighting. The thing is, Kate, I don't think that any of the people in that ring were there because they wanted to be there. I think they were there because they had no choice. The other weird thing is that it seemed that the *fight, fight, fight* screaming was a recording."

She looked over at Rodney, who was frowning as he listened in on the conversation. "But ..."

Simon replied, "I know. You have nothing to go on, and I don't know that this has anything to do with you guys either."

"In a way, I do though," Rodney interrupted. "I was just gonna tell Kate about one of the cases that came in. A body washed up downtown right off the pier where the aquabus lands," he shared. "The body was pummeled pretty good. We haven't got an autopsy on it yet, but one of the guys who pulled the body out of the river said the dead guy had been beaten from head to toe."

"What do we know about the victim?" Kate asked.

"No ID was on the body, and we still haven't figured out who he is, but the coroner did call this morning and said that he had a tentative ID. We're waiting for the dental records because there might be teeth left," Rodney added. "The body's that bad. It could be a man that the family reported missing approximately three days ago. Apparently he's a nice normal businessman, who goes to work every day, comes home to his kids, and all that good stuff. Then one day he just didn't come home, and nobody knew why, but now, if it's the same man, he's washed up in this condition, and we have no clues. However, maybe thanks to Simon's latest vision, we have an idea at least."

"Yeah, maybe," Kate muttered, staring at Rodney in shock. "Simon, you take care of yourself. Just because it was you in that ring—and often we think it isn't you—that doesn't mean that it can't be you."

"Same for you," Simon declared, "because, I swear to God, somehow I heard your voice in the middle of it." And, with that, he hung up.

CHAPTER 2

DETECTIVE KATE MORGAN walked into the morgue and stopped. It took a minute to adjust to the smell of death. It was always strong, yet at the same time overlaid with the scent of chemicals and cleanser. As she stood here, her name was called from the side. She looked to the left, and there was Dr. Smidge, busy at one of the autopsy tables. She walked closer, and he frowned at her. She frowned right back. She had learned that this was the only way to really handle him. Plus, it also suited her because she was no friendlier than he was.

He watched as she approached and then pointed to the body on his table. "I presume this is the one you're after."

She shrugged. "Possibly, if this is the one that came in from the harbor."

"It is," he confirmed.

"A floater?"

"He was found floating," Smidge corrected. "Yet no way in hell this was a floater."

"Meaning?"

"Meaning, he was beaten to death," he stated, followed by a shrug. "He didn't go easily into the night, but I don't think he was equipped to handle what was coming at him."

"They never are, are they?" she replied with a sigh, mentally reminding herself to get her sorry ass back down to the dojo for more regular workouts. If things like this were going on around her, she not only needed to know more about this but she needed to be well and truly in better shape than she was in right now.

It's not that she had slacked off, but living the easier life with Simon had made it seem as if she had. It was a good life, and so many extras made some things a whole lot easier. Yet this poor guy in the morgue had seen the opposite side of life. Staring down at the pounds of hamburger on the coroner's table in front of her, she was again reminded that sometimes shit happened. When it did, it brought all kinds of wrong into her world.

She shook her head, still focused on the body. "That's well beyond *beaten to death*," she declared, staring at it. The bruises, the cuts, the bloating was too much. "This is like rage."

"I think it's more than that," Dr. Smidge countered, with a nod, "but you're right. Whoever he pissed off didn't hold back. I found a few lighter-colored bruises, as if some attempt had been made to dissuade him from whatever he was trying to get into. Still, at the end of the day, he took a beating bad enough to kill him."

"Christ."

"And I'm quite happy to put down something a whole lot more definitive than *blunt force trauma* as the final cause of death. However, in this case, I'll just tell you flat-out that this guy was beaten to death. So, ... murder."

"*Great*, which is why I'm here."

"Of course it is," he stated, with a bright smile. "And you won't send me more, will you?"

"Wouldn't that be nice," she muttered. When he turned and glared at her, she nodded. "It will cease," she replied, raising a hand in a stiff and formal pose.

"It might take me a day or two to put all that in writing," he shared.

She stood here, hands on her hips, as she studied the body. The body had truly been beaten, focused mostly on the head, chest, and some on the groin. Thighs too, she noted. "It doesn't look like ... Obviously we wouldn't be looking at a professional fighter for something like this, but it does appear this dead guy was in one hell of a fight. His knuckles are bloody and bruised."

"I'm not even sure if it was a single fight or if there was more to it," Smidge suggested. "However, this man didn't survive the last blows to his head." He pointed to the severe damage around the occipital bone. "There's another equally rough one, which I would have said was from a hard kick to the back of the head," he shared, again showing her. "Ultimately these were the killing blows."

She nodded. "And it wouldn't take all that long at that point for death to occur."

"No, a shattered bone went straight into the brain," Smidge added.

She sighed. "Shit," she muttered. "We do have an ID on him, by the way."

"Good." Smidge snorted. "He didn't come in with anything."

"Any idea how long he's been dead?"

"Three days max," he stated, with a curt nod. "He wasn't in the water very long and had just started to swell. Not a whole lot else was going on there though. The fish weren't even nibbling yet."

She winced at that. "He was reported missing three days ago."

He looked up at her and nodded. "Yep, that sounds about right. If he was held captive, or God-only-knows what, maybe he got into a fight and holed up somewhere, then decided to go back and retaliate."

"Maybe," she murmured. She didn't see why or how that would appeal to anybody. If you got your ass kicked once, why would you return to get it kicked again? But she didn't understand a lot of people, so that thought wasn't a surprise.

Smidge looked over at her. "Just confirm you don't bring any more like it."

She looked at him, startled. "*Like it?*"

"Yeah, like it," Smidge repeated, his tone grim. "I've seen bruises like this before."

Her eyebrows shot up. "Do tell."

He shook his head. "I used to box ... a lot," he noted, with an eye roll. "And this just has that feeling to it."

"Boxing injuries?" She frowned at him and then back down at the body with interest.

"No, not so much boxing injuries but fights. This is a little more like ... street fighting," he pointed out. "That tends to be an environment where something hot, rash, and immediate happens. It has a different feel to it than traditional boxing."

"Point taken," she said, as she thought about it. "I'll keep that in mind."

"Maybe you should ask that boyfriend of yours," Smidge added, with half a snort, chewing on the word *boyfriend.*

Kate nodded. Being a man of science, Smidge was wary of Simon's gift and his ability to come through with such bizarre leads. Smidge didn't know the extent of it all, but he had some idea. She glanced at him and tried to keep her tone mild. "You and I both know how that will go over."

"Maybe," he replied, squinting at her. "As much as I hate to even consider it, there are times I do wonder …"

"Wonder what?" she asked, eyeing him closely.

"If there's something … *more* to him."

"Oh, I know something is *more to him*," she declared, her tone calm. The last thing she needed was the morgue to be gossiping about Simon and his strange abilities.

"Sure, but you don't talk about his abilities either," he countered, pointing a finger at her.

"Yeah, because I'm usually not sure if they are abilities or liabilities," she stated in a hard tone.

Smidge gave a crack of laughter. "Honest to God, if it were me, they would definitely be liabilities. I'm black-and-white. I thought Simon was too, until he started walking into the gray area."

"I don't think he's terribly comfortable with those walks either," she admitted. "It's also why he doesn't give us a ton of information. He can't get everything."

"Yeah, I think that goes for all psychics though," he muttered. "It's weird shit, if you ask me."

"Yeah, well, I won't ask you," she muttered, "because it's the same damn question I have to figure out myself. It's just weird shit all the way around."

He chuckled and nodded. "But Simon himself? He's a good guy."

She smiled. "I agree with you on that as well."

"You better," he said, with a smile. "You've got a good thing going."

"No, not necessarily," she replied, staring at him. "I don't think anything is a good thing when it comes to relationships."

"Maybe not, but, at least in this case, he seems to have an eye for keeping you safe."

She winced at that. "I'll never live down that my stepfather almost shot me to death, will I?"

"No, you sure won't," he agreed cheerfully. Then he frowned at her and added, "And now you're stopping me from my work, so time for you to leave."

She gave a snort of laughter. "Yeah, I hear you. You nag me so damn much I can't ever get anything done."

He rolled his eyes in mock insult, then waved her off. "Get lost."

With that, she turned and walked out, calling back to him, "I need that report."

"You'll get it when you get it," he snapped.

And, both of them happy with that snarky exchange, she headed back out to the car and joined Rodney, who was leaning against the vehicle, waiting for her.

He took one look at her smiling face and groaned. "How the hell can the two of you get along so well?" he asked. "You do know something is wrong with that man, right?"

"You mean, the fact that he works around dead bodies all day?"

"That for a start," Rodney muttered. "Yeah."

She laughed. "So, what is there to bitch about? He does a very valuable job, and we need him."

"That doesn't mean I have to like it," he muttered. "And I hate that place. It gives me the creeps."

"I know you do," she noted, smiling at him. "Which is why I took pity on you and went in myself."

He rolled his eyes at that. "You like it in there."

"Oh, I definitely find a certain amount of … I guess this will sound odd, but I find it quite … peaceful." He just turned and stared. She shrugged. "*Peaceful* in that they're all dead. It's not like anybody there can argue with me."

Rodney gave a snort of laughter at that. "Which is probably why Smidge likes it too. Nobody talks back to him."

"Maybe," she conceded cheerfully. She looked around at the hospital complex, where the morgue was located, remembering other cases and other people.

As if he read her mind, Rodney joined her, hooking his arm through hers. "Someday, hopefully a long time from now, we'll find out that everybody in this field is a serial killer. Like that TV show?"

She turned to him, startled.

"You think I didn't see what you were thinking?" Rodney quipped.

She shrugged. "It's just so weird, you know? You go to all these places, deal with all these people, and they seem so normal. Then you find out their secrets, and it's just … shocking, even to us," she muttered.

"And we'll likely see it again, but that's not our issue now," he stated, with a wave of his arm. "Let's just keep focused on what we have to do."

"Of course," she muttered.

"Off to the family next, I suppose?"

Kate nodded and got behind the wheel. "That's what I was thinking." It didn't take very long to reach the deceased's address in Point Grey. As she pulled up, she noted a really nice stately house. She looked around and whistled.

Rodney agreed. "I know, right? This is pretty amazing."

"It is pretty amazing. I'll give you that. But why would somebody from here end up getting involved in something that seems to be street fighting?"

"We don't know that he was involved," Rodney pointed

out. "It may not have been voluntary. Remember what Simon told us, and yet it could be something completely different."

"I suspect it was something completely different," she replied. "It's still strange to think that somebody who lives in this world, this neighborhood, ends up in the morgue, beaten to death."

"Maybe," Rodney conceded, "but we still have to investigate it regardless."

Kate walked up the front steps and rang the doorbell. Almost immediately a middle-aged woman opened the door. It was obvious she had been crying. The woman stared at the two people on her front steps. Kate smiled, pulled out her badge, and identified herself. The woman started sobbing in earnest. Kate winced and glanced at Rodney. "I'm sorry for your loss," she told the woman, "but we do need to ask you some questions."

The woman nodded, tried to get control of herself, and whispered, "Please, please, come in." And then she started to cry again.

"I know it's hard," Kate added, "but I don't have any way to make this any easier on you." The woman just sobbed, stepping back so they could enter. As Kate went inside, the house was an expensive, expansive, very beautiful home, and it looked to be very well cared for. "Mrs. Forbes …"

"Call me Kendra, please."

"Kendra, we know that your husband has just passed away," Kate began, "and that is why we're here."

"Of course," Kendra noted, trying to regain control. "I don't know what I'm supposed to tell you. He went to work on Thursday, and he didn't come home that night. I called his cell phone and got no answer, but a lot of times he just stayed late for work."

Kendra took a moment and then sighed before continuing. "Sometimes his work can get crazy, and he doesn't check in, and that's what I assumed had happened this time." Kendra led them into a small sitting area and motioned at the couch. She collapsed into the easy chair nearby, using a handkerchief to dry her face.

When she was finally calm enough, she added, "I never heard from him again."

"And when he left that morning," Kate asked, "did he appear to be upset? Did anything seem to bother him? Was there anything at all along those lines that you can pinpoint?"

Kendra shook her head. "No, I would have thought everything was totally fine."

"Is everything okay at work? Was there any reason to suspect a problem at the office?"

Again Kendra shook her head. "Outside of the fact that he works constantly, no. Other than that, I would have said that Dennison was totally fine." She sniffled into a tissue.

Kate studied her. "You do understand the way that he died?"

"No, I don't understand any of that," she wailed. "When they mentioned *floater*, I thought they meant that he had committed suicide, and that was tough enough, but now I understand that wasn't the case at all." She frowned. "I don't understand, Detectives. What could it be then? Did he have a heart attack? Was the bruising on his body from being bounced around in the waves?" At that, she started to cry again.

Kate hesitated, sharing a look with Rodney. Then she

got up, walked over to Kendra, crouched in front of her, and added, "There's no easy way to tell you this, but your husband, Dennison, was beaten to death."

Kendra stared at her in shock. "What do you mean, *beaten*?" she whispered. "Dennison wouldn't hurt a fly."

"That's what we have been told, so why don't you tell me about him?"

"You don't understand, Detective. … My husband was a typical businessman, his nose in the books, always thinking about how to improve the bottom line." She shook her head frantically. "Sometimes that alone was really frustrating because we wanted his attention at home, but he was always more focused on work. So he definitely wasn't the kind to get beaten up and certainly would never fight back. If he got mugged, he would have just handed over his wallet, then figured out how to address the financial damage later. I just don't understand," she whispered, staring at Kate.

Kate nodded. "I do realize this is all a huge challenge for you," she replied, "and at this point we have no way of knowing who may have done this. Obviously we're running tests and collecting data. As always, we're hoping for DNA of some kind to turn up somewhere, but even that is still only valuable if we have DNA to match it to."

Kendra blinked several times, as Kate went through her explanation. Then Kenda shrugged. "It still doesn't make any sense because he would never have hurt anyone. The idea that somebody would hurt him is just mind-boggling."

"Was he a fighter at all? Even to stay in shape? Was he somebody who worked out?"

"No, no, no," she stated, raising her hands in protest. "He didn't like any of that. He wasn't into being hot and sweaty. He wasn't into getting punched. He didn't like sports or anything physical," she said, with half a smile. "He was really very …" She sighed. "I know it sounds silly, but he was really just all about business. Nothing else."

"Was it his own company?"

"No, not just his, but he was a shareholder, and he took his job very seriously," she explained. "Did you talk to them yet?"

"That's next on my list," Kate said. "We'll find out when he left, where he may have gone, and see if they have any cameras."

"Yes, cameras would be good," Kendra agreed eagerly. "Honestly, I haven't seen him since Thursday morning, and I've just been beside myself. I was surprised when I heard he was found in the water. Are you sure you're not mistaken?"

"I don't believe so," Kate stated, her tone apologetic. "I've just come from the morgue."

At that, Kendra's eyes filled with tears. "Right," she whispered. And then she stiffened her back and looked at Kate. "When can I have my husband back?"

"Not yet," Kate told her firmly. "It'll be a little bit yet."

"I need to bury him," Kendra muttered. "I don't even know how one does these things. I've never had anything like that to deal with."

"What about your children?" Kate asked.

"Yes, we have two, but they're adults now. They've both been asking for answers, but I don't have any answers to give them," she whispered.

Kate winced at that because not having answers was always one of the hardest things, as she knew very well. She had long been waiting for answers regarding her missing brother for almost two decades now, answers that likely would never come.

She looked over at Rodney, who then had some questions to ask Kendra.

"Do you know whether he had any enemies? Or issues, like investments that went wrong? Any problem that somebody might have blamed him for?"

"I guess we're wondering if this is personal," Kate added, as she patted Kendra's hand.

"It can't be personal," Kendra declared. "You don't understand. He's literally all about business. There is no *personal* in his life."

"What about friends? What about family?"

"Sure, we had friends, and we do have family," she admitted, "but we're not close to any of them, other than our children, and we don't entertain. We live very quietly," Kendra noted.

"What do you for a living?"

"I'm an artist. I tend to spend most of my time in my studio," she murmured, once again looking as if she would cry.

Kate frowned, then continued with questions. "So, going back to Thursday. What time would you have expected him home?"

She blinked several times. "He was usually home by six, depending on the traffic—which, as you know, is getting worse and worse all the time in Vancouver," she muttered.

Kate nodded, then asked, "And what about the people he worked with? Did he ever talk about them?"

"Only in the sense that some of them did their jobs. The others? ... Well, they weren't very good at their jobs or didn't put in the effort, and that always really bothered Dennison. He felt somebody should have been fired, and the fact that they kept him on really riled him." Kendra smiled briefly at the thought. "He did get riled over injustice."

Kate nodded as she listened, forming an idea of who this man was. "And his age?" she asked.

"Fifty-four," Kendra replied, tears welling up in her eyes again.

"Fifty-four. Right."

Knowing there wasn't an easy way to end the conversation from here, Kate stood up. "Again, we are very sorry for your loss, and we may need to contact you again."

"That's fine." Kendra waved her hand about. "Yet I don't think I can tell you anything more. Seriously, ... he was just all about the business."

"Maybe so," Kate acknowledged, "but somebody apparently hated him enough to beat him to death."

Kendra gasped, a fist going to her mouth, as she stared at Kate. "Wouldn't that have been random? You know, somebody on the street, like a mugger or a junkie?" Kendra asked, again sounding completely bewildered.

"That is certainly possible," Kate replied, "but we have to look at all the options, all the possibilities." She pointed around. "While we're here, could we have a quick look at his home office, please? We need to see if he left behind anything that would indicate why this happened."

"Yes, of course you do," Kendra muttered, reaching up a tired hand to wipe her eyes. "God, I just want this to be over with." But she stood up and walked them to a small and extremely neat office. She even walked over and turned on the desktop, logging in for them. "I can tell you that he wasn't the kind to be involved in anything dubious. He was all about following the book." Kendra stepped out of the way and watched as they searched the office, filing cabinet, even his emails.

When Kate stood, Kendra stepped out of the doorway so they could pass.

"Thank you," Kate noted, with a smile to Kendra.

"I'm happy to help. I just want this to go away."

Kate nodded. "That's understandable, but the investigation is likely to take us a little bit of time yet."

"Of course, of course," Kendra replied, then rubbed at her tears once more. "Can you at least let me know when I'll be able to, … you know, have the body back?" she asked, stumbling over the phrase.

"As soon as we can, of course." Kate patted Kendra's shoulder. "We'll let you know."

"Yes, yes, … of course." Kendra stared at Kate. "It's just so hard to believe that anybody could possibly have hit him that much. You really don't understand. He was so very mild-mannered, easy to get along with, truly one of the good guys," she shared, tears filling her eyes instantly. "Definitely one of the good guys." And, with that, she started to cry in earnest.

"We'll let ourselves out," Kate murmured and headed to the door.

Just as she got to the door, it opened right in front of them, revealing a young woman walking in, looking distressed and in a hurry. She stopped when she saw Kate. "Who are you?" she snapped. "And what are you doing in my house?"

"I presume you are Sharlene. Is this *your* house?" Kate asked her.

With a wave of her hand, she completely nullified the question. "Fine, … my mother's house, my father's house," she clarified, tripping over that. "I guess it's my mother's right now. I don't know." Kate pulled out her badge, and the woman started to tear up. "God," she whispered. "Where is my mother? How is she?"

"We've just finished talking to her, so your return is very good timing."

"I don't live here," she clarified. "I live over on the island, but I had to come and help her," she whispered. "This is so awful."

"When did you last see your father?"

"Oh, goodness," Sharlene said, tucking back some stray hair. "Months ago. Maybe last September even. I don't think we've seen him since."

"So, you weren't that close?"

"We came over for a few days every month or so to spend time with Mom and Dad, but Dad, ... of course, was very busy," she stated, with an eye roll. "He was always busy, always had work to do, and was nearly always off doing work. I suppose, in his own way, it made him happy, but he certainly circumvented all the traditional family requirements by working all the time as he did," she pointed out, staring at Kate.

Sharlene grimaced. "By the expression on your face, I know what you'll ask me next. Do I hate him for it? ... God no. I loved him. I loved him dearly, and he will be sorely missed. But he was like—and don't take this the wrong way—a family joke because he was so conscientious and so focused on doing the right thing for the company. Yet the company didn't give a crap about him. Even now I'm sure they'll just hire somebody else to do his job without a thought, if they haven't already."

"That seems to be the way of the world," Rodney noted patiently.

"And I think in a way, Dad knew that. I think he understood that he was just another cog in the wheel, but, to him, he was an important cog, and that alone kept him going."

"Did you ever hear any indication of discontent at his job with anyone?"

"No, and I don't believe he would ever talk about it if there were," she stated, with a wave of her hand. "But then again, I never imagined he would be so despondent that he would take his own life."

Kate frowned at Rodney, then faced Sharlene again. "Your father didn't take his own life," she explained. "Unfortunately he was murdered."

SIMON STARED INTENTLY at his longtime banker in front of him and asked, "What did you just say to me?"

David harrumphed and muttered, "I was just thinking that maybe you shouldn't be quite so anxious to buy more properties, when you're already heavily invested in the ones that you have."

Simon slowly raised his gaze to study the man in front of him. "Are you telling me that I'm broke?"

"No, no, of course not. It's just that some of these build-ings"—he waved his hand all around—"they're hardly prime material."

"That's why I buy them," Simon replied, trying to mask his anger. "And I've never had an issue with this bank before. Are you telling me that I'm having an issue now?"

"No, no, of course not." David rubbed his temples. "I was just thinking that maybe you would do something a little less … touchy."

"I have no intention of doing that," Simon declared, with just the hint of a smile. "But if you'll have a problem with me and how I run my business, I can take my money elsewhere."

"That's not what I'm trying to do," he replied, glaring at Simon. "We've worked together a long time."

"Yes, but this is the first time you've questioned what I'm doing in my own business and the expenditures that I'm choosing to make. That's not your place."

"Yeah, well, … maybe there's a reason for that," he admitted, hunching over the papers in front of him. "The real estate market is down, and everything has just gone to shit in the world right now."

Simon smirked. "Maybe your own personal viewpoint is taking a tumble. Maybe your personal world has gone to shit. I don't happen to think everything is shit out there, and, by the way, I haven't lost money on a single building that I own. So I'm not changing my focus now, no matter what you think or say. And overstepping boundaries by giving me advice isn't appreciated," Simon pointed out, staring at his longtime bank advisor. David was a sharp, cunning, techy graduate from Harvard, and Simon liked him enough, at least until he opened his mouth today.

"No, of course not," David conceded, with a sigh, "but it's just not the same world out there today."

"No, it's not. Absolutely, it's not, but I won't sit here and get depressed because of it. Maybe the profit margin has shrunk …"

"Hate to point out the obvious, but it's not only shrunk"—David put down the sheet of paper in front of him—"in some cases, it's barely a margin at all."

Simon acknowledged that. "That's true, but, if I need to produce more money, I can do that."

David frowned at him. "I don't even know how the hell

you could consistently do that all the time," he muttered. "I just want you to truly understand what you are getting yourself into."

"I've been buying and rehabbing real estate successfully for years, longer than I've known you, in fact. It's never been an issue—up until now," Simon declared in frustration. "So, I'm a little concerned over this meeting. I don't get the intrusion, and it's not a meeting I called. So, tell me straight. What is this all about?"

David sank back in his chair. "Maybe I'm just having a bad day," he muttered, as he tried to backtrack.

"Maybe," Simon agreed, studying him carefully. "Problems in the banking world?"

"No, no, no." He rubbed his forehead. "Never mind. Just forget I said anything."

"Wouldn't that be nice?" He stared at David. "When you say that stuff, it does make people wonder."

"It's fine," he snapped. "I shouldn't have brought it up."

"That's definitely true," Simon muttered to himself.

They quickly finished their business, Simon signing some paperwork, then heading down to City Hall to address some issues with planning permits. One of his foremen was supposed to be down here dealing with some of them, but the city had given him quite the runaround, so Simon was about to go raise some hell and see if he couldn't get things processed faster.

As he went through the downtown area, heading toward City Hall, his mind was consumed with the boxing vision he'd seen earlier. He hadn't heard from Kate, so he didn't know whether anything was connected or she would even tell him. That was one of the challenges of having her around. Sometimes he got information from her, and sometimes he didn't.

He had no right to the official information, and he knew that all too well. The biggest challenge was always letting go of some of the things he got glimpses of, but generally, as long as he kept his psychic information flowing, the detectives kept their forensic information flowing in return. Yet Simon understood on a personal level if some people didn't want him to know anything. He was stuck in this weird loophole.

And yet, with Kate, he knew that reciprocal give-and-take was always available if her team needed help. It's just that Simon didn't always have something to help them with their cases. Getting that most recent vision, involving both Kate and him in that boxing scenario, was enough to terrify him, and he didn't like anything about it. The fact that it was somehow so strong made him wonder whether he was connecting with a person, a group, or something else. He didn't know what that *something else* could be. And yet the idea crossed his mind that maybe, because of the work he did, he was connecting to a building.

He snorted at that.

"If I wasn't loony enough to scare off people before, this would finally do it," he muttered. Still, he couldn't help but wonder if it was even possible. Was it even a thing? Did people connect to buildings?

As he looked around, he realized that he didn't even need to ask that question because that's how he determined which buildings he would be willing to take on. No matter the physical state of any property, whether the building's inherent heart and soul were left, made a project interesting for him. Did the will to stand and to still be something viable still exist, or was it a lost cause and just a crumbling construct? If the latter, he had much less interest in it.

He much preferred to have something out there just for him, that only he could fix, if he had that option. It wasn't always there with each property he reviewed, but, every once in a while, things did go his way, and he could see his potential rehab in a much better light. And the buildings that he did look after were ones that spoke to him in some way or another.

Speaking of which, that local persistent Realtor who continually stalked him was calling him—again. He shook his head. She wasn't his personal chosen Realtor, but that never stopped her. He let the call go to voice mail and focused on getting his business done at City Hall.

Once he was outside again and free to talk, he returned her call. He walked toward a little food stand, where he could pick up a coffee and a snack to keep him going for the day. "What's up?" he asked, when Ariel answered.

"I'll thank you again, for the umpteenth time," Ariel said.

"And I am telling you, for the umpteenth time, it's fine."

"I know that's what you say each time, but I'm not sure what you did or how you did it, but the fact of the matter is, Peter was found, and, for that, I owe you."

He winced. "You don't owe me anything."

"I get that too," she noted, with a playful tone. "You don't owe anybody or like being owed, and neither do I. So, I will do my best to discharge that as fast as I can."

He snorted. "I don't know how you plan on doing that."

"I can think of one thing. You know that one building we've been talking about? The one down on Georgia Street?"

"Yeah, what about it?" he asked, as he picked up his order and walked toward his next stop.

"They contacted me to say that they want to get rid of it,

and soon, so I'm telling you first. If you want it, give me a price, and I'll take it back to them."

His eyebrows shot up at that. "That's a pretty unusual way to do business."

"That's true, and the call certainly caught me by surprise because that has not been their usual position," she shared. "Apparently some family issues are involved, and I think they just want to call it quits and to get it done."

"Maybe," Simon replied, "but I'd need a little bit of time to consider that."

"I know that, and I did tell them that I had a buyer, a *potential* buyer," she corrected. "And that I would let you know."

"So, now you're telling me to just put in an offer for what I think it's worth?"

"Yes," Ariel admitted. "I can't guarantee that they'll take it because, knowing you, it won't be very high. However, I can tell you that they would at least look at it and potentially counter."

"They would have done that without your suggestion," Simon pointed out shrewdly. "So what's changed?"

"The wife has just had a cancer diagnosis," she shared. "So, I think they're gearing up for a whole different fight, and this really isn't the hill they want to die on."

"Right," Simon noted. "That makes sense."

"If it does, good luck to you," she added, "because some of this stuff never makes any sense."

He snorted. "I understand that too," he muttered. "I'll get back to you."

"Don't wait too long," she added, a warning in her tone. "I can't stall them for long."

"I'll see what I can do," he said. With that, he ended the

call, knowing she was hoping for a whole lot more. She wouldn't get it, so that's just the way the cookie crumbled today. Some things were good, and some things would just be a pain in the butt. So his mind was focused on everything else but his work today. Still, he was a man with more discipline than that, so pulling his attention back to the task at hand, he headed to one of his rehab projects to check on the progress.

After a fruitful meeting with his foreman at that site, and his customary rounds connecting with the workers there, Simon planned on heading home and just crashing, but something nudged him in a particular direction. So, feeling amiable, he kept going. As he got to one of the seedier warehouse areas, he stopped and looked around. A whisper in the back of his head spoke to him about one specific warehouse. He turned to it, frowned, and shook his head.

"I don't know who or what you are, but ain't no way I'm walking down there alone," he muttered. Sure enough, if you wanted to choose the epitome of a place to be mugged, this was the area. Dark alleys were all around, and this one particular warehouse had broken windows and showed numerous signs of abandonment—like some others nearby too. The poor warehouse in question gave off a feeling of abdication, a sense of giving up the ghost. That made sense here as Simon potentially had a ghost contacting him already. In his gut he knew something really ugly seemed to come with this warehouse.

He didn't know what was going on here, or had gone on here before, but he couldn't shake the feeling that his latest psychic nudge was definitely tied to this warehouse. He shook his head and resolutely tried to walk on by, but his feet couldn't walk past this one warehouse at all. He was stuck here, standing in one place.

He tried to shake off the feeling, but, for a minute, nothing gave. To say he was pissed would be an understatement. "That is not funny," he muttered, as he looked around to confirm nobody was nearby. But this ghost, or whatever, wouldn't let him move on.

He shook his head. "I don't have time for games right now," he called out. "Either speak up or let me be."

And then came the whisper in his head, *Make time.*

Simon looked around again and pointed out, "People have definitely died in this building."

The whisper came back, stronger this time. *Yes, and I am one of them.*

CHAPTER 3

AFTER TALKING TO Kendra and Sharlene Forbes, the wife and the daughter, Kate and Rodney headed to the workplace of the deceased, Dennison Forbes. As they approached the main office, they heard voices yelling back and forth, the hustle and bustle of a busy workplace in full swing. When they walked in, silence fell over the room, as they all turned to look at the newcomers.

Kate nodded and took out her badge. "We're here about your colleague, Dennison Forbes." Lots of people winced, and several of the women now wore somber faces.

One of the men came toward Kate at a quick pace. "We can talk in my office. I'm the managing director."

She and Rodney followed his lead toward his office, and, when he closed the door behind them, he introduced himself. "Alexander Foster. Sorry about the whole lot of them out there. Everybody is pretty upset."

"They didn't look upset," she shared shrewdly. "That seemed to be a celebration, if I'm being honest."

He winced. "The hard thing about a death," he explained, "is that, for everybody else, life goes on." He shook his head and continued. "For poor Kendra, her world has changed forever. I know Sharlene and Landon are devastated and are looking for answers, but, for everybody else, it's just another day. And I don't mean that to sound so terrible, but that's the truth of it. I had to make the decision as to who got Dennison's position and promoted someone this morning. What you heard as you walked in was the announcement."

"So, who got the promotion?" she asked curiously. "And why?"

He looked at her and flushed. "Rodger worked very closely with Dennison, being his right-hand man, so he was the best choice, the most knowledgeable to take over the workload," Alexander stated, with a pensive face. "He is also very dedicated to the company, so it was a no-brainer, and I had no problem giving him the promotion."

Rodney asked, "And would you have had any problem handing out that promotion if you thought that Dennison might have been murdered?"

He frowned at Rodney and stammered, "Murder? God, no." He took a moment, then shook his head. "Jesus frigging Christ, Rodger wouldn't have had anything to do with it. Rodger is not … Dennison wasn't murdered. Kendra told me that he was found in the water, so, … nope." He got up and then sat back down. "Didn't he commit suicide?" he asked. "I've been wondering if we just pushed him too hard, but he was always the first one here and always the last to leave. I have to admit, at times, we wondered if his home life was just so sad that he needed to fill his time with work. In the beginning I thought work was his getaway. Yet, the more time he spent here, I realized he was just a man who really enjoyed his job."

He made it sound as if enjoying his job to that degree was not normal. She looked over at him. "And the person who replaced him?"

"Yeah, Rodger," he repeated. "I would have absolutely

no issues or concerns if you did say Dennison had been murdered. But, thank God, that wasn't the case."

"Actually, it was the case," Rodney declared.

Kate studied Alexander and his reaction closely. The color drained from his face.

"Oh God, no," he whispered. "Suicide was bad enough, and I ..." He winced. "I know that all sounds terrible, and I don't mean it to, but what the hell? What do you mean, murdered? How? You mean, they drowned him?"

"No, he was beaten up first," Kate explained, still watching him closely. "He was beaten to a pulp and then thrown in the water."

"Not alive though, right?"

She turned to Rodney, and her partner shrugged. A curious question on Alexander's part, she thought, but she answered it readily enough. "No, not alive."

"Thank God for that," he said, then flushed. "I'll have nightmares enough as it is, but I lost a friend in college to drowning, and, ever since, ... drowning has always triggered me in a much bigger way."

Having worked a pretty-ugly case involving several drownings a while back, she could understand. "No, he wasn't alive when he hit the water. The autopsy found he died from blunt force trauma to the head."

Hearing that, Alexander sucked back his breath. "Dear God, just hearing you say it that way ..."

She nodded. "And yet there is no other way to say it."

"No, I understand," he muttered. "I'm sorry. I've never been in this situation before. If there's something I'm supposed to say, or some way I'm supposed to say it, I apologize. I'm probably coming off as completely nuts."

"Not at all," Rodney stated. "You're coming across as

authentically shocked."

"And I am," Alexander agreed. "I am shocked. Dennison and I weren't the best of friends in a personal sense, but we weren't enemies in any way either," he shared. "He was one hell of a worker and a good man. Given this office's scenario, that's one of the highest tributes I can give anyone." He stared around in the direction of the main room outside his office. "It does make it feel even uglier."

"But does it though?" Rodney asked, with a smile.

"What does that mean?" Alexander retorted, glaring at him.

Kate interjected, "To think that Dennison committed suicide and you promoted his underling right away, now that is ugly. I don't know what the protocol is here," she stated in a calm tone, as she focused on him. "However, it just seems a little quick to me. Particularly if the man was overworking himself to the point that even you felt suicide was the only answer."

"I just now realize how that'll look to outsiders," he admitted. "Damn, I've never really been in this situation, so I didn't have a protocol to follow."

She didn't say anything to that, just nodded.

"What can I help you with?" he asked, as he finally seemed to collect his thoughts and looked at the two of them. "Did you want to look at his desk or something?"

"Yes, thank you," Kate replied. "His desk, his space, his office, his locker. Anything and everything. And we'll need to talk to a few of his coworkers."

"Yes, yes, of course," he agreed, as he got awkwardly to his feet. "I'll make an announcement. Then you can do what you need to do."

As he stepped out into the larger main room, he called

for everyone's attention. "I've just gotten word that Dennison's passing ... wasn't a suicide. Dennison was murdered."

Immediately shocked gasps came from various cubicles around the room.

Kate watched their expressions change from shock to horror, as they realized how the unexpected death of their coworker had come about.

Alexander continued. "The police are here, and I'll give them access to Dennison's desk." He turned to a tall youngish man with curly hair. "Rodger, don't move anything yet."

Kate stepped forward and clarified, "Leave his office alone for a few days, please."

"Yes, of course," Rodger replied. "Do you know how or—?"

She looked at him and stated, "None of the details are being released at this time."

He just nodded and sank back into his chair. "God," he muttered. "That's awful."

"I gather you knew him very well."

He looked at her, startled.

Immediately Alexander stepped up. "Look. You can have my office for interviews, if you like. At least that would give you some privacy."

Kate nodded and motioned for the young man to come to the designated office with her. She entered first, and they stepped up to the desk. She asked him several questions about what he was doing for Dennison, when he'd last seen the victim, projects they were working on, but nothing felt out of place. She interviewed everybody else currently in the office, individually in the manager's office. Kate quickly realized that, chances were, nothing would be here. Still, Kate needed to go through the process anyway.

When she pulled in the woman continually drying her eyes, Kate eyed her intently. "You're the only one I've seen crying so far."

She nodded. "It's not that he was hard to work with," she began, "but he was demanding, and I've worked with him for a long time. So, we had found a rhythm in the work," she muttered. "Now I have to get used to somebody else."

"And yet that somebody else has already been working with you and Dennison for a long time as well, right? Hasn't Rodger worked here a while? That's what Alexander implied."

"Yes, yes, … he has," she confirmed, "and I shouldn't have any problem with that. It's just change," she muttered. "Change is hard."

"It is, indeed," Rodney interjected, as he leaned into the office and gave Kate a headshake, meaning that he hadn't seen anything suspect in the office.

After concluding her talk with the crying woman, Kate stood. The woman hurried out of the office as if her life depended on it.

"I guess I'll take a look at Dennison's office myself," she muttered.

"Nothing's there," Rodney replied.

"I need to look, just so I have an idea of who this guy was." As she walked into Dennison's office, she stopped and winced. Nothing was on the walls, nothing on the desk. The top surface was completely clean. She called Alexander in. "Is this how he would have left his desk?"

He looked around and nodded. "Yes, that was the way

he always left it. It was normal for him to confirm everything was spotless before he left from one day to the next."

"And what about logging in to the computer system for any of the information he needed?" she asked. "We'll need access."

He hesitated. After she raised one eyebrow, he nodded. "I'll get them for you." And promptly left.

She looked over at Rodney. "Does this Dennison guy just seem a little too ... perfect?"

He gave a quirk of his lips. "Maybe, but lots of these numbers people can be OCD."

"Really?" she asked, with a headshake. "He just seems so ..."

"*Perfect*," he repeated. "Just like you said."

When Alexander returned, he unlocked Dennison's computer, standing around to watch.

Kate sat down and went through the history to check on what he'd been doing. Then she went to the browsers and the emails. His inbox was flooded with messages, but everything appeared to be work-oriented. "How long had he worked here?" she asked.

"Seventeen years," Alexander stated, "and he would have been a lifer." At that, he winced. "Now that's a phrase I'll never use comfortably again."

She didn't say anything as she went through all that she could and then finally nodded. "Okay, I think we're done here for now." The relief on Alexander's face was so palpable that she smiled at him. "We really have to cover all our bases."

"Yes, yes, of course," he noted. "It's just so stressful, and, as I mentioned, originally I was all torn up, thinking it was the job and that maybe I'd been too hard on him—or maybe something that I just hadn't seen had happened. But now to find out that it's murder? It's an entirely different thing. The game has changed."

"It absolutely has changed," she confirmed, with a narrowing gaze. "And is there any particular reason why you used the term *game?*"

"God no," he said, staring at her. "It's just the word that came to mind."

She didn't say anything, nodding, not sure what anybody would even think about that usage in this context. By the time she walked out of Dennison's office, it was clear that the employees were all just waiting. She felt everybody waiting for them to leave. As soon as they stepped out of those offices, she looked over at Rodney. "That was fairly tense."

"Tense and odd," he agreed, shaking his head. "Did you get the feeling that, while people may have been celebrating the fact that somebody got a promotion, they were likely also celebrating the fact that Dennison was gone?"

"Yes. I got the same impression," she stated. "And that just pisses me off. Was his life worth so little that, the minute he was out of the picture, they couldn't think of anything else to do but cheer? Is that all we are to anybody?"

"I hope not," Rodney replied, "but you know all too well that we've seen it, time and time again. People do what suits them."

"I know," she muttered, "but I hadn't really seen such a universally odd reaction in an office environment before."

"Maybe he was tough to work with, had been here since forever, probably didn't like change, and most likely didn't take the time to make friends," Rodney suggested. "And that kind tends to cause trouble because they won't move forward in life. They stay right where they are because that's what they know. They oppose any change or progress, making life difficult for everybody."

"Maybe," she conceded, with a headshake. "But, Jesus, how would you like to be the bane of everybody's existence, where everything you've done winds up being part and parcel of what you represent, and, instead of earning their respect, they just can't wait until you're out of the office for good? That just sucks."

He nodded. "That would be awful," he agreed, "and I can't think of much that would be worse."

Together they walked back outside and stood in the sunshine for a long moment, contemplating Dennison's life of nothing but work and the way he ended up.

Kate asked, "How the hell does a meek and mild businessman wind up getting beaten to death and tossed into the harbor?"

Beside her, Rodney sighed. "We don't know the answers yet, but I can tell you one thing …"

She smiled over at him. "I already know what you'll say."

He laughed. "That's because I learned it from you. *We will find out.*" And, with that, he walked to the car. "Come on. Let's get out of here. It's lunchtime."

CHAPTER 4

THE NEXT MORNING Kate walked into the office and noted Reese was already there. Kate took one look at her face and muttered, "Ah, crap."

Reese nodded somberly. "Yeah, in a way it's *Ah, crap,* but, in another way maybe not."

"Why?" Kate asked curiously.

"It just occurred to me that this case was unusual enough that potentially something else could be going on, just beneath the surface."

"Of course something else is going on," Kate agreed, rolling her eyes, "but what?"

Reese handed over three files.

"Three more related deaths? Are these beatings too?" Kate looked up to see if Reese was serious.

"Yes," Reese confirmed. "Three other deaths, all the result of beatings, their bodies dumped. One is out in Coquitlam, another in Burnaby, the third in West Vancouver."

Kate frowned at that. "They could be completely unrelated."

"Maybe," Reese conceded, as she shrugged. "The cases were reported from different coroners in different jurisdictions, but one similarity remains. They all were beaten to a pulp. None of them had records either. None of them were the type you would expect to be into boxing, street fighting. If you ask me, I would say that makes it all very unusual."

"Interesting," Kate murmured, as she thumbed through the files. "We can't really think somebody is going around, picking up men, and just beating them for no reason though."

"You and I both know there'll be a reason," Reese stated. "I did my job and found these cases. The issue now is whether you can figure it out or not."

Kate snorted. "Well then, since I'm tasked with the job of figuring it out, I guess I'll have to try."

Reese laughed. "See? … That's why I decided to find these other case files for you."

"*Great.* So how did you come up with that idea?"

"Lilliana suggested it," Reese shared, with a wry smile for Kate. "Isn't it great when a team really comes together?"

Kate shrugged. "Yeah, it took a bit," she added, staring at the files in her hand, "but I'm hoping we're there."

"Oh, I think you're there," Reese confirmed, "and what one member doesn't quite get, the others do. So we're all good."

"If you say so," Kate muttered, as she walked over to her desk with these new related files.

Rodney frowned at the folders in her hand and asked, "What are those?"

Kate sighed. "Yeah, that was my reaction to seeing them too." She hooked a thumb over at Lilliana. "Apparently Lilliana asked Reese if she could find any other similar deaths."

And Lilliana, her phone in her hand as she was about to call somebody, looked up at the mention of her name, saw the files, and winced. "Sorry. It was a casual comment because we've had so many connected murders lately. I figured that you might find some threads to follow with another one."

"Me?" Kate repeated, raising her hands. "How is this mine?"

"Anything weird, bizarre, and connected to Simon is generally all yours," Lilliana pointed out, with a laugh.

"*Crap*."

"It is connected to Simon, isn't it?" Lilliana asked, studying Kate, then raised an eyebrow at Rodney.

"Maybe," Rodney acknowledged, with a grin.

At that, Colby walked in, took one look at the folders, then frowned.

"Yeah, I know," Kate muttered, glaring at him. "Not what we wanted."

"No, we sure as hell don't," he confirmed, staring at the folders as if they would blow up in her hands.

"On the other hand," Kate noted cheerfully, "maybe we can get to the bottom of something here and prevent some crimes."

"I hope so," her captain replied, "because lots of other cases need your attention."

"Oh, I know," she acknowledged, staring at him. "Lots of other cases and never enough time."

He nodded at that. "If it doesn't move, we have to move it along," he said, his jaw working.

She nodded. "This one is definitely still on the books because we just came from the victim's office."

"And seeing his wife," Rodney added.

"Right, so what did you find?" Colby asked.

Kate shook her head. "We spoke to his daughter while we were there with the wife, and nobody has any idea who, what, why, or anything else." She dropped the files on her desk and turned to look at her boss. "I plan to take a little time and see if I can come up with something that connects our victim to this mess," she shared, frowning at the files Reese had just brought her. "We searched the victim's home but found nothing."

"Keep at it," Colby replied, "but then—"

"I know. I know," she grumbled. "If I don't find anything soon, I'll move on to something else, or at least drop the possibility of its being related to these. And, just so you know, I'm not the one who brought up the idea that it could be connected to other homicides," she pointed out, with a wave of her hand. "You can blame Lilliana for that."

Lilliana got off the phone, frowned at her, and asked, "Did you just throw me under the bus?"

"I absolutely did," Kate admitted, with a smirk. "You're welcome."

Lilliana snorted at that. "Yeah, there'll never be a good time to have this crap happen," Lilliana muttered.

"No, there isn't, which is one of the reasons I said that." Kate then asked her, "What are you working on?"

"A dead child," Lilliana shared. "I figured I would take this one."

"Are you sure?" Kate asked, turning to her. "You were part of the last one too."

"The problem is, we're all part of all of them," she stated, "and sometimes we can handle them and sometimes? ... Well, they get a little bit harder. I suspect this one doesn't belong with us, so I wanted to go to bat over it."

Kate frowned. "What do you mean?"

"The child had multiple health issues, and the police seem to think that the mother killed her daughter in order to bring peace to her."

"Oh, crap," Kate muttered. "Yeah, you can have that one. It will be tough no matter how it comes out."

"Yep," Lilliana agreed, "because, if she's guilty, a court of law would have to settle that. Maybe it's not related or her daughter just died of natural causes"—she winced and shook her head—"or it could be a result of all her medical treatments, which is another issue entirely. So, it's pretty much just as you said. It'll be difficult regardless."

Kate grabbed a cup of coffee, happy to leave that one to Lilliana, then sat down at her desk to look through the three possibly related files. The team had worked together long enough for Reese to know that Kate absolutely preferred paper copies. Then, when she did more research, she always went to digital, which she could search easier on the computer. But, for the initial reading, she definitely wanted a paper copy in her hand.

And, with that, she settled down to read. It didn't take long for her to get deeper and deeper into the mess, and she realized just how many similarities there were.

Rodney stopped in front of her. "You're scowling," he noted. "So?"

"I've gone through all three reports, nothing else," she replied, turning to him. "There is definitely a pattern, and definitely something is there, but we need to prove they're all from the same killer," she added. "They occurred in very different jurisdictions, and the victims appeared to be very different, from all walks of life. So, finding common ground that ties them together won't be easy."

He nodded. "I guess I'm not surprised by that either," he shared, with a headshake. "This shit is never easy."

She smiled. "On the other hand, we do have to follow up."

"Yep, we do," he agreed. "So where do we start?"

She tossed him all three folders. "You could contact all three coroners and confirm we have autopsy reports on all three. We also need to contact the families and see if we have the same issues, such as workaholics or people who aren't athletic, or if something else was brewing under the surface."

"You think somebody is targeting people who are pretty defenseless, in a way?" he asked, surprised.

"I'm not sure about that, but let's just see what kind of people they were and get a feel for what they did with their lives."

"A lot of that should be in the files already."

"It should be," she agreed, "but I didn't get that far. So that's where you can start."

"And what will you do?"

She hesitated, then frowned. "I feel this nudge to talk to my mother."

"Your mother?" he asked, turning on the spot.

She shrugged. "I know it's bad timing to do this, but when would it ever be good timing? Plus, she took off, and she doesn't want anything to do with me. Yet, after I had to deal with Ken recently, I still have that weird sense that maybe my mother and I need to connect more."

"It's probably not a good idea, since she continues to blame you for Timmy going missing."

"I know that," she muttered, sagging back in place. "I keep going around the bend on it."

"She left for a reason," Rodney stated.

Kate's expression flashed with anger. "You do what you need to do or give me the damn files back, and I'll do it myself."

"Why don't you set up a whiteboard?" he suggested,

with an understanding smile, returning the files to her for that project.

"Now that I can do," she conceded, trying to mask the anger that had come out of nowhere. Yet it would probably always be there, until she found out what happened to Timmy.

Rodney nodded. "Meanwhile, send me the digital copies, and I'll make some calls to see if we can get any more personal information on these three victims."

She did that and got up and headed into one of the conference rooms with these paper files to set up a board. Then they could each post their findings, to help them figure out if they had one killer who had done this to more than one person. The thought that anybody would want to do this much damage to another human being was mind-boggling, but, typically in this line of work, Kate always found way more shitty stuff than good things.

It didn't take long for her to set up all three victims on the board from the data found in each file. When she turned around, Rodney stood there, his arms crossed, glaring at her.

Her eyebrows shot up. "What is that look for?"

"All three were businessmen. All three were a little on the pudgy side, and all three had zero fighting experience."

"Okay," she replied, "and that look on your face means what?"

"They're all connected, all three to each other," he declared, frustration in his tone. "Damn it to hell, I think they're all connected to our victim too."

WHEN SIMON GOT home, he'd walked in literally right behind Kate. He called out to her, and she turned, just as she went to enter the elevator, then held it for him so he could join her. "How are you doing?" he asked, studying her intently.

"I'm fine," she muttered. "I dealt with my insurance company on a few things today, but I'm hoping the worst of it will be over now."

"That'll be nice," he noted, with a smile. "It's not your fault some asshole shot up your place."

"According to them it is my fault, and it's completely related to my job."

"Of course it is, but that doesn't mean they shouldn't pay."

"They're thinking about it," she noted, with a frown. "I didn't know they could actually consider that."

"Oh, they'll take their time regardless. Even if you are denied," he suggested, with a headshake, "appeal immediately. Once they realize you won't go away, they'll come up with an answer that will make you a lot happier."

"That's a stupid way to do business."

"I understand," he replied, "but, if they can get away with not paying you, trust me that they will. You just always have to be ready to appeal these things. That's what I do."

"Let's hope they don't have any issues with it in the first place," she muttered, "because I'm not the one who's responsible."

He chuckled. "You might not think you're responsible, but, in their eyes, you're a bad risk. Which means they could choose to not insure you afterward. The damage isn't all that bad, considering what it could have been," he pointed out. "A new door and some dry wall repair in the hallway where the bullets entered, some more inside where the bullets landed, but, other than that, it's really pretty minor."

"That's true too," she agreed, "so you would think they would be okay with it."

He smiled at her. "Nope, it's an insurance company that sells policies, telling people how quick they are to hand out money whenever someone hits a bump in the road, then does the opposite when a claim is filed."

She groaned. "Why is everybody so concerned about money?"

He laughed. "Because those who don't have it, want it, and those who do, want to keep it."

"And yet"—she frowned at him—"I don't sense those same issues with you."

"Oh, I have the same issues," he declared, "but I've learned to deal with them. I find that, if I give away money and help others, it helps me to feel a little more secure with the money I have."

"You do know that makes no sense, right?"

He chuckled. "No, to you, it probably makes no sense," he corrected, "but, to me, it works perfectly, and that's what matters. You have to find out what works for you."

She smiled. "I agree with that part for sure," she confirmed, followed by a chuckle. "But how giving away money is supposed to make you feel better about what you have, I don't understand."

"It doesn't matter," he replied, as he walked to the hall closet, took off his jacket, and turned to look at her. "I am absolutely starving. What about you?"

"Me too," she agreed. "It's also freezing cold out there, so I don't want to go back outside." She blew on her hands as she took off her coat, hung it up, and looked around. "I don't suppose we have any food here though, do we?"

He laughed. "Half the time we order in anyway."

"I know, but that means waiting," she muttered, with a groan.

"Are you that hungry?"

She thought about it and then nodded. "In a way, yeah. I've been fighting that whole *I should try to contact my mother* thing all day."

"Oh God, no," he said, shaking his head vehemently.

"I know that it's a bad idea, I just—"

"You don't need to open that can of worms again. And she disappeared for a reason," he pointed out.

"I know, and Rodney told me the same thing."

He smiled. "I'm happy to know that Rodney and I are on the same page here."

She glared at him. "You guys are on the same page all too often, and it feels as if I'm the one living in a completely different world."

"No, not at all," he replied, giving her a gentle hug. "It's just a matter of coming to terms with the new reality."

"It sucks."

"You mean, the fact that you don't have any contact with your mother?" he asked.

She frowned, shook her head, and explained, "No, not that. I really don't want anything to do with her at all, but … I guess I don't even know what the *but* is."

"But you don't want her to go kill herself or to do anything stupid like that."

"No, of course I don't. Whether I have anything to do with her or not, it doesn't mean that I want to see her so despondent and trying to get rid of whatever is going on in her world that she takes her life. We've seen enough suicides to last me a lifetime, and every single day there's another one."

"I hear you," he said, "and the job you're in really doesn't help, does it?"

"No, or, hell, maybe it does in a way," she admitted, with a groan. "I don't want to think that I'm becoming complacent, but …"

"But you're becoming complacent," he noted, with a nod. "And, as much as that might be difficult to acknowledge, it's also understandable. You are turning off your emotions to deal with it, to protect your own mental health."

She laughed. "You're always so accepting."

"Maybe," he conceded, with a wry smile, "but we still really do need to get food."

"I agree." She nodded, as she stared at him.

"Suggestions?" He grinned.

And she groaned. "You just want pasta again."

"We could order something different for a change," he suggested. "We have a lot of other options."

"Maybe, but I'm really too tired to care. You order whatever you want," she stated, "just get lots of it. I'll go get a hot shower." And, with that, she quickly disappeared.

That was the one thing that Simon found very unique about her. If it was food, and it was sustenance, that was good enough for her. She didn't want the fancy restaurants, the five-star service, or the whole nine yards that went along with it. She wasn't interested in any of that. What she really wanted was enough to confirm she wouldn't be hungry and wouldn't have her appetite disrupt her later.

With a smile, he quickly placed an order, but completely switched it up and ordered several big platters of ribs. He left the rest of it to Mama to sort out, mentioning how Kate was really hungry, so he had her orders to get them in some food.

Mama was already clucking in the background, like the mother hen she was, promising to send something over within twenty minutes. And he believed her. He quickly sent a message down to Harry, the doorman at the post now, letting him know. Yet Simon already knew the notification wasn't even needed. Harry knew the drill and was very good at his job, and Simon appreciated that.

When Kate came back out in something warm and cuddly, he grinned in appreciation. She frowned and pointed. "I don't even remember seeing this before," she admitted, "but it seemed about right for my mood." He didn't say anything, making her eye him suspiciously. "Did you get it for me?"

"I might have," he noted carelessly. "If I did, I don't remember."

She looked at him intently and then shrugged. "That's the way our world works, isn't it?"

"It absolutely is," he stated, with half a smile in her direction. "Anyway, food is coming."

"Good," she muttered. "I'm literally starving."

He shook his head and sighed, not understanding how she could forget to eat, no matter how busy she was. "So, tell me about your day."

"I'm not even sure what I can tell you," she muttered. "We've got this case, which you already know about, since you're the one who brought it up."

"About the fighting?" he asked, studying her intently.

She nodded. "Yes, so I have a body in the morgue that doesn't fit the fighting scene, and phone calls in to three other precincts, coroners, and families basically because we have the possibility of another three—"

"Three what?" he asked, startled.

"Three other men who seemingly died in fights."

"Sure, but ..."

She smiled at him and nodded. "Exactly. Sure, *but.* These cases were classified as muggings, murder in the obvious sense. In all three cases, nobody was caught."

"That seems to be the biggest issue all around, all the time."

"Yeah, and now you have a much better idea why we have so many challenges in that area."

"Yeah, sure I do," he confirmed. "This stuff just never quits, does it?"

"No, it sure doesn't," she muttered. "On top of that, the victims all appear to be a similar type of person."

"Meaning?"

"They were all businessmen, all not in the best physical shape, and all considered to be more workaholics than family men. Not that they had anything against family. It's just that they were always working late. From what we can tell, they were actually working late, not just hooking up with their secretaries—at least so far, in these cases that we've seen. There have been no known suspects, no recordings of the incidents, and, in each case," she added, "and this is really the clincher. ... Their bodies were found three days later."

"And that's when you found your current one as well?"

"That's exactly when we found this one of ours," she stated, with a nod. "So, that brings us three extra and very similar cases. So, I started a board today, and, of course, Colby came in and just about blew a gasket when he realized what we were looking at ... again."

At that, Simon winced. "Yeah, I'm sorry about that myself."

"Me too," she muttered. "But not for the sake of the work ahead of us. But more so because these other people were in other locations, different venues and jurisdictions, with nothing to put it together as being a single killer. One was in West Vancouver. One was out in Coquitlam. Plus, we have one in Burnaby. Now we have the most recent one downtown, in our jurisdiction."

He just stared at her.

She nodded. "In each case, the victim appeared to have been thrown into the harbor."

"The same harbor?"

She frowned. "That's a good question. They were all found in the water. Were they all put in at the same place? I don't know. Were they all meant to float to the same location? I don't know," she admitted, still frowning as she thought about it. "I have to bring that up with the team—or Reese. We might have to take a look at tidal patterns to know exactly where the bodies came from, see where they would have been put in, and see if anything was caught on street cams thereabouts." She immediately starting texting on her phone.

He continued to frown at her, and she nodded. "I know. So, as much as I don't want to think that some serial killer thing is going on, apparently we have to consider the potential that something connected is definitely going on." She threw herself down onto the couch and then frowned. "Do we have any wine? I could really use a glass."

He laughed. "Do we have any? *Come on.*" He walked over to the sideboard to the temperature-controlled wine cupboard. He opened it up so she could see twenty-odd bottles.

Her eyebrows shot up. "I don't think I've ever even looked in that cupboard before," she shared, as she got up and walked closer.

"Of course not," he noted, "because you would consider it *not yours.*"

She looked at him, then nodded. "Of course it's not mine. But now that you have it open—" She grinned, as she eyed several of the bottles. "We should have something, depending on what would go well with dinner, of course." Then she looked over at him and frowned. "The problem is, I have absolutely no idea what's for dinner."

He chuckled. "I'm not even telling you what's coming for dinner."

Just then Harry called out on the intercom system, "It's here."

"Apparently," Simon noted, turning to her, "you're about to find out anyway because our dinner has just arrived." He reached for a bottle of red and brought it out.

"Good," she muttered. "I always sleep like a log after a red."

He nodded. "It doesn't have the same effect on me, but I do know other people who have the same issue." He walked over to the elevator, just as it opened to reveal Harry with the bags of food. "Thanks." Simon took the bags and handed him a tip. Harry just waved him off, refusing the money, then headed right back down again.

"See what happens?" she pointed out, with a laugh. "You tip him so often, he's just like, … *Leave me alone.*"

"Everybody can use a little help sometimes."

"Sure," she confirmed. "I won't argue with that. I think a lot of times people could use a whole lot more than *a little bit.*"

He smiled and nodded. "Agreed. Let's dig in, shall we?"

She walked over, opened up the bags, and froze, sniffing the air. Frowning, she tore into the packages.

He laughed, absolutely loving her reactions to each food delivery.

When all the food was revealed, she looked down at the ribs and pointed. "I keep forgetting they have these things. We order pasta so often that we should add something else sometimes. What a treat."

"I agree," he replied. "I just wanted something a little heftier in the protein department today."

With her mouth already full, she just nodded. When she finally could speak, she said, "I'm totally okay with whatever you order," she muttered. "I'm just so hungry that sometimes I lose track of the fact that food is a necessity and that I need it."

"I know," he replied, frowning at her. "I would be a hell of a lot happier if you wouldn't forget that quite so often." She just rolled her eyes at him, making him laugh. When she slowed down, he noted that the first wave of insatiable hunger had been calmed somewhat. He smiled. "Now maybe you can enjoy your second helping a little more."

She nodded. "When you're that hungry, it's so hard to slow down. Even though you know you should, but I find things that I *should do* are easier said than done."

He chuckled. "Yes, that's true," he muttered, "but you're doing fine."

By the time they finished dinner, they still had tons of leftovers. She just sat here and looked at them happily. "I'll be more than happy to eat these tomorrow." She picked up her wine and moved to the couch, where she sprawled on her back, taking up the bulk of the space. She patted her tummy and said, "Okay, that was way too much food ingested in a short amount of time, but I'm so grateful to have had it."

When he sat down on the floor beside her, she tried to

shift to give him space, but he refused. "It's all good," he told her. "Just stay as you are."

As she relaxed, he could see the stress dropping off her in waves, and he realized what another one of these cases would do to her. He also knew that no way she would ever change jobs or would even consider doing anything different. Yet it was hard to watch her fade away with effort every time. It always came around to justice, and she ended up with some pretty-crazy cases solved, but the toll on her was excessive.

"I'm fine, you know," she muttered, without opening her eyes.

He snorted. "You're completely crashed on my couch," he pointed out, "so forgive me if I don't believe you. It's hard for me to see that as *fine*."

"Let me rephrase it then. I am currently in a food coma, after having a fantastic meal that I didn't have to worry about cooking or picking up or paying for," she clarified with a smile, as she opened her eyes and faced him. "And that is not something to worry about."

"That sounds better at least," he murmured.

After a few minutes of silence, she asked, "For what possible reason ... would somebody want to beat people to death? Particularly people who are not likely to have much fight in them or to present much of a challenge?"

"Dominance and control," he stated.

"Sure, dominance and control, but you must have something more than that. Why would you pick these people if that was the only thing?"

"It probably isn't the only thing."

"What I get out of this," she added, not sitting up, "is somebody who's been treated the same way and is being publicly or privately mocked in such a way that he can't let it go."

He looked at her and nodded. "That's an interesting idea."

She just smiled and shrugged. "I do get them every once in a while."

He laughed. "You get them all the time," he noted. "And I would agree that it's probably got something to do with that, but there also has to be a particular reason why *these* specific victims were chosen."

"I know," she conceded, with a groan. "And I think it's … the businessman element. Well, that is one thing, but the lack of physical fitness, lack of fighting ability, or something along that line, is a completely different thing altogether."

"I think that just ensures that it's a victim he can subdue, a fight he can win. So, maybe this isn't about dominance as much as it's about winning," he murmured.

She thought about that and nodded. "That makes sense in a way. It sucks, but, if so, then he should have this entire world full of people who aren't in the best of shape and who could potentially be his victims."

"So, why choose these ones?" Simon repeated.

"Exactly. I have to see if there's any connection between them. I've got Reese on that, looking to see if she can make any connections between the businesses they worked at, between where they lived, or even hotels they stayed in when traveling, or that kind of thing," she murmured. "But also a mess of other points could be involved here too."

"Of course, but if you already see a connection …"

She nodded. "Yeah, I just wonder about the psychology of that."

He hesitated and then spoke. "I know you really don't want to, but you could contact your local untapped shrink on staff and ask." She frowned but didn't dismiss the idea, so he would take that as a win. "Do you still see him?" he asked.

"Sometimes," she grumbled, "but not if I don't have to. Why would anybody want to go see him on purpose?"

He smiled. "Because it makes them feel better."

"It doesn't make me feel better," she declared. "It's more like nails on a chalkboard, and they're scraping the inside of my skin. I don't want to experience that feeling any more than absolutely necessary."

He winced at the description and shook his head. "That's a particularly unpleasant way of looking at it."

"Yep, it sure is," she muttered, her eyes closed.

"And you'll leave all this alone tonight, won't you?"

"Well, … I will," she said, "when I fall asleep. In the meantime, I'll just see if I can sort out in my mind what kind of psychopath would do this."

He laughed. "There's no end to those who will do it, but the reason why differs with each killer."

"Yeah, it does," she agreed, her eyes opening, turning to him again. "Motivation is everything. But in order to figure out the motivation for this, I still need to know what happened to him to trigger it."

"Maybe," Simon replied, "and maybe you just need to know that the same person is doing it and figure out what you need to do to stop it."

CHAPTER 5

K ATE ROLLED OVER and curled up tighter to Simon, her arms around him, tucking in for a bit more sleep, right when one of their phones rang. She groaned, opened her eyes wider, realizing it was her phone. As she reached over to answer it, Simon snagged her around the middle and pulled her closer.

"You could just spend the day here."

She laughed. "Wouldn't that be nice," she muttered. "On the other hand, if somebody is calling me—"

"Yeah," he winced. "It means somebody is dead." And, with that, he let her go.

She reached for her phone and read the Caller ID. "Reese, what's up?" she asked, wiping the sleep from her eyes.

"Looks like another beating victim."

"What?" she asked, bolting upright. "When did this happen?"

"The body just washed up. The coroner is down there right now, and word came back to me that we're supposed to call you in for it."

"Meaning Smidge has probably noted something about it. I've got to go."

"Exactly," she said in relief. "He wasn't very pleasant about it."

She laughed. "No, he wouldn't be."

"You okay with that?"

"Yeah, I get him just fine," she replied. She ended the call, rolled out of bed and into clothing almost as fast. By the time she was dressed and out in the kitchen, Simon called out his goodbye. She called back a goodbye to him and moments later was downstairs and heading for her car.

It took another ten minutes on the empty roads to get to the crime scene. She pulled off to the side, next to where the aquabus normally docked. She parked her vehicle on the sidewalk, so she was out of the way of the emergency vehicles. As she walked closer, Dr. Smidge looked over at her and glared.

She nodded as she approached. "Yep, seems we've got something ugly happening." She added, "We found three other cases similar to your two."

"Fuck." He stared at her, his hands on his hips. "Where's the crime scene?"

"One in Coquitlam, one in West Vancouver, one in Burnaby."

He shook his head. "So not mine."

"Not yours, not yet anyway, but"—she looked down at their current victim—"if this is the same thing, this makes number two for us, and the list is escalating."

He nodded. "It looks to be number two for me," he confirmed, "and that just pisses me off."

"You and me both," she noted glumly, as she stared down at the victim's facial features, barely recognizable. "I don't understand what our killer gets from this."

"The same thing they all get," Smidge grumped. "Power."

"That's what I was thinking too. Power, control, some

return to whatever sense of control he needs," she muttered, as she stared down at the body. Then she frowned at the coroner. "I'll need that autopsy soon." He just glared at her, and she nodded. "Glare all you want," she said cheerfully, "but I can't do shit until I get your report."

He groaned. "I know. I was just hoping you wouldn't keep me quite so busy in the meantime."

"I was hoping that too," she muttered, "because this one … Shit, what am I saying? They're all ugly as fuck."

"No," he countered. "This one will be more than ugly." He pointed at the body. "I'm not sure what defines one versus another and what degree makes it worse, but I'm not liking anything about this one at all."

"No, I'm not either," she muttered. "Age, name, date, anything?"

"No ID," he replied, looking back down at his victim. "Male, I would say forties, maybe fifties, I don't know," he admitted. "I'm not too sure on that point yet, but I'll find out."

"We should get an ID fairly quickly," she noted, sorrow in her tone. "Unfortunately somebody is probably already missing him, and, if the pattern holds, he'll be a business-man, workaholic, who kept to himself." Smidge raised his eyebrows. Kate nodded. "They're all mild-mannered businessmen. No fighting, no martial arts, no fitness buffs to be sure."

"So, easy targets," Smidge muttered to himself, as he looked down at the body.

"And obviously," she added, "no fair fight for whoever is doing this."

"Yeah, our killer doesn't want competition. He just wants to win."

"And yet these are easy wins," she stated pointedly. "There's no build-up here, no challenge. What happens when he figures he needs a bigger challenge?"

Smidge frowned at her. "It means more victims," he noted, as he pointed at the victim by his feet. "I'll take this one back and get to work on it now. I'll do *my* job ..." He looked over at her.

She nodded. "Then I'll do mine."

"Promise me," he began, frustration in his tone. "I really don't like being dragged out at this time of night."

"Neither do I." She sighed. "So, let's do what we can and get this asshole off the street."

"Too late," Smidge noted. "I think he's tucked in for a nice long visit."

Unfortunately she was pretty sure Smidge was right. She hung around until the body was removed, and then, with the help of several cops, questioned onlookers and the person who found the body. Afterward she approached a crowd of curious people still hanging around and talked to them. Several of them moved away as she neared, but she was more concerned about a certain criminal who just stood around and watched, sometimes even getting involved in the actual investigations. It was apparently more fun for them that way.

As she joined the first two men still standing here, she asked, "Have you ever seen him before?" Both men shook their heads.

"Another drowning?" asked one man, staring down at the black water. "That is not how I would choose to go."

"Yeah, you're not kidding," the other one agreed, with a shudder. "I don't even swim, so no way you would catch me over there."

"I do swim, and you still would never catch me over

there either," added his buddy.

They both worked close by and were just coming off the night shift in the commercial district. She got their names and let them go on their merry way, once again reminded how life and death can change in a heartbeat.

As she walked over to a lone man standing off to the side, he looked at her and said, "I didn't have anything to do with it."

Her eyebrows shot up. "I didn't say you did," she replied.

"So why are you talking to everybody?"

She smiled. "It's standard practice. For all I know, you knew this guy."

"No, I sure didn't," he stated, with feeling. "But it's got to suck to hate your life so much that you're willing to throw it all away—and worse in a place like this."

"If he committed suicide, I'm not sure that this is any better or any worse than any other place," she murmured. "And, with the currents around here, I would think that he would still end up here no matter where he went in."

"I don't know about that," he countered, staring out at the black and angry sea. "It still sucks." With that, he turned and walked off. She called out to him to try to talk to him some more, but he quickly disappeared.

She knew that he would be on the cameras, so that wasn't necessarily an issue. His demeanor was interesting, not so much that she was afraid he was suicidal himself but that something was off about him. Making note of it, she quickly moved on, and by the time she was done with the next few bystanders, the first responder vehicles were all dispersing, and so was the crowd.

She joined Rodney, who was on his cell phone. "Texting

your girl already?" she asked.

"Nope," he declared, "but I did catch images of everybody standing around though."

"Good." She nodded. "I want to talk again to that last guy in particular, who wasn't all that excited about seeing me."

"Yeah, I saw that one," Rodney said. "He'd been here for a while too. You think he's involved?"

"I don't know whether he is or he isn't," she acknowledged. "I just know that he was … odd."

Rodney nodded. "It's a great world we live in when somebody doesn't say the things we expect them to say, and, all of a sudden, we consider them odd."

She smiled. "Sounds like you didn't get enough sleep last night."

"Nope, I sure didn't," he agreed, a yawn escaping. "Rough night." He looked over at her. "You?"

"Mine was okay," she murmured. "We brought in food last night, and I ate a ton."

He laughed. "When did you *not* bring in food? You're just lucky he's wealthy and can do it all the time."

She frowned at that comment several times throughout the morning, as they processed all the reports and interviews coming in, even as she waited to hear from Smidge. She was just heading off to grab some food for lunch when she got a phone call from him.

"It's the same," Smidge greeted her, his tone bitter. "Blunt force trauma to the head, multiple blows, and over multiple days from the looks of it. The most recent hits—though I hesitate to guess—were probably about two days ago, so that's how long he's been dead. Some of the wounds are still pretty fresh, so it might even be within a twenty-four-hour window."

"In other words, he's escalating."

Silence came from the other end. Then Smidge groaned. "Yeah, that would be my take on it."

"*Great*," she muttered. "Thanks for the heads-up." She ended the call and turned to look at the others. "This one hasn't been dead as long, and the body was found faster. We don't know whether that was deliberate or not, but Smidge puts the death between twenty-four to forty-eight hours ago."

Just as Kate finished, Reese walked into the room. "And I may have an ID on our victim," she interjected. "I have a John Hobert who went missing after work two days ago. The family contacted the police and got the standard response that maybe he left on his own and maybe the family should wait and see, before filing a report. Sounds as if they were about to post a missing person's report."

At that, Kate walked over and took a look at the photo she had with her. "Where did you get the picture?" she asked.

"His driver's license."

"Right, of course." She sighed and looked over at Rodney. "Same body type, same basic everything."

"Well, shit," he muttered. "We really don't need another one of these."

"No, but it looks as if we don't have a choice." She looked back at Reese. "Did you ever do another dive to check and see if you can find any other similar victims?"

"I have." She nodded. "I didn't find any, but ..."

"You sound hesitant."

"I want to take another look at a couple. They aren't identical, but I wondered if something might be there."

"If you don't have time to do it today, pass them my way," Kate suggested. "I can then either rule them in or rule them out."

"Good enough." Reese turned and walked away.

Kate stood here, holding a file on this John Hobert. It held little info. She looked back at Rodney. "Seems we have to make a death notice."

He winced. "Or we can send the black-and-whites."

"We could, but then we won't learn anything about the family, or personally about the victim. We'll have to talk to the wife anyway, although we don't have 100 percent proof yet."

Rodney was already up and grabbing his jacket. "I know, but they're the roughest."

"They absolutely are, and, in this case, the family will be irate that they were told to wait to see if he just showed up again." Kate shook her head. "If they'd filed a report earlier, maybe he would still be alive."

"Maybe, but how many times have we had people who just walked away for a bit, looking for a few minutes to themselves? You know, just to rethink their life or their job and felt they needed five minutes alone? We would have so many cases that really aren't cases if they all filed a report that first evening or whatever."

"I know." She sighed, as they both left the building. "It still sucks for the family who's waiting for answers, and they are just told to keep waiting for more time to pass."

"And we also know," he added, as they walked out to her car, "that time is of the essence. For us, the first twenty-four hours are so important. Yet we often don't even hear about a case until then or later."

"Unless it's a child," she noted, looking back at him. "At

least then it's all hands on deck, right away."

SIMON DELIBERATELY WALKED through the back alley of the scary warehouse, wondering if he could trigger whoever had been calling out to him earlier. But nothing came this time. He was doing everything else he could to avoid entering that warehouse. Call him a chicken, he didn't care, but something was damn creepy about that place. He did have fighting skills, but nothing that would have an effect on gangs or ghosties. And he had to admit, ghosties had the power to frighten him. He shook his head even thinking about it.

This was not exactly the life he'd expected for himself. And why the hell wasn't his grandmother ever popping through? That was a damn mystery to him, though he knew she deserved a rest and a chance to be free and clear in heaven. But still, this was one of those times when he really could have used somebody here for backup during all these years.

Still getting no response from his grandmother or from his most recent ghost, he realized that his feet were taking him to the one place he didn't want to go. The one building that was stuck in his mind as being off-limits. And yet, even as he got closer to the front entrance, he recognized that he was almost being led there by the will of another. He stopped walking and waited to see what would happen. His feet were urged to move again. He let them carry him a little bit farther, then he stopped. "I'm not going in there," he declared.

A sense of frustration surrounded him. He wasn't sure what this entity—spirit, ghost, or whatever—wanted, but

Simon wasn't really impressed with the idea of being pulled back to this place. And, if something were here, he really should get a cop to come check it out. Better them than him. And yet what would he say? "Oh, yeah, so a ghost stopped by my place one day and told me that you needed to go in and check out this warehouse."

That would go over like a ton of bricks. Particularly if people knew his connection to Kate. He could see that, for her, this was a way bigger challenge, just because of who she was, but also because of who he was. They were still working their way through so many different things in their lives, and it was very much on her watch that so much of this depended.

He stared up at the building, realizing his feet were still trying to take him inside. He swore and took a couple hesitant steps in that direction. And just when he was contemplating whether he should enter or not, his phone rang. Immediately whatever had been driving him seemed to groan in exasperation, and Simon stepped back with a smile. He changed directions and headed off, as he pulled his phone from his pocket. It was Ariel, his stalker Realtor again. "I haven't had a chance to consider the offer," he muttered. "You'll have to give me time."

She paused, then stated, "I can't hold it forever."

"Yeah, I know that," he said, trying to keep his voice calm. Negotiations 101, never let them know how much you want it. "But, as always, shit happens."

She laughed, trying not to show her frustration. "Fine," Ariel replied, "get back to me when you can."

He realized he owed her for shifting whatever psychic energy was happening at the time, but he still didn't want to talk to her at this moment. Not about something he hadn't had a chance to do a serious cost analysis on. He absolutely loved the building she had for sale, but it might not be one that he could make work.

He realized he wasn't that far away from it right now. As he looked around, he saw that he was even closer than he thought. He walked around a couple blocks, and there it was. The Queensborough. He stopped to look up at the once-beautiful hotel that had been turned into a million other things in the last few years. Sometimes he wondered what his attraction for these places was, but usually he didn't even bother to figure it out. He just knew, and this one was glorious in her old age—yet showing so much of that age, as he soon realized, just by walking around her. It would cost a fortune to rehab this building, and it might really be better if this one was dropped.

He kept walking, checking it out, looking back and forth. When he turned around again, he saw Ariel, standing on the front steps, a smile on her face.

"Hey," she greeted him. "I didn't realize when I called that you were already over here."

"And I didn't realize that I was so close," he replied, with a shrug. "I'm just doing a basic analysis on it right now, but that's not enough for me to make a decision of that magnitude."

"I know," she noted. "It has quite a pull though."

"It does. I'm just not sure that it's a good pull." When she frowned at him, he shrugged. "It'll be a very expensive rebuild. ... I basically have to take it down to studs."

"But it is steel."

"I know," he confirmed, turning to her, "but steel ..." Shaking his head, he wouldn't let her bug him as he turned and walked inside. It took him quite a few minutes before he stopped. His heart was still tugging at him to say yes, but he just wasn't sure what was driving that.

She looked over at him. "You're really not sure on this one, are you?"

"No, I'm really not," he conceded, with a smirk, "and I want a whole lot more surety before I make a decision."

"You've got a little bit of time but not a whole lot."

"You mean, before you go to other people."

"Right," she admitted. "And that's not necessarily the same thing. Just because the owners are ready to sell doesn't mean that anybody else is ready to buy. But considering the price they've dropped it to, and the location, if you just dropped it and rebuilt something completely different, it would be hard to lose money on this venture."

He looked at it from that point of view for just a moment and nodded. "Which is exactly what somebody else would do."

"Sure, and you could too," she pointed out. "I know you don't build from scratch very often, but at times you can take the same concept of whatever it is that you're trying to salvage or save, then rebuild it that much better."

"I know," he murmured. "I'll think about it."

She laughed. "I've heard that a time or two."

"Yeah, you sure have," he acknowledged, "and it will still be the same answer. *I'll think about it.*"

"I can give you another forty-eight hours, but that's it."

He nodded and didn't say anything.

Ariel turned and walked away.

As she left, he suddenly had that same weird feeling he'd had before. It usually came from one of these buildings when it was one he should buy. He looked around, feeling that sense he'd been looking for before but had yet to feel—until now—and smiled.

Because he never bought one of these buildings without that sensation of knowing it was right, of knowing he really could make this happen. Knowing that whatever was wrong was something he could fix, or, as Ariel noted, could rebuild completely. That might be a good project to do here because this old hotel certainly had a lot of years on her. But that didn't mean those years would go to waste, even if he did a full redesign.

Thinking about it, he pondered the money involved and then contacted his accountant and made a couple requests to get something on paper to take a look at.

Quinn, his accountant, laughed. "I've already done a cost analysis on this building, and you and I both know it."

"I know," he replied, "but we're talking about a much lower price now—or at least I am."

"Why would they take it now?" he asked curiously.

"It's one of the things I've just been talking to the real estate agent about," he shared. "No guarantee they'll accept it, but it's more likely now than it was before, as their lives have changed."

"Right," Quinn muttered. "I'll take another look."

"Also take a look at it from the point of view if we dropped it and rebuilt something bigger and better on top of it."

"If you got it cheap enough, this location could do well. I can tell you that right now. It's problematic when you want to rebuild what's there, keeping a lot of the old structure. As you and I both know, that's where a lot of the expenses come in. But if you'll take it back down to either the steel or the foundation," Quinn stated, "still, you can't lose money on it."

"Yeah, that's what I thought," Simon agreed. "I'll make an offer tonight then."

"Make sure it's low enough though. Just because you can make money doesn't mean you make enough for your trouble." With that, he was gone.

Half laughing over that, Simon turned and looked back at the old girl. Somehow she seemed to have lightened up, almost smiling at him. "I know. If I get you, I promise I'll do something to make you proud," he vowed.

It would stretch him if he bought the property, then let her sit. That's what had been happening to her all these years. At the same time, he also knew that he might just have to let her sit for a time while he figured out what he was doing with her. Plus, he needed the manpower for it, which meant one of his other rehab projects had to get finished up—or at least to the point where he could get his framing crew back again.

And, with his thoughts full, he headed home, only to realize that his feet had once again taken him to that damn creepy warehouse that he didn't like.

"I should just buy you and drop you flat," he muttered, as he stared up at the old building. It was another derelict, probably mostly a drug-addict-inhabited building, not his favorite by any means. Although it would certainly be spectacular if somebody took the time and the effort to redo her as well. He just wasn't necessarily sure he was up for the job. He forced his feet to walk past, but he soon hit an invisible wall.

He groaned, turned to look back at the building, and asked, "Why?"

He got no audible answer, yet he felt this weird sense, and soon a whisper came in the back of his mind.

Because we need you.

He didn't know what that meant, but, as he walked hesitantly outside, he heard a weird whine inside. He wasn't sure what it was. As he headed toward the building, he called out, "Hello. Hello."

He heard a faint groan, followed by swearing. He went inside, knowing it could literally be a trap to get somebody like him to go inside and then get pounced on. With his guard up and all the psychic energy he could muster at the ready, he moved forward. He hadn't gotten very far inside when he recognized a form on the ground, not in very good shape. He raced to the man's side.

The old man looked up at him and whispered, "You need to leave. You need to get out of here."

Simon nodded. "Probably, but no point in leaving you behind."

"They'll come back, and, if they do, they'll likely be done with me today."

"Maybe," he murmured. "Is this where you want to end up?"

"Not like this," he said.

As the old man reached up, Simon bent down and scooped him up. When the old man called out, a dog appeared from nearby and followed them outside into the sunlight. The old man looked up at the sky and smiled. "Now that," he whispered, "makes it worthwhile."

"What happened to you?"

"I don't know," he replied, a sad smile on his face. "Feels like I hit my head or something," he muttered.

"We need to get you to the hospital and get you some care."

"That ain't gonna do no good either," he shared. "I've

been dying for a long time."

"Dying from what?"

"Cancer, and I refused the treatments. I don't want to go that way either," he said, his gaze on the sun. "It's just me and Elsie." He pointed to the dog following them.

It looked to Simon as if Elsie was just as old as the man in his arms. Both of them had quite aged features.

"Where do you want me to take you?" Simon asked, as he shifted the weight of the man in his arms, the dog at his feet trembling in the cold. "Can you walk?"

"Barely," he muttered.

"Is there a shelter you go to normally?"

"Some won't take me, saying I have to be ambulatory," he muttered. "And other places won't let me take the dog." He swore at that, and then the man smiled. "See? That's why you shouldn't have come in."

"Yeah, maybe," Simon admitted, "but I did, and now the question is, what do I do with you?" He walked over to a bench and slowly sat the man down.

The man laughed. "Yeah, this is good. At least I'm in the sun."

Simon phoned Kate and asked, "Is there a place for homeless people who have disabilities?"

She thought for a moment and muttered, "I'm not sure about that. There are places for seniors."

"He has a dog."

"Yeah, that's where the problems begin," she muttered. Her tone seemed distracted.

"Never mind. I'll figure it out." And he ended the call, looked down at the man, and sighed. "Surely there's a place for people like you."

"There is no place for people like me," he muttered. "If I

didn't have Elsie, I could probably go to some shelters. But she's so old, and she's been with me this whole time, so I don't want to desert her right now."

"Well hell, any idea …"

"You mean, any idea of our life expectancy?" The old man laughed. "You can say it. I don't mind, and neither does Elsie."

"It just sounds crude," Simon said apologetically. "That's not a nice thing to ask somebody."

"No, it's not a nice thing, but it's the truth, and the truth can be bitter," he noted, with a groan. He took several gasping breaths. "Honest to God, both of us are goners. We were just looking for a place to finish it, preferably somewhere safe."

"And what if you die before Elsie?"

"She won't last much longer," he replied. "She's been with me a very long time. We just need a place out of the cold for a little bit."

"Yeah, and, when you say, *out of the cold for a little bit,* what does that mean?" His mind said, *Don't do it, Simon,* but something inside him said that he had to. He had no choice in the matter. He frowned as he looked around and then asked, "Have you got any place, any family?"

"No, no family, … at least not anybody who gives a crap about me anymore," he added. "I lived pretty rough for a long time, so just leave me here. The cops will tell me to move on. I'll tell them I can't. Then they'll try to put me in a shelter, but I won't leave Elsie, so they'll end up leaving me here."

"Well, crap." Simon stared at the old man. His skin appeared paper thin. "When did you eat last?"

"Not eating much anyway," he murmured. "Food

doesn't sit well, doesn't travel through the system as it should. Seriously I'm just days away from croaking."

"You can't just sit out in the street like this, just waiting to die," Simon argued.

The old man looked up at him and smiled. "You haven't seen enough of the city side of life to realize that's exactly what happens, day in and day out," he murmured.

"That may be, but I'm hoping I don't ever see that," Simon snapped. "Look. I've got a place where you can stay for a couple days, but I don't want you bringing any of your neighbors with you."

"You mean, other homeless folk? No, I wouldn't do that," he stated. "Would you really give me and Elsie a place to stay out of the weather? We just need a few days."

Simon hated to do it, not because of potential damage to his place but because he couldn't properly look after the old man. Yet Simon didn't want to be old himself and in a similar situation and not have anybody give a crap. Swearing to himself, he asked, "What's your name?" Then he called a cab.

"I'm Arnie. Where will you take us?" he asked. "I can walk a little bit, you know."

"We'll have to go to the opposite side of downtown," he replied, "and I'm not carrying you. I need to get you settled, so I won't worry so much about where else you could end up."

"I don't think I've ever met anybody who gave a crap where I ended up," Arnie pointed out, looking at him curiously. "Don't you care that I might steal something?"

Simon shook his head. "I would be pissed if you broke things, but I'm not too worried about your stealing any-thing. ... I'm more concerned about the lack of humanity in the world when somebody is in your situation."

"Ah, you can't blame them," he suggested. "Everybody tries to do something, but there isn't a whole lot of space in this world for people who can't provide their own keep or who don't do whatever it is that the world expects."

"Which is no excuse," Simon declared abruptly.

The old man laughed. "No, it sure isn't," Arnie agreed, "but it does make people feel better when they can't do anything."

"I can do something."

Just then the cab arrived. He helped Arnie into the back, Elsie beside him, as Simon took a seat and gave the driver instructions to head back toward his penthouse.

"I don't think you should take me in," the old man argued. "I'm sure people in your world would much prefer you had nothing to do with me."

"Maybe, but, if that's the case, they're not people who should be in my world, are they?" As soon as the cab got to the location he wanted, he helped the old man out.

Arnie looked around at the harbor and smiled. "Now this brings back memories," he murmured.

"Yeah, what memories?"

"I used to have a boat myself, way back when," he shared and smiled. "I lost my wife and my children in the divorce, and afterward I never seemed to make good decisions." He shook his head. "I lost everything at that point. So, it doesn't even matter."

"What is everything?"

"Way too much to say. I did the things you do because you don't know how to cope," he explained, with a head-shake. Simon urged him on, and, with the little dog now in his arms, directed Arnie down to the *Running Mate.* As the old man stood on the wharf and looked around under the graying sky, he whispered, "Good God."

"What?" Simon asked. "Don't you like her?"

"Of course I like her," he declared, grinning from ear to ear. "You giving me a place to stay for a day or two, aren't you?"

"A day or two while I try to figure out what the options are," he shared. "I know about women shelters because I help them out, but I don't know that I've ever seen anything for old men."

"No, I don't know that there is anything. It's not a sexist thing. It's just that we're supposed to always look after ourselves," he noted, with half a smile. "And we can, … right up until we can't."

"And that's the hard part," Simon murmured.

"It's very hard because we don't try to *not* look after ourselves," he clarified. "It's something else entirely."

As Simon got him into the boat and down into the cabin and explained how everything worked, the old man turned to him and nodded. "I just want a place to lie down. I swear to God I'll be dead in forty-eight hours anyway." Simon stopped to stare at him. He nodded. "I'm not kidding. I really am done."

"Your willpower might be done," he countered, "but that doesn't mean your body is."

"Isn't that the truth," the old man muttered, staring at him. "Okay, we'll do it your way. See if you can find a place for me and Elsie here."

Elsie was already curled up on the couch against the blankets, still shivering. Simon walked over and couldn't help himself from tucking the little dog in. He looked back at the old man. "When did you eat last?"

Arnie shrugged. "Neither one of us eats much anymore. It's one of the ways that you can tell that you're getting there," he murmured. "We just don't really care a whole lot for food."

"Maybe Elsie here does."

"Nope, Elsie really doesn't. She just wants a place to curl up and die too."

"Jesus," Simon muttered, staring at him.

"You're angry, and I get that. It's kind of nice, young man."

"You can call me Simon."

Arnie smiled. "It's a surprise to see anybody angry about something like that," he said, "but life is really simple at this stage. We really just want a place to be safe."

"So, what was happening in that warehouse? You said, *they would come back.*"

"Yeah, some assholes," he muttered, with a careless wave. "The world seems full of them when you're run-down and out of luck. But they were ... I don't really know what they were doing. I don't think they saw me, but I figured, if I stuck around, they would eventually run across me. They were doing some fighting."

Simon lit the gas fireplace and sat down beside him. "When you say, *fighting,* tell me more."

"Yeah, I don't really understand." Arnie shrugged. "It seemed they were fighting, but it didn't seem to be a fair fight." He yawned at that and rolled over, so he could curl up to the warmth of the little fireplace. "You're a blessed man, indeed," he murmured.

"Maybe now," Simon noted, "what I do know for sure is that, if you can do something, you should do it."

Arnie looked at him, his aged face shivering, and he

smiled. "And again, that's the young idealistic part of your heart. Most of the world doesn't give a crap."

"I'm not most of the world," Simon declared. "Now, get some rest, and I'll make sure some food is here when you and Elsie wake up." And then he waited, while Arnie closed his eyes and fell into a deep sleep.

Simon got up, grabbed blankets from one of the cupboards. When he turned around to cover up Arnie, the poor shivering dog was now tucked up and sound asleep beside her owner. Simon put the blankets around them both, smiling. "Not exactly the rescue I expected today," he whispered to himself, "yet why not?"

And with a self-satisfied smile on his face, he turned and headed toward Kate, knowing that her reaction could go either way. Regardless it wouldn't matter because Simon meant what he had said to the old man. There was no room in his world for people who weren't on board with helping others.

He highly doubted Kate would have an issue with it. She might have an issue trying to find Arnie and Elsie a place to go because it didn't seem any such place existed. Simon found that a difficult aspect too. But that wasn't today's issue. Right now, it was all about making sure he got home and got some of the leftovers before Kate ate them all.

CHAPTER 6

KATE STARED AT Simon and blinked, then blinked again. "And you took him where?" she asked cautiously.

"He's down at the *Running Mate,*" he replied. "I didn't know where else to put him right now."

She just nodded, but inside her mind was still drawing a blank. "I'm really surprised you took him to the *Running Mate.*"

"In a way, I am too," he admitted, eyeing her intently. "I wasn't sure what to do with him. I did ask you about shelters, but there didn't seem to be an easy answer for him."

"Yes, of course. ... While there are shelters for men, you're right. They don't seem to allow pets," she agreed.

Simon frowned, adding, "So, there's a business opportunity."

Her eyebrows shot up. "I don't think anybody would consider a shelter for homeless men and their pets as being a business opportunity," she noted carefully. "I think, in most cases, that would be considered financial suicide, assuming it's run the same as the women's centers."

"Which is also wrong," he snapped.

She nodded. "From your perspective I can see that, but, short of good citizens willing to step up and to do something more, it's definitely an issue." He grumbled about it but didn't say a whole lot more. She stared down at the leftovers he was serving up. "Did you take him food?"

He turned to her and steadied his gaze. "Not yet. Honestly, I'm not even sure he'll be alive when I get back there."

Her face was almost a mask, and she knew it, because she was still trying to figure out how to react. The fact that he had done this was so very much *Simon*. It was the part of him that she didn't see very often.

"Are you upset?" he asked, turning to look at her.

"No, not it all. It's you being *you*, and I like that. I was just thinking back and remembering how much of you I don't necessarily know."

He stared at her and then went back to serving up the food.

"I realize this is something you would do," she shared, "and I think, the farther along in life that you get, the more of this you'll do. So, I was thinking that you might want to set up something a little more … official."

He turned to her. "What does that mean specifically?"

She shrugged. "I don't know about these buildings that you rehab. I don't know anything about your financial situation," she began, choosing her words carefully, "but …"

"But what?"

There was almost an aggressive note in his tone. She took a step back and added, "But maybe you would want to consider setting up something that would be available to men like him."

He stared at her, then brushed back the damn lock of hair from his forehead that just drove her crazy. "That would also be very typical of *you*," he said finally.

"What's that?" she asked, as she sat down across from him and reached for the plate he handed her.

"Instead of moaning and groaning or complaining about

the system and just helping where I can, you're telling me to step up and to do more." He gave her a wry look. "When you first started talking, I was afraid you would be upset."

"I'm not upset, and I shouldn't even be surprised because it is very much you," she stated, with half a smile. "But I have to admit that I was surprised to hear that you took him to the *Running Mate*. ... That felt like it was just *ours*. So, I didn't know what to say."

He nodded. "And I won't argue with that because I had some qualms over that aspect as well," he shared and grinned at her. "But it's still ours, and, in a way, Arnie and Elsie taking refuge there makes it ours even more."

She laughed. "I can see that too," she stated, with a smile. "Does he need to see a doctor?"

"He says he's well past a doctor. He's dying and so is his little dog," he told her. "Honest to God, ... I won't be at all surprised if they're not alive when I go check on them."

She nodded. "In which case, you gave them a nice warm place for their last night on earth."

"Yeah, I was hoping you would see it that way."

"I'm not an ogre," she muttered, "not at all, and I know your heart is a whole lot bigger than you're allowing other people to know about."

"People take advantage of you if they know your weakness," he pointed out.

"They can, but that doesn't mean they will, because not everybody is out there to take advantage of others."

He laughed. "Is that really you saying that?"

She winced. "Yeah, it's me," she muttered. "It's funny how something like this brings out such different reactions. ... I have no right to the *Running Mate*." She shook her head. "It's yours, but it's felt kind of special, as if it was ours. And you're right. It shouldn't make a difference that you're helping somebody in a big way for whatever time period he has left, as long as you realize that it could be months."

"It could be—or even longer than that. For all I know, he lied, and he's not sick at all."

"But you don't believe that."

"No," he replied, staring at her. "He did look quite ill."

She didn't say anything for a bit. "I'm not sure what is available, officially at least. I know the shelters don't allow for pets, so, depending on the state of his dog, that could change Arnie's outlook fairly quickly."

Simon nodded. "Elsie didn't look like she would make it through the night at all. She seemed so cold, although she was looking better when I left her snuggled up against him."

Kate nodded. "It's a tough world out there for the homeless, and it's even tougher for those who have pets. They want the pets because of the companionship, and, in some cases, they've had these pets for a very long time. Then their circumstances changed, and they found themselves homeless," she explained. "So, for him, it would be a heartbreak to lose his beloved pet."

"And yet I think he almost feels it would be a kindness for Elsie to die because things have been so rough."

"Of course," she murmured. She took several bites, wondering at the softness of a man like Simon. "I guess you'll just have to do something about it then," she declared, with a shrug.

He tilted his head at her. "It won't be easy."

She smiled. "Maybe not that easy, but I don't think it'll be that hard, not for you."

Frustrated, he shook his head. "I think you expect too

much of me."

She laughed. "I don't know that I expect too much from you," she argued, as she looked across the table. "But, when we see a problem, something that needs to be addressed, we need to look for a solution. And, if this is a problem that you see as needing to be addressed, then we need to find a solution."

Glum, he nodded. "And I can clearly see from your point of view that's exactly what you're thinking," he replied. "I'm just not sure I'm at that point."

"No, of course not," she said, with amusement. "That's because you're still thinking that, when you go back there, you can send him on his merry way, and everything will be hunky-dory. Like he'll heal overnight, and the dog will be fine to go out in this terrible weather. You do realize we have a storm coming for the next few days, right?"

"I didn't even check on that," he muttered, as he stared down at the table.

"Nor should you," she added. "Your heart is always in the right place, and I'll never argue with that. You might just want to see if we can find a long-term solution for him."

He smiled over at her and added, "That would make more sense, wouldn't it?"

"You gave him a place, a safe space in a rough world," she noted, "so don't ever feel bad for that. Now it's a matter of finding a long-term strategy that would work for him, for Elsie, and for you."

"And I have no idea what that is," he admitted, sitting back and staring at her. "I really didn't expect to run into this."

"You could contact some people for ideas, and your women's center might very well be one of them."

"Yes, that's true. I could contact Lisa and see what she knows about options for men."

"Exactly. I'm sure something is out there," she murmured. "I'm just not sure it'll be the answer to what you really need right now."

"Of course not," he said. "I didn't even think about Lisa as a possible avenue for more info."

"And that's fine," she murmured. A smile drifted across her face. "You really are all heart, aren't you?" He glared at her, and she chuckled. "I know. You don't want anybody to know that."

"And yet you already do know it apparently," he muttered in disgruntled disdain, as he worked at his food. "Why aren't you eating? You are not even tasting it."

She patted his hand. "I really do love everything that I pick up from you," she shared. "I don't particularly care if the powers that be agree or not. There isn't enough heart in the world as it is, so, anytime I see a little bit extra, it makes me happy."

"You better watch it," he teased. "Otherwise your coworkers won't understand you either."

"Not sure they do now," she stated, with a smirk. "I admit we're definitely dinosaurs in a world that doesn't quite understand. Yet that's okay too."

He laughed and looked better. "I knew that you came from the heart," he admitted, "but I wasn't sure how you would feel about helping a stranger."

"How about that old line," she noted, "*a stranger is just a friend I have yet to meet.*"

He laughed. "The world doesn't function like that."

"I know," she agreed, "but, the more I'm around you, I realize that's too bad and that we need more people to function like that. We need more heart in this world," she stated. "I won't argue with that. But I do think you have potentially addressed a need that we as a community might want to take a look at. The problem for me is that I don't make the kind of money you do," she pointed out, with a laugh, "so I'll offer ideas as I get them."

"You don't make the money I make is so true." He rolled his eyes. "You don't make any money. I don't know how anybody would even decide to do the work you do when the pay is so poor."

"That's because you're coming at it from a very different point of view, remember?" She chuckled. "We're not doing it for the money. It's more of a calling."

"A calling where you're broke all the damn time? You live paycheck to paycheck. The only reason you probably even function at all with the money you make is because of the fact that you don't have any time to do anything to spend it on," he offered, shaking his head.

"Maybe not," she agreed, "but it never bothered me."

"Until now?"

"Not until I consider wanting to do something to help others," she shared, "and then a bit of extra money would come in handy."

"It would," he agreed. "It's not required because people like me do make money. As such, I know plenty of others who make money too. Besides, any time I got low on funds, I could just gamble a little to boost things up again." He laughed as she eyed him curiously. "I haven't had to do that for a while, not since the last building sale went through."

"I'm glad to see that you do sell some of them," she added, with a snort.

"Only some of them. The others I keep for rentals, and,

as long as I can make it cost-effective, I'm happy to work on those," he explained. "It's just not always cost-effective, and that's when my heart and my emotions get caught up in it, and that's a death knell for a business."

She smiled. "I don't know about that, not with you anyway. I think, when it comes to business, you're pretty shrewd."

He grinned. "Just don't tell anybody else that. Now"—he sat back, a wineglass in his hand—"did you want to tell me about your day?"

She shrugged. "Let's just say it was a strange day." She hesitated, then asked, "Did you pick up anything else on this fight mess?"

"Nope, nothing," he replied. "The whole reason I even found Arnie is because of that strange inclination I didn't want anything to do with."

"Yet you went into that spooky warehouse, even after you knew something awful was inside. … Well, classic you, I guess." She just shook her head.

"He did say something about fighting though." He frowned. "I forgot about that."

"What did he say?" She stared at him intently.

"Just that some discussion was going on about fighting, like an unfair fight," he replied, with a shrug. "I know that's very nebulous."

"That would be beyond nebulous," she declared, still studying him.

"Maybe we need to talk to him. He had been outside and needed to get in out of the cold, even though he didn't like anything about this place because of some guys that he'd seen there. Also needing to get his little dog out of the cold, he went in and figured, if they killed him, it was nothing off his back. To some degree they would just be putting him out of his misery, so it didn't really matter either way. At least that's the impression I got from him."

"Maybe," she muttered, "but if there's more to it than that …"

"I know. We can go talk to him, if you want."

"Yes, because if illegal fighting is going on anyplace, or if people are being taken to fight," she noted, "I do need to know about it."

"Right," he agreed, with a smile. "In that case, let's finish up here, and we can go talk to him."

"You think he'll be awake?"

Simon frowned at that and shrugged. "I'm not sure whether he will be or not, but, if you need to ask about what he overheard, we need to go regardless. Besides, I need to get him some food anyway." He looked over at the leftovers and pointed. "What do you think about this?"

"I think it would be fine," she replied. "There's probably about the right amount, though we don't really know what his stomach can handle."

"He did say something about not eating much anymore, so food wasn't a big part of his world right now. Same for Elsie, his dog."

"Of course not," she muttered. "What about the dog?"

"I was wondering about that. What do dogs do in this situation? What do they eat?"

She looked at him and grimaced. "Probably anything … because they don't have a choice. When you're hungry, it just doesn't matter."

He nodded. "And both you and I have experienced that, haven't we?"

She smiled. "A very long time ago, thankfully."

"Right, sometimes it's easy to forget the rougher times, isn't it?"

"Sometimes. Yet sometimes there's no forgetting it either," she stated, her tone odd. "Some of these cases just bring it all back up again."

"Let me take this with us, and"—he looked around and then walked over to the fridge—"a little bit of sliced meat is here. I can bring some of that for the dog." He quickly packed up what he thought the dog would eat, or at least a few options.

As they walked down to the boat, she surveyed the weather and noted, "It's about to get really ugly."

"I know," Simon noted, "but I won't kick him out when that happens."

"Of course you won't," she stated, with a smile. "You won't kick him out at all at this point." When he glared at her, she laughed. "You might as well just give it up. Until you find him a place, he'll be here. So no point in eyeing me like that."

"Maybe," he muttered, "but I wasn't thinking long-term."

"You weren't thinking," she clarified. "You were reacting to your feelings." When they reached the *Running Mate,* she motioned him on. "Go on in and see how he is. See if he's awake and if he needs anything, before I come in. He might be pretty terrified of the cops."

"I didn't consider that," Simon admitted, stopping as he went to board.

"Doesn't matter," she said, "because now he's somebody I do need to talk to—if only to rule out the possibility that he has heard something that could be relevant."

Simon nodded, and, with that, he turned and boarded the *Running Mate.*

SIMON WALKED DOWN the stairs to the low berth, where the old man was curled up in a ball. He was sleeping, but he woke up with a start.

He stared for a long moment at Simon. "Are you here to kick me out?" he asked, his voice raspy.

"No," Simon declared in a forceful tone. "I'm here to bring you food."

Genuine surprise appeared in Arnie's gaze, as he stared at him. "That was mighty kind of you." He shifted upward, and Elsie whimpered in her sleep. She'd been tucked up beside him and reacted to the cold air from his moving the blanket. He quickly wrapped her up again. "She doesn't have much longer in this world," Arnie noted, as he looked down at his dog. The tears weren't evident but they weren't far away, and it was obvious from his tone.

"I guess I've been selfish, keeping her with me, but, when times are tough and ugly, you don't always have the answers or the comforts that you want. In this case I thought maybe it would be nice to have her with me. Yet she's suffered for it too."

"Maybe," Simon replied, "but that doesn't mean she would have wanted to be anywhere without you."

"Maybe," Arnie agreed, as he shuffled to sit up comfortably.

Simon added, "Look. My partner is a cop."

Immediately Arnie looked worried. "*Uh-oh.*"

"It's all right, but I mentioned to her what you told me about the warehouse and about the fighting."

He just nodded, staring at him, as if waiting for the shoe to drop.

"She just wanted to ask you a few questions."

The old man relaxed back and sighed. "She can ask questions, but that doesn't mean I'll know the answers." He spoke as if he'd spent way too much time dodging questions in his life.

Simon laughed. "No need to tell a lie in this case," he stated, amused at the way Arnie spoke. "She just needs to know about the fighting."

"Not about anything else I might have seen?" he asked, his gaze narrowed.

"Unless it's criminal," Simon clarified, "and then she would like to know. She has a case that has some peculiarities, and it might have some fighting involved in it."

He sucked in his breath at that. "There's been some rumors for a while."

"Rumors about what?" he asked and then held up a hand for Arnie to wait. He opened the cabin door and called out to Kate.

Moments later, she appeared in the berth down below. She looked over at the old man and smiled. "I'm Kate."

He looked at her carefully for a moment, then relaxed. "I'm Arnie," he murmured. "At least that's what they've called me since forever."

"Arnie," she murmured, "you mentioned something about hearing sounds of fighting or something along that line to Simon here."

At the mention of Simon's name, the old man looked at him intently. "Are you Simon?"

"I am," he confirmed, "and I did tell you that in the beginning."

He shrugged. "Ain't no use for names in my world. Generally we don't have them, or we make them up as we go along," he shared, with a sigh. "I don't remember what my name was."

"Yet you would remember if you needed to," Simon pointed out, "but we also know how easy it is to let some of these things slide because it's easier and a whole lot less … painful."

"Yeah. At one point in time," Arnie shared, "I had a wife and children. My oldest died, suicide. Never knew he was so … fed up with everything. God only knows what happened to the others. I think … she remarried and headed off. I don't know about my daughter."

Simon wondered what it took to end up with such a drastic life change as that, but he knew it wouldn't be a good story, and that's not what he and Kate were here for right now. Besides, Simon didn't want to bring up any more torment for the old man. Arnie was obviously suffering physically, and emotionally as well.

"If I can get your name," Kate began, "I could track them down and let them know …"

When she didn't finish that sentence, he looked over at her with a nod. "I would be grateful. They may not have wanted to know much while I was alive, but I want to let them know if I'm not here anymore."

"I can do that," she said.

He sighed. "Don't even know what to tell ya about the warehouse. … It's not as if I have any answers for you," he suggested, eyeing her shrewdly.

"Nobody has answers," she declared, "at least not all the time. I just want to know what you heard."

He thought about it and nodded. "It didn't hear much, just the sounds of somebody getting beat up," he muttered, "and something about, … just voices, urging, taunting someone to fight."

"Right," she replied. "Did you recognize the voices?"

He shook his head.

"Did you ever see any faces?"

He shook his head again. "I try hard to stay away from everybody," he explained. "Most of them are much more likely to send a boot in my direction than any act of kindness. Simon appears to be very different."

Kate nodded. "He is because he comes from the heart."

"That will get your ass kicked," Arnie muttered.

"And it might," she agreed, "but, if that were to happen, I would be the one right at his side to make sure that I punished that person."

Arnie looked at her and laughed. "I know what you think you'll see," Arnie stated, with an odd look, "but it's an ugly world out there."

"I know, and I deal in it every day. I'm in the trenches with all kinds of ugliness that you don't even want to think about. Although you've seen a lot of it, you haven't seen all of it, and you don't see the level that I see, any more than I've experienced what you've seen," she shared. "Back to the fighting, any idea who?"

"No, I don't know," he replied. "Honestly, I don't want to know. Something damn scary is going on in that building."

"Why that building?"

"I don't know," he admitted, "except it's was slated for demolition at one time but nothing happened. It's really not safe to even be in there. I guess maybe half of me was hoping it would come down while I was in there, and I wouldn't have to worry because the old girl and I could go at the same time." He looked over at Elsie, a sad look on his face. "We'll go pretty close to the same time but not the exact same."

Kate nodded and just sat here and waited.

He frowned and then shrugged. "In theory I won't be around in case somebody ever does get caught for this. So no good reason not to tell you what I heard. The last time some man said he wasn't a fighter and didn't understand why he was there. Somewhere around that statement I eased out of the building and left. No good can come from hearing comments like that."

"No, of course not," she agreed. "It does imply that somebody was being coerced."

"People are always being coerced," Arnie declared, staring at her.

She nodded. "True, but I do have an interest in this," she stated, "and it's something I can't just let rest."

He frowned. "Might be better if you did."

"Maybe," she acknowledged.

"You can get killed yourself too, you know?"

"Maybe," she conceded, sending a wry smile in his direction. "Still doesn't mean I can stand by and let other people get killed as well. So, what's the talk on the street? You seem to be doing a good job of avoiding telling me something."

He frowned. "I don't know about the rest of the street," he began, and again that same tone creeped up. "I just think some weird person out there is wreaking havoc."

"Have you seen him?"

He hesitated, then sighed. "I could say, yes, but, in truth, … I wouldn't recognize him. He always wears a hoodie pulled up over his head, always looking like a ninja—you know, black hoodie, black sweats, black shoes, and black gloves."

He shook his head at that. "I swear to God those damn gloves always give me nightmares. I try to avoid him, but I did get stuck inside that warehouse after a storm broke. It's not a good place for us to be." He looked over at Simon. "You've been very kind. This is much nicer."

Simon nodded, giving Arnie a smile.

"It's a lovely boat and …" Arnie hesitated.

Simon added, "You aren't leaving today or tomorrow."

The old man relaxed visibly. "Seriously? Elsie and I can stay?"

"Yes, I'm trying to find a place where you can go permanently."

"They won't take my girl," he reminded him, patting Elsie. "So, I've just been waiting."

"I understand," Simon replied, "and she's suffering while the waiting is going on."

"I thought maybe she would just not wake up one morning," he explained, tears coming to his eyes. "And I know that's probably not something I should wish for. I just thought it would be easier on her."

"I'm sure it would be," Simon noted, "but that doesn't mean that's the only answer available to you."

"As long as I don't want to leave her, it is," Arnie declared, staring at him. "There's really no place for those of us with pets."

Simon frowned, as he stared off in the distance. "There's really not a whole lot of places for you anyway, is there?"

"There's the shelter," he replied. "If I get in early enough, I can get a meal and a bed. But there's never enough beds, so you have to line up. As soon as you're moved back out, you have to start lining back up again. And, most of the time, I'm okay to do that because the food is there, but not everybody in that line is decent."

"Does the line give you trouble?" she asked curiously.

He shrugged. "Sometimes lots of people are down on

their luck, lots of people who haven't had an easy time of it," he described. "That makes people desperate. I'm an old man and easily picked on. I just don't want to get picked on by the wrong people. I know I'm dying, and I was just hoping to go out on my own."

"Of course," she murmured.

"You say *of course*," Arnie noted, with half a smile. "Yet it's tough out there, and that makes it almost impossible for some of us."

"Right now," she pointed out, "you're doing okay, and we'll see what the morning brings."

He looked at her and asked, "You won't tell your guy here to not help me?"

"No, of course not. The *Running Mate* belongs to him," she replied. "I would never interfere."

He looked at her for a long moment and then nodded. "In that case, I really want to stay for a few days—until I can at least dry out enough to handle the weather again, plus for Elsie here. I don't think she'll make it even that long."

Simon looked over at the dog, sleeping at Arnie's side. "And then you'll have to decide if it would be a kindness to not have her sleeping like this."

"Thought of that too," he muttered, "but there's really no money to help her out in that way. And, honest to God, part of me is jealous. Why can't we have something like that for people?"

"There is in Canada," Kate shared, studying him, "and that is something you could pursue if you wanted to, but it won't be fast and easy."

He laughed. "Nothing in the medical system is. I'll be dead beforehand."

She smiled. "Or maybe not. Maybe you will make it past

all this."

He looked at her and shook his head. "No," he stated forcefully. "I already know my time is coming. The question is whether I can make it until after my girl goes first."

CHAPTER 7

KATE GOT UP the next morning, her mind full of the old man sleeping in the *Running Mate*. As she headed out to the kitchen, she looked at Simon. "Will you check in on Arnie today?"

"Of course." He nodded. "I'll confirm there's some food for him this morning."

She suggested to him, "You could always offer to pay for euthanasia for his dog."

"I've thought about it," he said, with a sad smile. "I think, in his mind, he wants Elsie to go on her own."

"Sure, and maybe that's an option. I don't know. As long as she's not in pain, that's fine, but at some point in time ..." She left it at that because she was already late for work and only so much she could say in this case.

As she walked out, he snagged her into a hug and just held her. She hugged him back, and then he leaned down, kissed her, and added, "Look after yourself out there." And, with that, he turned and headed back into the kitchen.

She walked outside, still thinking about Simon as she got into her vehicle and headed to work. They'd come so far, and yet, in so many ways, they still had a way to go. But she was definitely learning to understand who he was and what he was up to. When she walked into the office, Reese was dropping off information on her desk. "What have you got?" Kate asked.

"It's more information on the three other cases I gave you," she replied. "I contacted the detectives in each one. Everybody more or less said that they were muggings and really not worth another look. However, when I told them that we had two similar cases on our desks, that got quite a bit of interest from all of them. So, these are a few answers to my follow-up questions for you." Reese stopped in the process of turning back to her desk and added, "None of them were much of a help except that it establishes a pattern."

"Meaning that nobody knows, nobody sees, nobody was around in any of those three cases?"

"Exactly." Reese gave her a sad smile. "Nobody saw anything." With that, she returned to her office.

When Rodney walked in, Kate stood up, grabbed her coat, and announced, "Come on. We're heading out."

"Okay, where are we going?" he asked, even while in the act of taking off his jacket.

"Downtown to a warehouse area, where someone says they heard somebody crying out about not being a fighter and not wanting to get involved."

Rodney's eyebrows shot up. "You have a witness?"

"Nothing so clean or simple as that," she replied, with a wry look in his direction.

"Simon?" he asked in delight.

"No, God no," she muttered. She punched her partner lightly as she passed him, still heading to the door. "And you shouldn't be so happy if it was."

"Hey, if we can get information, I don't care where it comes from."

"Oh, I hear you, and sometimes I agree. In this case, although the witness is involved, a completely different scenario is happening. Just don't ask me how it all came about because I haven't quite figured that out yet."

"Good." He smiled. "Let's go, and you can fill me in on the way." As they walked outside, he added, "You better let me drive."

"And why is that?" she asked, looking at him with suspicion.

He grinned. "Because you tend to be a little more preoccupied these days."

"I am not."

"Are too," he noted, with an equally childish response. She rolled her eyes as she got into his vehicle and gave him the address for the warehouse in question. As they pulled up to the derelict building, he found a place to park. Approaching the old building, she walked up the front steps.

He looked at her and muttered, "This is a pretty interesting area."

"Is that what you call it?" she quipped, as she stared at it. "It looks pretty dodgy to me."

"Me too," he agreed, "which is why I'm fascinated that we're even here."

"If there was another location, I would be there," she declared, "but, in this case, it looks as if we're supposed to be here." As she walked into the main part of the warehouse, she heard the echoes of the empty hollowness all around her. "Is there anything more dead than a deserted building that has sat unloved for all these years?" she muttered.

"I think this one is slated for demolition," Rodney shared, as he pulled it up on his digital files. "It's also a bad area for drug deals and prostitution."

"Of course it is," she muttered. "It's really free housing, and everybody will treat it that way."

He looked over at her. "You're in an odd mood this morning."

"Yeah, you could be right," she conceded, and then she told him about the old guy that Simon had brought home.

"He took him to the *Running Mate?*" Rodney asked in astonishment.

She looked over at him and nodded. "Yes, and the old guy, Arnie, he's waiting for his beloved pet to pass on before he tries any of the shelters."

"Good God," Rodney muttered. "Poor guy. What a way to die, waiting for you and your pet to cross over."

"I know, but, not having had a pet all my life, I don't necessarily understand, although I'm not against it," she added. "It's obvious to me that the dog is very important to him. Plus, Elsie looks as if she may not make it through the weekend."

Rodney nodded. "I tell you though, some of those old dogs, they may look that way, but they keep going for years."

"And that is a real concern in this case because I think Arnie's counting on her passing first, so he can get a little more comfortable somewhere. And, of course, Simon is chomping at the bit to change the world because there doesn't appear to be any decent housing for men, not the way there is for women."

"But this guy wouldn't qualify anyway." Rodney shrugged. "He's not abused, he's just homeless, and that's an entirely different story."

She nodded. "Agreed, but the whole thing has sent Simon off in a couple different directions."

"If he's got the money, I guess he can always start something."

She laughed. "I pretty well told him the same thing."

"I'm sure he loved that."

"Not necessarily, but he does understand why we would say it because we see the problems. Still, it's really hard to find anybody who'll help."

"You're not kidding, especially not the government. Shelters are around here, and I think one for men is nearby," he pointed out, "although it might be privatized."

"I'm not sure that anything like that can be privatized, but I can understand it being private," she clarified.

"Exactly."

"So, the question that remains is whether there is a place for this guy to go to, or is he stuck on the streets until … ?"

Rodney stared at her as they walked through the lower levels of the building. "He's stuck if he can't get into one of the shelters. They obviously have an overcrowding problem, and we never have enough places for anybody who needs a shelter. Still, we have somewhere he can go, but he must sign back up the next day to get a hot meal, then turn around and carry on over and over again. At least until the weather warms up."

"God, what an existence," she muttered, shaking her head at it.

"And it's not just him," Rodney added.

"No, it isn't. Quite a few people live like that."

"We see them in our work all the time," he noted. "It's interesting that this one really got to Simon."

"He got to Simon—or maybe it was the pet. Arnie seems pretty taken with Elsie," she noted, with a smile. "Last I saw Elsie, she was tucked up in a blanket and looked as if she was in heaven."

"Probably warm for the first time in many days," Rodney noted. "People forget about how the pets don't have an easy time of it when their owners are homeless."

"I can see that," she said. As they walked through the building, she looked around, taking in the interior. "Empty, derelict, and yet not, somehow."

"What does that mean?" Rodney asked.

"A spooky atmosphere hangs over the entire place," she shared, still looking around, frowning.

He grinned. "I love how Simon is rubbing off on you. You could yet end up being a psychic yourself." She turned and stared at him in horror, making him burst out laughing.

"God, why would you even say that to me?" she muttered. "Don't I have enough issues already?"

"You sure do," he confirmed, with a big grin. "On the other hand, maybe those issues are things you can deal with in a different way."

"*Sure,*" she muttered, with an eye roll. "Enough talk about psychics." But just then came a slight crash upstairs that made them both freeze. She looked at him and whispered, "Meet you at the top." And, with that, she took off running.

He swore behind her, as he tried to catch up, but he was huffing and puffing when he finally reached the third floor. He almost slammed into her.

She held out a hand and pointed. And there, off to the side, was what appeared to be somebody crawling on the floor. She called out, "Hello, we're the police."

A quiver came from the form on the floor, and the man whispered, "Help me, please. Dear God, please help me."

She walked over, her weapon ready, as Rodney did a quick search around them. As she approached, she looked at the man and asked, "Are you in need of assistance?" When he looked up at her, she winced. His face had been pulverized and so swollen that she was certain he could barely see. She holstered her weapon and dropped down beside him. Calling out to Rodney, she said, "Get an ambulance in here now."

The man at her feet whispered, "Dear God, thank you, thank you."

"You want to tell me what happened?"

He shook his head. "I'm not even sure," he said, half sobbing. He made several attempts to get up, and then, with a cry, collapsed back down beside her, unconscious. It was twenty minutes later before the paramedics arrived, and he was loaded up and taken to the hospital.

Rodney looked at her grimly. "What the hell is going on here?"

"I don't know," she said, "but that could have been just a mugging."

"Just a mugging? Are you fucking kidding me? He was worked over pretty good."

"Yeah, I hear you loud and clear, but we also don't know exactly what happened."

"Yeah, damn it," he muttered. "So, off to the hospital now?"

"Off to the hospital for sure, but I want to continue searching around here first."

"What are we searching for?" he asked, as he looked over the gloomy interior of the building.

"Our man didn't give me any specifics," she noted, "but considering that we were talking about coming here and looking for information about fighting, it does interest me as to whether anybody was here with him. Maybe, if they were, they took off. What we don't know is whether or not they were planning on coming back. We've got to find a way to be sure of what's going on here." Then she frowned. "I really want cameras."

"Yeah? I want a Ferrari," Rodney muttered, turning to face her.

She rolled her eyes. "Thanks, that's really funny. But what would it take to set up a camera system in here to see if anybody came back?"

"Too much for our budget. So you expect them to come back?"

"I don't know," she admitted, with a shrug, "but, if our killer was looking for this guy to beat up again, or to dispose of his body, it would sure be nice to find out."

"So, you really think it's connected?"

"How can I not? Just think about the whole damn mess here. There's got to be some connection," she stated, staring at him. "Right now we already have five dead men, severely beaten up, and we just found another who's been beaten to a pulp."

"Sure, but we don't know if it has anything to do with it."

"But how will we ever find that out if we don't have cameras set up? It's not as if we can set up a security guard here for round-the-clock surveillance or anything."

"No, we sure can't," he muttered. "We need a small re-cording device even, but at least one on each of these three floors."

She nodded at that. "We should talk to Colby and see if we can get at least that. In the meantime, we've got people out canvassing the area, looking for anybody who might have seen or heard anything."

"And you know how that'll go."

"We can always hope," she said, as she looked at him. "It

is a unique location in town." As she stepped to a nearby window, she saw a group of homeless men standing off to the side. "I see some people I want to question."

"I'll come with you."

When they walked over toward them, they stepped back. She asked them, "You guys see any activity around here?"

Immediately they shook their heads.

"You guys seen anything that scares you around here?" she asked, thinking about Arnie, the old man in Simon's boat. Immediately they shook their heads again. She nodded. "I guess you wouldn't tell me even if you did, would you?" And once again they all shook their heads.

At her side, Rodney whispered, "I don't think anybody here will talk to you."

"They might," she declared, yet a weariness filled her tone. "It all depends on if you use the right method of persuasion." She looked at them and asked loudly, "Anybody interested in talking for a hot meal?"

Immediately all three men lifted their hands.

She nodded and added, "But I want the truth, nothing made up."

The hands stayed up.

Rodney frowned at her. "You know you shouldn't be doing this."

"What?" she asked. "Taking some people for a hot meal and hoping they have information that might help? It's not illegal."

"No, but it's probably ill-advised."

"Ill-advised is something I do on a regular basis," she declared, giving him a lopsided look. "So, *whatever*."

A coffee shop was around the corner, so, with the three homeless men slowly moving behind her, she walked there, looked at Rodney, and asked, "Do you want to go in and get stuff, or do you want me to?"

"You can," he muttered, rolling his eyes. "At least Simon will reimburse you."

She snorted. "I wouldn't even ask."

"You should." He grinned at her. "He wants to start dealing with the homeless, so maybe this is a good place to start."

Shaking her head, she looked at the men and asked, "Coffee?"

They all nodded, smiles on their faces. They were so alike it was hard to tell them apart. They all had the same messed-up clothes and looked as if they hadn't had a shave or a shower in days. Her heart went out to them.

She knew it was a bad idea, but, as she walked into the coffee shop, the waitress looked at her, held up a hand, and pointed. "They can't come in here."

"That's fine," she replied coolly, as she held up her badge.

"Oh, okay. Hopefully you'll haul them away with you," the waitress stated, her tone reflecting her attitude. "It's bad enough that they rummage through the garbage all the time, but, when they come around, they make a mess and keep the customers away."

"I understand that," Kate noted, then ordered enough food for all of them.

The waitress just shook her head and muttered, "If you don't make sure they eat it, they'll go trade it for something."

"Maybe," Kate acknowledged. "We'll see."

When the food was ready, she paid for it and took it outside. She'd picked up coffees for her and Rodney, as well. As the three men settled in to eat, she winced as she realized just how hungry they were.

When the first guy lifted his head, he looked at her, sheepishly. "That building is very scary," he began, almost a whine to his tone, and then he rubbed his nose several times. "We avoid it."

"Meaning you never go inside, even for shelter?" He nodded. "You ever see anybody around it?"

He shook his head. "But there's often voices, scary-ass voices coming out of that place," he muttered. "It's just bad news, a bad woo-woo place."

The second man lifted his head and nodded. "Any time we hear noises, we scuttle to the other side."

"You ever been attacked by anybody around here?"

The third man lifted his head and stared at her. "We try to avoid trouble when we can, but there are always punks, always somebody who thinks the way to make themself feel better about life is ..."

She was visibly surprised at his diction.

He shrugged at her reaction, then continued. "I used to teach school," he muttered.

"Sorry," she replied.

He raised rheumy eyes her way and nodded. "Me too, but sometimes life happens, and you take a turn, and there's just no coming back from it."

She winced. "I guess it depends on how bad the turn is and how much you want to come back from it."

"Again, that sounds easy and simple, but it's not." He shrugged.

"Look. I don't intend it to be ... This building, do you ever see anybody coming and going?"

Two of the men shook their heads, but the third one, the homeless schoolteacher, stared at her. "Why do you care?"

"Because of the man who was found inside that warehouse this morning. He's in pretty bad shape." She'd taken a picture of his face and held it up. "Do you recognize him?"

As they peered at it, squinting in order to see it, she realized they all probably needed glasses. If they didn't have decent vision, they probably wouldn't have seen anything outside either. She nodded as she looked over at them. "Do you guys need glasses?"

"I can see," the first guy said, "but he's pretty banged up so can't see much."

Kate nodded. "He is pretty banged up, and that's why I'm here asking questions."

"Nobody around here cares though," the first one added. "They just want us to keep moving on. Just like these guys." He pointed to the coffee shop.

"Are you guys the ones making a mess in their garbage?" she asked him, a smile on her face.

He flushed and shrugged. "Maybe, but they throw out food, and we need the food to survive out here."

"I get that," she stated, with a smile. "So maybe don't make such a mess, and maybe they won't have such a problem with it."

He frowned and looked over at his buddies, who just shrugged as if that was a foreign concept, but maybe they could give it a try.

She smiled. "I understand. They probably do throw food out, and you probably could really use that food," she acknowledged. "But, if you don't want them to get angry at you, maybe don't do anything to piss them off." They just stared at her, and she continued with her questions. "Is there anything else you can tell me about the building? Have you seen any businessmen-looking types there? Have you seen anything suspicious?"

"A businessman, … yes," the first guy replied, "but it's been a while."

"And you didn't see this man there before?"

"No," he said.

"Another old guy stayed in there all the time," the third guy shared. "He didn't like staying there, but he was trying to keep his old dog out of the weather. So, he would take the chance and go in some nights."

She nodded. "I know about Arnie, and he's warm and comfortable right now."

The third guy frowned at her. "More than we can say," he replied.

"At least you have food now."

He nodded. "Thank you for that."

She didn't comment on their situation, as it would be cruel. "Does anything else come to mind that might help me?" They again shook their heads, and she brought out business cards and gave one to each of them. "If you hear or see anything going on there, let me know."

"Why do you care?" the first man asked, frowning at her.

"Somebody has to," she said. "And I care about a lot of things."

"If you really cared," the first guy declared, with a snort, "you would see that the restaurant here doesn't chase us away all the time."

"That's what she just told us though," the third guy reminded his buddy impatiently, frowning at him. "If we didn't make such a mess, they probably wouldn't care, but we pull out all the garbage out and just leave it."

"Why would we throw the garbage back in?" the first guy asked. "We can't use it."

"Sure, but then we leave a mess that they have clean up, so they get mad at us."

The second man nodded. "It is something we could do."

"I suggest you do that part, and I'll talk to them about it," Kate suggested. "Maybe with a little effort on your part, they might change their attitude a bit and see you a little differently."

The men looked at her and then nodded. "We can try that," the third guy admitted.

"Good," she murmured. She looked back at Rodney and asked, "Shall we?"

Rodney stood up from where he'd been sitting, listening to everybody talk. "Can I get your names?" he asked.

"No," the three of them replied, almost in unison.

He smiled at them and added, "I'm not here to harm you in any way. I'm just hopeful that I don't end up in the same position." And, with that, he turned and walked toward where their car was parked. "Come on, Kate. Let's go."

She smiled at the men. "Have a good day." As she walked away, she heard them muttering behind her. She had taken several steps when the more articulate man called out. She turned to him, then took a few steps toward him.

He added, "If you can talk to the restaurant, about being nicer about us, we could tell you something."

"Good," she agreed. "Tell me something then." He hesitated, and she just waited, not saying anything. "Sometimes we've seen a vehicle parked around here, a van. A dark gray van."

She nodded. "Okay, and?"

He shrugged. "No reason for it to be here."

Kate suggested, "Drugs, prostitution, a mobile shack to

rent by the hour."

He shook his head. "Lights off, quiet, one guy skulking around all the time."

She stared at him. "And does skulking mean to you what it means to me?"

"It means exactly what it's always meant in the dictionary," he declared, staring at her.

"Good enough. A description?"

He shook his head. "No, none."

"Okay, and how about anything else to help identify it?"

He shook his head. "Just a dark gray color … to the point that it looks black."

"Smoked windows?"

He shook his head. "No, I can see inside."

"But you don't look inside," she guessed.

"God no, that's scary."

"Right." And, with that, the three of them stumbled backward.

"Ever hear his voice?"

He shook his head.

"What does he wear?"

"Black, always in black."

"Good enough. License plate?"

He shook his head.

"Didn't see one or doesn't have one?"

He looked at her, shrugged, and replied, "I don't know."

"Okay. When did you last see it?"

He frowned, then shrugged. "Maybe a couple days ago. Maybe last night." He looked at the others, and they just nodded.

"And when you say *last night*, is that a *maybe* or are you sure of it?" Kate asked.

He shrugged. "It was last night."

"Good enough," she said. "Where do you guys usually hang out, in case I want to talk to you again?"

They all shook their heads.

"If it helps to put your minds at ease, it comes with a meal," she added, a smile on her face. They just stared at her, and she nodded. "Just if I have more questions." All three of them, almost like the Three Scrooges, frowned at her. She smiled. "Hey, it wasn't too scary today, was it?"

They looked at each other, and one of them seemed to shuffle his feet bashfully, and finally he nodded. "You can usually catch us a couple blocks from here," he shared, "at Norman Square." And, with that, they turned, moving as fast as they probably could, and took off.

The fact that they were slow enough that she could watch as they left just made her smile. And, with that, she walked back into the coffee shop and talked to the waitress, who stood there, watching. Kate explained, "I've talked to them about not leaving you a mess when they dig in the garbage."

Her eyebrows rose. "And you really think they'll do that?"

"I would like to think so," she said, "because they really do want the food you're throwing out. And, when I explained to them what your problem was with that, they thought maybe they could be a little neater."

She snorted. "What a way is that to live?"

"Maybe it's just nice that it's not the way you and I have to live." And, with that, Kate turned and walked out.

SIMON WALKED TO the *Running Mate*, stopping to admire

the morning view. When he got to where his two guests were sleeping, and were both still alive, Simon was relieved.

The old man opened his eyes, looked at him, and smiled. Then he thought of Elsie. "Is she okay?" he asked.

Simon nodded at the dog, curled up beside Arnie. "You tell me," he said. "She's right beside you."

Arnie reached out a hand, felt her breathing, and sighed happily. Then he frowned. "I shouldn't be happy."

"Of course you should be. Every day you have with her is a gift."

The old man's eyes filled with tears, and he nodded. "Honest to God, it's been such a long time for me that I tend to forget decent people are out there."

Simon nodded. "I've seen some of the scum of the earth myself," he admitted, "so I do understand what you mean."

"I'm sure you do. You don't necessarily look like you've had the easiest life."

Simon laughed. "No, but I don't sit around and cry about it."

"No, you don't." Arnie shifted in the bed, then got up and stumbled to the bathroom.

When he came back out, Simon suggested, "While you're here, if you want a shower, go ahead." The old man looked at him gratefully. Simon also reached into his pocket for the disposable razors he had brought and added, "I don't have a shaver to give you, but I have these if you want them."

Arnie smiled at them in delight. "That would be lovely," he said, rubbing his chin. "It's been a long time, and I know I won't maintain it, but hey …"

Simon laughed. "Let's just go one day at a time." Then he held up the bag of food.

Arnie frowned at him. "I still have leftovers from yesterday."

"Yeah, maybe you do," Simon noted, his gaze intense. "And maybe you're just saving them, in case Elsie needs food."

The other man winced. "You saw that, *huh*?"

"Sure, I did," he murmured, "but I won't fault you for making sure the dog is fed, even if you go without."

"She's had such a tough life," he explained, "but she's made every day of mine easier."

"Which is why you do what you do," Simon said, with a gentle smile. He sat down and made sure that the old guy ate. Meanwhile, perking up at the smell of the food, Elsie came over and had a few bites, but only a couple. Simon looked over at Arnie closely.

He sadly studied her. "Her time's coming, I know."

"Her time's coming, and she'll be happy when it is time," Simon noted. "However, in the meantime ..."

"In the meantime," Arnie stated, "we are warm and dry, and, for that, we have you to thank. It's a hell of a boat."

"I bought it because I needed a way to get out and to release my soul to the wild," Simon shared, with a one-arm shrug.

"Oh, I get it," the old man replied. "And truly you are blessed."

"I am blessed," Simon agreed, with a smile, "and life has been good to me overall." He sat and visited for a little longer, then he said, "Okay, I have to get up and go to work."

"Good enough," Arnie replied.

"In the meantime, you enjoy your time here with Elsie." And, with that, Simon got up and headed downtown to his rehab projects. When he walked into the first jobsite, he looked around, frowning.

"Now what's that frown for?" his foreman called out.

He smiled and shook his head. "Oh, … just thinking."

"Yeah, but when you *just think*," his foreman noted shrewdly, "plans have a way of changing."

Simon nodded. "Yeah, they sure do. … I've just been thinking about the fact that there's really no place for the homeless."

"Oh, good God," his foreman muttered, staring at him. "There are places for the homeless, but just never enough places for them."

"And nothing for the seniors either."

"I don't know about that," he countered, facing Simon. "Where's all this coming from?"

Knowing that his foreman wouldn't be as accepting as Kate, Simon sighed. "Just seeing how pathetic it is out there sometimes."

"Sure, it is, but remember, if you don't make a profit, you can't turn around and do the next project. You will have tied up your money in an endless pit that you won't have any idea how to make up for."

"Oh, I know," Simon replied. "Speaking of which, I have to check in with the Realtor."

"You'll get the Queensborough?" he asked curiously, but an underlying excitement filled his foreman's tone.

"What do you think about it?" Simon asked him.

"Hell, I've been wanting to get my hands on that property for a long time," he shared, with a smile. "I really do think it would be a good one for you."

"Even if I decide to build a homeless shelter in its place?"

His foreman shrugged. "It's not a bad location for that, but a lot of people would be pissed off if you did."

"Maybe," Simon conceded. "It's probably not the right

location, given the district, but it would be ideal if we wanted to get into the hotel business."

"Or you could demolish it and then decide what will go there later," his foreman offered. "I'm not used to seeing you buy something that really needs to be dropped though."

Simon nodded. "I know, and that's why I'm still hesitant."

"Put in a really cheap offer because you know all too well that one will cost you."

Simon laughed, but he agreed with his foreman. This one would cost a bundle. But that didn't mean it would cost so much that it wasn't doable. As soon as he stepped outside, looking to contact Ariel, she was already calling him.

"I need an answer today," she stated impatiently.

"And I was just about to give you one."

"Good," she said. "I can't hold this much longer. They're getting very impatient and just want to get it done with."

"Yeah, well, they might not like what I'm about to offer though."

"Give me a price, and I can at least go back to them with it. If they don't like it, then you're off the hook. Unless you decide you want it anyway, and then you'll have to negotiate, the same as everybody else."

He laughed. "That's not happening."

"I know," she muttered, with a groan. "Anyway, what are you thinking?" When he gave her the price, dead silence came from the other end. "Wow," she finally said, "that is really low."

"It's a complete drop-down."

"You can't save her?"

"I don't think so," he said. "Believe me that I've been

looking at that. If anybody could restore her, it would be me. This would be the first of these grand old buildings that I decided would be better to drop. It's not my preference."

"I know, and that's one of the things the owners were really hoping for."

"I've taken it into consideration," Simon noted, "but she's had no care to even keep her in a safe condition while my people are working on her, so I'm not sure it's even doable."

"Do you want to put that offer in writing?"

"Do you think they'll go for it?"

"I don't think so, no," she declared, "but I'm not privy to their thought processes, especially considering their circumstances. I know that most people would say you're taking complete advantage of them, but that's also the industry."

"It is the industry," he confirmed, "and generally I don't take advantage, but this building is definitely no good as is."

"But, even if it would be a drop-down," she pointed out, "the land value alone is worth it."

"Yes and no," he argued. "You also have to consider what it'll cost not only to drop it but in taking care of all that asbestos, which will be a very significant expense."

"Oh God, death knells on my heart."

"Yeah, the minute we start talking *asbestos*, you and I both know that it can run hundreds of thousands to mitigate that."

"If that's all it is," she muttered.

"Exactly, so run that figure past them and see what they say."

"Will do." With that, she ended the call.

Simon turned to see his foreman grinning at him.

"At that price," he noted, "you can do whatever you want."

"Yeah, if they go for it," Simon reminded his foreman. "You and I both know that just because that may be what it's worth, it still doesn't mean they'll be willing to let it go for that."

"No, they shouldn't," he agreed, with a headshake. "Damn, it takes balls to make an offer so low."

"It's not so low," Simon argued, with a wry look. "It'll just feel that way to them. But the thing is, it completes something that they have held on to, and it also still makes them a ton of money. They left her too long without taking care of her, and it's gotten bad enough that she's more of a liability than an asset to them at this point."

Later that afternoon, when he got a phone call back from Ariel, the answer surprised him.

"They're willing," she stated abruptly.

He froze for a moment. "Seriously?"

"Yes. I don't know what the hell it is about you, but you're just completely shot with good luck."

"I wouldn't say that," he muttered, "and it's not a figure I came to lightly."

"No, and because I had already explained who you were and what you did with these old buildings, they were much easier about it. I also told them that you weren't sure it could be saved because so much structural damage has evolved, and that, with the asbestos throughout the whole building, would be an even bigger issue. I think in the end, the husband basically just decided they would take it. I got the sense that he didn't want any more headaches or hassles and probably knew they were on borrowed time with the city."

"Good for them," Simon said. "Draw up the agreement,

and I'll work on getting the financing in order."

"Good enough," she replied, and, with that, she rang off.

Distracted by the details of the transaction running through his head, when he stopped and looked around at where he was, he realized he stood right in front of the Queensborough. He smiled up at the building and muttered, "It's okay, old girl. You're in good hands now." And, with a smile and a jaunty step, he started to walk onward, when a voice stepped into his mind.

Help.

"Oh no, no, no," Simon muttered, as he turned around and looked. "I already helped, and the guy is safe." Then he winced because he didn't know if the guy was in the hospital or not. But, as far as Simon was concerned, he had done what he could do. The fact that he found the guy alive meant something.

He just didn't know how to get out of all these people calling on him all the time or whether he should even be trying to get out of it. Ariel was right, he begrudgingly acknowledged. In many ways, much of his life had been filled with luck. And then there were the other times, when it seemed as if everything and everyone had been against him.

It occurred to him that he should take notice when his life looked good and when it looked bad. Because maybe, if things were aligning, and he needed to help people in order to have his world move smoothly, then maybe that was a sign, and he should listen.

The voice was insistent, asking for help.

Hesitant, Simon slowly moved, once again urged back to that same damn warehouse where he'd found Arnie. As he got closer, he didn't expect to see Kate, hands on her hips, having a conversation with Rodney. She looked up, glanced over, and smiled.

His heart calming down after that last message for help, Simon walked toward them. "Hey," he murmured.

"Problems?" she asked, staring at him.

He shrugged. "Maybe."

At that, Rodney's eyebrows lifted. "*Uh-oh*, there can't be any *maybe*s."

"I know," Simon agreed, "but I just got … a call."

"What kind of a call?" she asked suspiciously.

He glanced at her and said, "Three guesses."

"So, one of those. *Great.*"

Simon asked, "Why? Has something else happened?"

"Yeah, we already found somebody this morning, when we came to look at the warehouse, after talking to Arnie."

"Found somebody?" Simon repeated.

"Yeah, and I don't know if he'll make it or not." She shrugged. "I haven't checked in at the hospital."

"But you already found him," Simon confirmed in delight.

She frowned at him and asked, "Is that who you think you're here for?"

"I don't know," Simon admitted. "Wouldn't it be nice if I could tell you?"

She smiled, then looked over at Rodney, who just stared at Simon.

Rodney nodded. "I guess you don't always know, *huh*?"

"No," Simon muttered, his gaze shifting around. "It would be nice if I did. It would be nice if I had any clarity at all," he shared in frustration. As he turned, he added, "I'll head out and get back to work."

The voice popped back up. *No.*

Simon stopped moving. He groaned, looked back at

Kate, and shared, "The voice won't let me go."

She straightened and asked, "Is he here?"

"I don't know," Simon replied, staring at her, misery in his eyes. "All I can tell you is it's not letting me move."

"Okay, does it want you to go inside?"

Almost immediately the weight on his feet was removed, and he relaxed. With a sigh, he smiled at her. "The weight lifted, so I guess that is what they want me to do."

"They?" she asked.

"I don't know. I can't say if it's a he, she, or they, so, ... did you check everything here?"

"We've done a quick run-through, and so did the patrol units who came out with the ambulance and all."

He nodded, as he listened to the voice in his head. "Based on the way they are going on about it, you probably missed someone."

"Someone or something?" Kate asked.

He frowned at her, heard the voice again, and declared, "Someone."

And, with that, they all bolted inside, Simon bringing up the rear.

CHAPTER 8

KATE DIDN'T WANT to put too much credence in Simon's psychic input, but neither could she ignore it. She hadn't personally done a full walk-through of the warehouse yet, delaying that when she had seen the three homeless men from the window and had gone outside. And now she was here once again, going step by step, room by room, floor by floor of this warehouse. The three of them had decided to split up to check out everything faster, but Simon remained close to her. She looked over at him with a scowl. "Any particular reason for the hovering?"

"Yeah," he declared, with a shrug. "It makes me feel better."

"Why is that? I've never known you to be the hovering type."

"I don't like this building," he snapped.

She stopped, slowly turned, studying him. "The three homeless guys I just spoke to thought it was more or less haunted too. They mentioned seeing somebody with a dark gray van who came through here often."

He nodded. "I don't know anything about the dark van, but I can tell you that this place has seen some ugly shit."

"*Great*," she muttered.

"Let's just see if you do have another person here," Simon suggested. As he waited for her search to complete, he kept steadily abreast of her.

When Rodney rejoined them from his side of the building, he shared, "Nothing is here."

"Good," Simon snapped. "I really don't want there to be any more."

"Of course you don't," Rodney said. "All the ghosts are talking to you."

As Kate walked through the top floor, she noted a bunch of garbage tossed off to the side. She raised an eyebrow as she looked over at Rodney.

He nodded. "Yeah, I checked. It's literally garbage."

She nodded and kept going, but she kept glancing back. Then finally, not allowing herself to even question her urge, she backtracked to the pile of garbage for a closer look. Definitely old tarps and paint cans, fast-food trash, and generally just a mess of leftover stuff had been thrown here. When she bent down to take another look, she noted something didn't belong.

Pulling gloves from her pocket, she put them on and lifted one corner of the stiffened tarp, and right there in front of her was a set of toes. She lifted it higher and found the toes were attached to a body, and the man who was here couldn't care less about anybody getting his toes. The body was cold. He was dead, and, by the looks of it, he had been dead for a very long time.

Rodney bent down beside her. "Damn, I was going by volume," he shared in disgust. "As in there couldn't be anything here because there just wasn't enough space for a human body to be here. I wasn't thinking of an old skeleton."

"It's not quite an old skeleton," she clarified, as she looked at it, "but it's not far off, that's for sure. The problem is, it's not been decomposing as much as it's been here long enough that it's pretty well been eaten down to nothing."

"And when you say, *eaten down?*" Simon asked, turning to look at her.

"Rats and anything else that needs food and sustenance. This is a body, a body that people will be quite happy to have the smell of its decomp limited," she noted, her nose scrunching. "It's January, and, although there is some decomp, this body has been here for a very long time."

Rodney stared down at the body and swore. "That's a hell of a way to dispose of a body."

Simon nodded. "The voice is quiet, so that's got to be what they were so adamant about."

"Good," she replied. "I would hate to think someone else was here."

Simon frowned. "I think that's it."

Rodney swore as he stood up and started making phone calls.

Kate still looked around at the rest of the area. "It's a very strange area for a dumping ground. Yet we don't even know if it's connected to my other current cases, so, for the moment," Kate decided, her tone glum, "we'll just treat it as a separate scenario."

"It's connected," Simon muttered.

"Yeah, I hear you," she murmured, as she turned to him. "But I, … I need to be as open about it as I can. So, for the moment, we'll treat it as a completely separate issue. Separate case, everything except for location. What I can tell you is, this one's been here for a very long time. I don't suppose that voice in your head"—she gazed him intensely—"wants to clarify how long or why he ended up here?"

"I don't think he has any idea," Simon noted.

"Is it a he?" Kate asked.

"I really can't say, but that voice skipped into my mind. Like so many of the voices I hear, they have no idea where they are or why they're there," he explained. "It's been the same as always, as you well know."

"I do know," she noted. "I know you get told what you get told. I just keep hoping that one day we'll have somebody who can say something more."

"Well, … Peter did."

"*Puppy*," she repeated, with a smile. "Yes, he did remember the puppy, didn't he?"

"Yes, he did, and that led to exactly what you needed."

"It did, indeed," she muttered, as she looked up at him. "And, for that, I'm very grateful for Peter."

"And he's grateful to both of us," Simon replied.

"And do you know anything about this guy, our skeleton?"

"No, I don't know anything." Yet he frowned, and his eyes turned glassy for a moment, and then the fog cleared. "Jay."

"Who's Jay? His name is Jay?" she asked Simon. "Or are you asking me to check something?"

He shrugged. "I don't know. He may be Jay, … which could even be Jacob or John, who the hell knows? … Or maybe it's the guy who killed him. I have no clue."

She filed that away for later and waved to Simon. "You might as well leave, as we'll be here for a while. We'll handle this. We'll have to wait for the coroner to show up for one thing. Smidge will love this."

"He can't blame you for this one, can he?" Simon asked her.

She smiled. "He doesn't blame me for any of them, but,

if they stay on the docket too long as unsolved, believe me that I'll get a talking to because I'm *not doing my job.*"

Simon shook his head. "I'm sure that goes over well."

"It hasn't happened to me yet, but it's happened to the others. So I guess they keep waiting for it to happen to me."

"Not happening," Simon declared. "You're closing an amazing number of cases."

She gave him a sideways glance. "And so are you," she added, her tone wry. "I wouldn't have even known about this one. I was hoping to get back around and through here, but it wasn't exactly high on my priority list either," she admitted. "So that's on me too."

"It's not on you at all," Simon countered, shaking his head. "You can't be expected to do everything."

"Nope, I can't, but I can tell you one thing. An awful lot of people are out here who seem to think I should be doing more than I am."

"Christ," he muttered, "that's not fair."

She laughed. "Nothing is fair. When you think of all the cases we still haven't solved, of all the people looking for answers, hoping beyond hope that we're doing our jobs, you know for a fact that nobody really gives a crap when we say we are doing our best."

"But you do," Simon stated. "I know you do. I see you inside and out."

"You're right. I do," she confirmed, as she looked down at the sad remains of a life cut short. Sadder still that this was someone who had apparently gone missing some time ago and seemingly hadn't triggered a response that generated any answers. "We'll find out who this person is, what the story was, and continue from there. But I suggest you get lost before the chaos ensues, and you get caught up and can't leave."

Simon winced. "I'm out of here." He gave a wave to Rodney, as Simon quickly disappeared down the stairs.

Rodney walked back over to Kate, with a long face.

She looked up at him and nodded. "I was still planning on doing a walk-through here anyway," she added. "So we would have seen him at some point."

"But I looked at this garbage," Rodney admitted, "and dismissed it as garbage."

She nodded. "I hear you, and I understand why it's upsetting you, but don't let it get to you. We all make mistakes, and it's easy to get callous and to lack care at times, but that wasn't the situation in this case. It's just that sense of constantly being pushed to carry on and to get to the next thing."

"That's always the problem, isn't it?" Rodney muttered, as he stared around. "This was supposed to be canvassed today by the patrol units."

"And they probably walked right through and took one look, realized it was just garbage, and kept on going, just like you did. But now," she noted, as she looked down at the body, "we know this isn't just garbage, and we have another soul whose life and death we need to unravel."

"You also think it's connected, don't you?"

She hesitated, then turned to him. "I'm afraid it is. So, the question is, has our killer been operating all this time—since this guy's death one year or however long ago? Or has something brought him back out of retirement? Was he happily married, and then something blew up? Was he in prison?" she asked, shrugging. "We won't know until we get to the bottom of it. But, right now, it'll be all about finding the bits and pieces to get there."

In the distance, they heard the emergency vehicles approaching.

Rodney said, "Here they come. I guess we'll be here for a while, won't we?"

"Yeah, I'll be here for Smidge."

"Good," he declared, smiling at her. "Better you than me."

She shook her head at him and laughed. "He's really not that bad."

"No, he's way worse," Rodney declared, with feeling. "I'll go outside and direct traffic or something."

"Direct traffic?" she repeated, laughing. "I have way better things you can do."

"What's that?"

"Why don't you go dig up the history on this building? See if we have any idea when it became derelict and who may have been interested in it in all these years."

"You don't really think somebody who has a history with the building would have done this, do you?" he asked, staring at her. "Isn't this more a case of motive and location?"

"It might be," she admitted. "I don't know, but until we get there—"

"I know. I know," he muttered, raising both hands. "Jesus, I need to go clear my head before I start throwing things."

She laughed. "Yeah, you do that. If Smidge sees you pulling something like that, he'll be all over me."

"Are you kidding? If he finds out what I just did, he'll be all over me for that too."

"I'm not telling him," she stated, with a smile. In the distance, she heard a voice snapping in her direction.

"Not telling me what?" Smidge asked, as he walked toward her. "And what the hell are you doing bringing me more clients?"

She smiled at him. "Oh, good, it's you. Glad we got the best man for the job."

He stopped and glared at her. "Compliments don't work with me. You should know better by now."

"Maybe so," she conceded, keeping a knowing smile on her face. "But this is something that we've seen, yet in many ways, we haven't."

"What is it?" He stopped as he got to the tarp, and his face lit up with curiosity. "Now this is interesting. That's a lot of animal activity." He looked around and asked, "Derelict building?"

She nodded.

"Weather, probably completely stripped by animals," he pointed out. "Teeth marks along the bones. Bones have even been separated to a certain extent." As he lifted the tarp farther, he noted, "Somebody's been in here, working on this a little more than you would have expected."

"Possibly," she noted cheerfully. "That's why I'm so glad to see you."

He just nodded, his head tilting. "I'm definitely not happy to be here, but at least this one's interesting," he muttered.

She laughed. "They're all interesting," she declared, "but this one'll be a little more than the others."

"The others?"

"We found a man here, ... alive, beaten badly, almost to death it seemed. I'm hoping that he isn't on your table already," she said. "I haven't checked in with the hospital."

"When was that?"

"Early in the morning."

"It's not on my table yet," he stated. "I got two women

in overnight, and a car accident with three seniors in the back seat, but I don't have any new able-bodied males."

"I wouldn't say *able-bodied*."

He stopped, eyed her slowly, and shook his head. "Oh no, no, no."

She nodded. "Oh yes," she declared, "and, as far as I can see, it could very well be connected."

"But that doesn't make any sense. That extends the timeline beyond one year, at least."

"Our killer may have been interrupted in the process of his serial killing mode," Kate suggested, "or he could have changed his MO. It could be that he has multiple dumping grounds."

"That would make it very unusual."

"It would, but there has to be a reason as to why one versus another."

He shook his head. "You know what I'll say."

"Yes, I do know what you'll say," she said, with a smirk. "And because I do know what you'll say, let me go get to my job, so I stop bringing you more bodies." And, with a laugh, she got up and walked farther away, so she could take a look at the world outside the windows and get a lay of the land. It still looked very much like an opportunity to dump some-body. But was it important? Outside of the location, was this important to the other killer, if two separate murderers had been dumping here?

Did her killer even have any idea that this dead guy was hidden here?

SIMON WAS HAPPY to escape the chaos that was about to ensue before the police and the coroner finally arrived. As he walked to the next jobsite, his mind was still thinking about the insistent voice he heard that led to the decomposed body. Was it really the voice of that dead man, his soul speaking to Simon? Was it really that easy for these beings to contact him? Was it easy to just say, *Hey, Simon, my body is missing, so get over there.*

Because that wasn't something he really expected from his psychic gift. Maybe if his grandmother were around, he would have some traction with the dead, although that thought just raised the reality that, if she were here, she would be laughing her fool head off at him for not having listened to her in the first place.

"Right, Grandma," he muttered out loud. "You were right. I was wrong. But I really wish you were around to help me right now."

He didn't understand why, if she had abilities, she couldn't give him a hand and come back. But then she probably needed as much of a holiday as he would need by the time his life was over, so there was that too. That almost brought a smile to his face because who the hell got a holiday from life? Is that what death was? Was it an escape? Was it something else entirely? He didn't know and found it all pretty damn confusing.

His foreman walked up to him and asked, "Are you okay? You look like you saw a ghost."

Simon winced. "I ran into my partner outside of a warehouse. I guess some guy got beaten up over there last night," he began.

"No way."

"I went along while they were wandering through, checking out the rest of the building, and we ended up finding an ancient body," he added, keeping the explanation simple.

His foreman's eyebrows shot up. "Seriously? You're not kidding, are you?"

He shook his head. "No. And believe me that it wasn't fun."

"Good Christ," his foreman muttered. "If that were me, I do love my wife, but, in that case, I think I would be telling her to keep her work to herself."

Simon laughed. "Wouldn't that be fun," he muttered, with a shake of his head. "It is something she tries to keep to herself, but, every once in a while, I get mixed up in it."

"That would only happen once with me," his foreman declared. "I can barely go to the hospital to see sick people, and, even then, it's just not a place I want to be." He shook his head. "Can't stand hospitals, can't stand funerals, won't attend them," he declared, with a strong headshake. "Nope, not having anything at all to do with the dead."

Simon smiled at that. It wasn't exactly an option in his case. Or, at least, he didn't think so. Maybe he could shut it off, but he figured that option was no longer available to him now. He could be wrong, but, so far, it didn't appear that anybody was listening to him.

As his foreman started to walk away, Simon added, "I need to know if there are any issues today."

The foreman shook his head. "You go deal with your dead guy woo-woo stuff. I'm all good here," he muttered. "Just keep that crap away from me."

Simon snorted. "It's not as if I was planning on bringing any bodies over."

"God, can you imagine?" he asked, turning to look at him, with a horrified expression.

"We have to acknowledge that, chances are, something like that could be found on our projects. We keep opening up all these ancient buildings, and you've got to wonder how many we're disturbing."

And, with that, his foreman shook his head. "Oh no. … Hell no. … Everything's fine on the job here, boss. If I have any problems, I'll text you." And, with that, he turned and headed off, shaking his head, mumbling to himself.

Simon stared after him for a long time, realizing that they had been blessed so far in that they hadn't had anything of that nature happen at any of their projects. They hadn't opened up anything and found something they weren't expecting, which was a godsend as far as Simon was concerned, and something he didn't want to even consider now.

But over time, quite likely it would happen at some point. He was buying derelict buildings. He frowned at that as he hurried on with the rest of his day, wondering at the different thoughts and beliefs people had when it came to the dead.

When Kate called him a little bit later, he asked her how her day was going.

"Better now," she replied. "I'm back in the office. We don't have an ID on our latest victim yet, and he's down at the morgue, getting a full workup." She hesitated, then went on. "It's way too early to tell, but …"

"But," he repeated cautiously.

"According to the initial examination, it does appear that he's been brutalized. We can't tell yet if that's just a lot of animal activity or something different. I know that the longer Dr. Smidge looked at it, the quieter he got," she shared, "and that's always a bad sign."

"I thought he was always silent to everybody but you."

"I don't know about that," she noted, "but he definitely tolerates me better than the others. We're not exactly bosom buddies though."

He nodded. "Will you be in the office for the rest of the day?"

"We need an ID on this skeleton guy, and I still have to get to the hospital and check on our other victim. I did phone this morning, and the staff expected him to come around today. They were supposed to call me, but I haven't heard anything so far."

"Right," Simon agreed, "that should be a priority, as he might tell you something."

"He should, but he was also in rough shape." She paused, waiting …

Simon groaned. "You're wondering if I have anything else, and the answer is no."

She pondered that and added, "If you're not that far away, maybe pop in, and we'll at least get a statement from you on the skeleton we found. I should have done that right at the beginning."

"You should have, but you already had the information, so it wasn't much of an issue or a high priority, based on other things that needed to get done."

"Exactly," she said, "but you're right."

He looked down at his watch. "Give me about twenty minutes or so." He ended the call and headed back toward home. Going to Kate's office meant he needed a vehicle. Then he wondered whether there would be time to sneak her out for a meal or something. She wasn't exactly the easiest to pull away from work, but, given her rough morning, maybe she could be persuaded. He wasn't so sure she would agree with that, but he had hopes. To her, it was probably just a normal morning.

When he got to the police station, he sent her a quick text, saying he was here. She walked out to the reception area and opened the door for him. He followed her to the back, where he greeted Rodney, who looked up with a confused expression.

"Need to get a statement for our records," she explained.

"Oh, right," he muttered, then frowned. "Let me write it up."

"Good idea," she replied, then pointed out the spare chair at Rodney's desk.

Simon sat down and waited. Giving a statement wasn't difficult, but he wasn't exactly sure how much he should say. He looked over at Kate and asked in an undertone, "How much do you want officially recorded on that sense of … knowingness?"

She looked over at him and smiled. "We can keep most of that out of your statement. Just say that you were out there, looking at derelict buildings you might want to purchase, and this just happens to be another that you were curious about. You went in to have a look and get an idea of what work would need to be done."

He looked at her and then nodded. "Something I do on a regular basis."

Rodney shuddered. "You may want to rethink that, after being with Kate and finding a body."

"I had that conversation with one of my foremen today," Simon shared, looking over at him.

"What exactly?" Rodney asked.

"He told me that I looked like I'd seen a ghost, so I told him where I'd come from and about the body and all. That led to a discussion about how lucky we are that we haven't had anything like that come up on our jobsites yet."

"*Yet*," Rodney noted, with a shudder. "I'm not sure I like that."

"No, I don't either, but it's certainly something that is entirely possible. We've come across drug overdoses and things of that nature, but never something like this."

With that, Rodney ran him through a series of questions to help get the information they needed. When he was done, he nodded. "Okay, seems we've got everything you've got to offer."

"Is that it?" Simon asked, with a smile. "That didn't seem too bad at all."

"What were you expecting?" Rodney asked, studying him curiously.

"I don't know, bright lights, no heat, hard chairs, you know? … A generally uncomfortable setting and the same questions over and over."

He snorted. "You know, we could have some fun with something like that, but I don't think that would wash in the end."

"Maybe not," Simon noted cheerfully, as he got up and looked over at Kate. "Any chance I can convince you to go out for lunch?"

She frowned at him, then checked the time on her phone. "Oh."

Simon nodded. "Yeah, it's lunchtime."

"It's past lunchtime," Rodney pointed out. "I'll go as far as saying it's way past the lunch hour, and my stomach feels as if it's been cut off."

She nodded, then turned to Simon. "We can go catch a bite around the corner, if you want to."

"Sure," he replied, with a smile at Kate. And, with a wave of his hand, he said goodbye to the rest of the team and left with Kate.

As soon as they got outside, she stopped, looked around,

and pointed up the street. "A little hole-in-the-wall Thai food place is up here, I think," she said. "I went there a few weeks back."

He looked at her and chuckled. "That was probably a few months back."

"Maybe," she muttered. "Time goes by so quickly."

"Especially when you're having fun."

"Or not," she muttered. Then she looked at him and stated, "You really could end up with a body in one of these buildings of yours."

"It's probably quite a normal thing to consider," he noted. "I'm not too bothered about it, but obviously it is a possibility."

"Right," she murmured. "I can't say that would be something I would be terribly impressed about."

He laughed. "I wouldn't be all that happy about it either, but realistically it's a possibility, probably grows more likely with each project, statistically speaking," he added, giving her a lopsided grin. "But it's not something I'll worry about because, if it happens, it happens. What am I supposed to do? At least let's be happy that this body's been found."

She winced. "So many times nobody says anything."

"And have you considered that?"

She stopped and frowned at him. "Actually ..."

"What?" he asked, turning to her. "I'm not sure I like the sound of that."

"I just wondered about Arnie."

His eyebrows shot up. "You mean, whether he knew the body was up there?"

She nodded. "I'm just not sure that he would have said anything. Everybody tries to avoid the police if they can, and the homeless doubly so," she murmured. "But there is a chance that Arnie knew."

"And maybe he didn't," Simon suggested, yet frowning, thinking about it.

"But it wouldn't be fair to think any less of him because of it," she added. "It's a big ugly world out there for him."

"Right, I agree," he said, putting hands in his pockets. "I guess I can ask him, but he's just as likely to say hell no either way."

"And, if he did know, it's not likely he would have said anything. He wouldn't have wanted to get involved," she suggested. "Knowing his situation, I can't really say that I blame him."

Simon pondered that thought as he headed back to work after lunch. Unable to let it go, he decided when he got back to that corner of the world, he would pop in to see how Arnie was doing. As he walked down the stairs on the boat, he found Arnie sitting there, holding Elsie in his arms. Simon looked at Arnie, saw the tears flowing down the old man's face, and sighed. "You gave her what you could," he said.

"It wasn't enough," he whispered.

"I don't know about that. ... She's quite old."

"About fifteen, as far as I know," he muttered.

Simon nodded. "That's quite old when it comes to dogs." He looked at the old man and asked, "Did you wake up to find her this way?"

"No, she just had her nap after breakfast, and that was it," he said, tears running down his face still. "It's like she was telling me that she wouldn't go out in that cold anymore."

Simon smiled. "I'm not surprised. It's a cold world for her."

"Yeah," Arnie agreed, his voice husky.

Simon watched as the old man rocked Elsie in his arms and asked, "Do you want me to take her down to the vet?"

The old man looked up at him and shook his head. "I don't want you to, no." Then he frowned. "But I don't have any other options, do I?"

"We don't exactly have acreage to bury her on," Simon noted, as he sat down across from him, seeing how shattered the old man looked. "And this would confirm she gets taken care of properly and not just dropped in a Dumpster around the corner."

At that, the old man winced. "And that would be about the only thing I would have as an option," he admitted.

Simon looked down at Elsie, then got up and made tea for both of them.

A little bit later, still sipping his tea, Arnie looked over at him. "Please, can you look after her?"

Simon nodded. "What about you?" he asked curiously. "What will you do?"

The old man shrugged. "I'm not long for this world either. I can't really do anything to move it along, but I can go to a shelter now," he admitted. "And I know that's what Elsie would want me to do."

Simon stared at him.

"She really loved the shelters. People were always around. It's just … she was never allowed to stay, so I never stayed either. I really, really appreciate the fact that you gave her this," Arnie said, waving a hand around the *Running Mate*.

Simon nodded. "Do you want to stay another night, to give you a chance to catch your breath?"

"No, I couldn't enjoy it without her. I'll be on my way."

"Can I at least give you a lift somewhere?"

He looked around and nodded. "If you wouldn't mind, I want to go back to my old stomping grounds. I know my way around, and my friends are there."

"As long as you go to a shelter where you'll get meals and a bed for the night."

"I'll huddle around the place and become one of the regulars," he noted. He got up and carefully handed the blanket with Elsie to Simon. "Please look after her."

Since he had the car, it didn't take very long to get the old man loaded up. Once Elsie was delivered to the nearest vet clinic, he took Arnie down to where he'd first seen him. As he looked for a place to park, he asked Arnie, "We found a still-alive but beaten-up man in that warehouse where I found you and Elsie."

"Yeah? That's a really ugly place to be," he muttered.

"During a full search the cops found another body," he added.

Arnie stiffened and looked at him, with that *knowing* in the back of his gaze.

Simon sighed. "A body you knew about apparently."

"No, it's not one I knew about. It's one I heard rumors about," Arnie clarified. "And believe me, that's not something I would ever go looking for. A bunch of kids were around at one time who used to talk about it, and it's always been one of those whispered rumors. Always in the background, always somebody talking about it, but never anybody really knowing if it was truth or not."

"So even though you haven't seen it, you knew?"

"I didn't go looking for a body, that's for sure. But if you found one—or that partner of yours—in a way that should put another ghost to rest. And that place has a lot of ghosts to put to rest."

"And you don't know any details about it, right?"

He stopped, looked at him, and shook his head. "I've spent a long time just trying to stay out of trouble," he murmured, "so I won't do things that create problems. Anything going on in that building has just been plain bad."

"Why don't you tell me about it?"

"What do you want to know?"

"Anything and everything."

"It's got a history of its own, and it needs to be dropped so something new, something invigorating, something inviting can go back up," Arnie shared. "There are just times when a building needs to not stand any longer. I know it sounds like crazy talk, as if I think a building has a soul, but I've seen a lot of buildings in my time. And I swear to God, a lot of them, they either don't have a soul or lost whatever soul they once had. Buildings like that should be dropped."

Arnie was out of the vehicle before Simon could even park properly. "I'll just carry on from here," he murmured. "I do have some friends here, and they won't take kindly to my coming up with a cop, or at least with somebody who's a little too … well-connected." He started to walk away, then stopped, looked back, and added, "Thank you. You are a redeeming person in this very dark world." And, with that, he turned and walked away as fast as his old body would allow.

Simon let him go, knowing nothing would be easy for Arnie now that Elsie was gone. Simon was filled with a certain sadness to think Arnie was going back to that life, even lonelier now, where really nothing around him was available to help him very much. Regardless, Simon wasn't even sure that Arnie would accept the help.

Once Elsie was gone, Arnie felt he had to get up and to move on. Simon wasn't sure if it was because Arnie knew that he was next or if Arnie just wanted to move on quickly through this missing-Elsie stage.

Either way, instead of parking, Simon kept on driving and ended up outside the warehouse where they'd found the skeleton. He swore as he stared up at it. Police tape was still all around it, and off to the side were most likely the same three men Kate had taken for a meal earlier. He doubted if they would be open to talking to him, but he found himself parking and walking over to them anyway.

The men just huddled together, looking at him warily.

He nodded. "You spoke to Detective Kate earlier," he began, "about the beaten-up man who was found here."

They looked at each other, and their gazes narrowed.

"She's my wife ..." he explained.

Their eyebrows shot up, and still they assessed him and the vehicle. He shook his head. "My partner, anyway," wondering why he'd even used the term *wife*. "They found another body in the building this morning, and this one had been there for years, was basically a skeleton."

They didn't say anything, just stared at him, ... waiting.

"I just wondered if you knew anything about it."

"Who's asking?" one of the men asked. "You or the cop?"

"Whatever you say to me would go to the cop, unless you tell me that you don't want it to go to the cop," he stated. "I just hate to think that somebody languished in that building all these years and that nobody cared."

"Nobody ever cares," one of them declared. "It's evidence of the sad deterioration of our society."

He looked at him and nodded. "That could be, but it

doesn't have to always end up that way."

"It sure seems like it," he muttered. "We don't know nothing about that skeleton. We heard talk of one in there, never saw one, never went in to look. Really don't want any more of that stuff in our world. Living out here on the streets, we see dead people all the time, from overdoses, beatings, car accidents."

The homeless man shook his head and continued. "No shortage of that side of life in our world," he noted. "But bodies that have been there for a while? Hell no, but there have been rumors. I can tell you that. Plenty of rumors."

Simon nodded. "I just spoke to Arnie, if any of you know him." Again that blank stares turned his way. He nodded. "Arnie and Elsie. Elsie passed away this morning."

All three of them winced.

"Arnie is heading to the shelter, at least I hope so. I'm also hoping he has some friends who might rally around him right now. He's pretty upset."

The men just looked at each other, then back at him, still not saying anything.

"Of course, if you don't know the old man, that won't be an issue for you. But, if you do, and can do anything at all to make his day a little bit better, you might want to consider getting in touch with him." And, with that, he headed back to his vehicle.

"How do you know Elsie died?" one of them called out behind him.

"I just took her body to the vet," he shared, turning to look back at him. "I gave Arnie a place to stay while she was in the worst way."

Surprise lit his dark gaze, then he frowned.

"I know," Simon explained. "It's not the usual thing to

happen, but all of us haven't lost our humanity."

"Are you sure?" he asked. "It seems as if the whole world is lacking all signs of humanity."

Simon smiled. "And you would be correct in some ways," he admitted, "but I couldn't *not* help Arnie." And, with that, he turned and headed for his car.

CHAPTER 9

THERE WAS JUST something about the smell of a hospital. As Kate walked through the halls, she could see how that would be rough for people dealing with a loss. That brought to mind the text message she'd gotten from Simon about Elsie. Not exactly an easy thought either, but she was happy that Arnie was on his way back to a shelter, or at least to the world that he knew. She was sorry for Elsie, but the poor dog looked like death would have been a relief for her. The end-of-life stage was one of those things that was difficult for everybody, but, since Kate didn't have pets, she'd always sat back and wondered at the emotions the loss of a pet seemed to generate.

But now that she was a little more connected to Simon, and her heart was definitely involved, she could see how a pet could become family very quickly. And, for Elsie, she had hung on as long as she could, but, once it was her time, she was gone. It was also typical of Simon to handle things efficiently and to take care of Elsie as well as Arnie. There was an awful lot to love about that man.

As she walked toward the room number she had gotten for her beating victim, she found a doctor standing outside, looking at his notes and frowning. When she identified herself and asked how the patient was, he shook his head.

"Not good," he muttered. "He's in pretty rough shape."

"Are we talking *not good* as in not making it or *not good* because no signs of recovery are seen at the moment?"

"Not at the moment, no," he replied. "I'm really hoping that we get there, but, so far, it's not showing up."

She nodded. "Can you tell me exactly what happened to him?"

"God no," he said, with a shudder. "All I can tell you is that multiple blows were all over his body, including a major head wound. That's the biggest concern."

"Of course," she murmured. "Any sign of when …" She stopped at his headshake and didn't even get a chance to finish her question.

"He's in a coma right now. It's medically induced. He had surgery last night to repair the crushed rib as it had punctured his lung, plus to reorient the bones in his skull," he shared. "We're only doing what we need to in order to keep him stable. All the other surgeries will happen after that."

He looked at his notes again. "While they were in there, they did fix his leg. It was broken back on itself." She winced at that, and the doc nodded. "That should tell you something about the level of beating this poor man took," he stated, staring at her.

"There's always that one asshole out there who will push it, isn't there?"

"I don't even know that I would say *asshole* in this case but maybe *psychopath*," he murmured. "This beating was severe. If he does come out of it, I can't see it being without brain damage. Did you find next of kin?"

"No, we haven't got an identification on him yet," she replied, "but we're working on it."

"Work faster. I hate to see anybody die alone." And,

with that, he turned and walked away.

She stepped into the man's room, thinking about the doctor's words and how every conversation seemed to end up with someone telling her to work faster.

Wouldn't that be nice? The problem was that these killers she was up against were often so hard to deal with, things just didn't make any sense, no matter how quickly she worked. These murderers were already off doing something else to some other poor person, while she was chasing her tail on the last victim.

As she walked to the edge of the bed, she looked down and winced. The poor man's face was completely swollen and puffy. He had bandages around his head, and his leg was in a cast and lifted. His arm appeared to be full of needles. Honestly, there didn't appear to be anything about his poor body that hadn't been beaten.

She shook her head and whispered, "I don't know who did this to you, but I will find him." She put a hand on the hospital bed. "What I don't know is whether I can do that before you pass," she murmured, "and I know that's not what anybody wants to hear. I also need to find out something about who you are."

She kept on talking to him. "No ID, nothing was on you. We've taken your fingerprints, but, so far, nothing's come up in the database, which just means that you probably have no record and are some nice clean businessman. So, the question is, has somebody not even reported you missing yet?"

She sighed. "Were you visiting someone here in town?"

"Were you on a holiday?"

"Do you not have a job any longer?" she asked, as she stared down at the poor victim. She shook her head as she looked out at her world.

For this guy, to survive this would be a pretty-rough struggle. To live with these injuries afterward would be even worse. It would also be a rough struggle for whatever family he had, since, at the moment, they didn't even know what had happened to him. Just then her phone rang. It was Rodney.

"We've got a possible hit on your victim in the hospital."

"I'm here with him right now," she said. "Who is he?"

"We have a missing person's report that just came in. Some woman reported it. A businessman was heading out, or about to head out, catching a flight back to Toronto in the last couple days. She mentioned how they didn't worry when he failed to check in right away, but, when they called his hotel to see when he had checked out, they found out he hadn't even checked in. And that fact started the search."

"Of course," Kate muttered, her heart sinking as she stared down at him. "Did she provide any description? Not that I'll see much to match, not considering his current condition."

"Right," Rodney replied, his voice heavy. "I suspect it's him, but we'll have to identify him using scars or DNA or the like."

"Even if the woman who made the missing person's report came in, an identification would never fly, as he's too badly banged up."

"She's on the way to the hospital right now," Rodney told her, his voice heavy. "So, you might want to talk to her."

"Yeah, I will, as soon as she gets here. Anything else happening?" she muttered, as she stared at the victim.

"No. I got as much from her as I could over the phone,

and we'll just keep working on it," he told Kate. "But this is really getting ugly."

"What do you mean, *getting* ugly?" she asked, with a sigh. "This is way past ugly, if you ask me. If we find out that our other body from the warehouse was also beaten to a pulp, we'll have to consider that he may have been our first victim."

"I know, and I was thinking about that."

"You better go update the board because this one'll get even bigger."

Just then came a cry from the hospital room door.

Kate quickly ended the call with Rodney and turned to see a woman standing there, staring at the man in the hospital bed. Kate walked over to her, with her badge out, as the woman's eyes filled with tears.

"Is this Sonny?" she asked.

Kate winced. "We were hoping you could tell us."

"Oh my God, how can anybody tell anything?"

"And that is exactly our problem right now," she murmured. "Are you a relative?"

"I'm his wife."

Kate led the woman closer to the hospital bed, explaining, "He's in pretty rough shape. We can get you a conversation with the doctor, but I can tell you that they had him in for surgery last night. Luckily he's stable for the moment, but he seems to have been very badly beaten."

"What was he even doing at a warehouse?" she cried out. "He was supposed to be at the airport, flying to Toronto."

"And he may well have been on his way to the airport. Did he take a cab?"

She frowned at the man in the hospital bed and nodded. "Yes, he always does."

"Okay, good. Do you know if he got picked up at the office?"

She stared at her. "Yes." Then she frowned. "Do you think the cabbie did this?"

"I have no idea who did this yet," Kate admitted. "What I need is every detail that you can tell me about when he was due to leave, when he left the house, and when you last saw him."

Her name was Anna Hilton, and her husband was Sonny Hilton. By the time Kate got that information from Anna, the woman sat down beside her husband, or at least the man she assumed was her husband. Anna added, "He does have a couple birthmarks."

"Good. We'll get a doctor in here to see if we can find those and can determine whether this poor man has them or not." It took Kate a few minutes to get the doctor back.

When he showed up, his questions were all about whether the man had any allergies and what diseases he'd had. By the time Anna had answered his questions, she was shaking and asked, "Can we please just check for the two birthmarks?"

It didn't take long for the doctor to check the body over, and they concluded that this was indeed Sonny. Anna was sobbing beside her.

Kate waited until Anna had a chance to breathe, patting her on the back. "I know you don't want to talk about this, but I do need to learn a lot more about him, and we need to do that now."

"What do you want to know?" Anna asked.

"When was his flight? I need to get the details of his flight and any other plans because I need to establish a timeline."

"That was yesterday." Anna stopped and shook her head. "No, no, no, it's already been yesterday." She rubbed her face. "I have an email." She quickly pulled out her phone, brought up the email, and sent it to Kate.

She quickly opened it. It was his flight reservations and travel plans. "Good, this gives us at least the start of a timeline."

Anna looked at her. "But a timeline doesn't help him now."

Kate took a deep breath and nodded. "No, a timeline may not help him at all. I won't lie to you. His injuries are pretty serious. All I can tell you right now is that we will do our best to find out who did this to him."

"Don't do your best," Anna snapped, her tone harsh and raspy. "Just find him and kill him. Please, just take him out, remove him from this world, because anybody who could do something like this to my poor Sonny should not be allowed to live," she murmured. And then she started to sob again.

Kate got up and, after sharing her condolences and trying to comfort the woman one more time, quickly exited the hospital room. When she got outside, she contacted Rodney. "The wife confirmed that's him."

"How?"

"She was able to describe some birthmarks, and, with the doctor's assistance, we were able to find them, exactly as described," she explained. "So, it looks to be that's exactly who we have. He took a cab from the office, and I have his flight information here. I'll forward it to you right now. The wife's name is Anna, and our victim is Sonny Hilton." She quickly emailed it over to him.

"We'll need to know what cab it was," Rodney noted.

"Anna didn't know, but maybe his office does," Kate

suggested. "They might have an account with somebody."

"I'm on it," Rodney replied.

And, with that, she got off the phone. She stood outside for a moment, taking in a couple deep breaths as she contemplated her next step.

Lilliana called her a few minutes later. "Hey, I hear you've got another victim."

"Maybe," Kate replied. "It's a little early to know if it's the same deal, but I would bet on it."

"In that case, we'll go with it," Lilliana stated. "If you need my help …"

"I'll call," Kate stated. "Right now Rodney is looking into the cab that picked him up. I'll make a phone call to Reese next."

"Good idea," Lilliana noted. "Stay in touch." And, with that, she ended the call.

Phoning Reese next, Kate asked for a rundown on every one of the victims that they currently had, looking for any similarities, any clubs, medical issues, suicide watch groups, and anything else that came to mind. She only added the suicide watch groups because of the one case recently where it was all connected through a group like that.

Reese snorted. "Do we add that to all our lists now?"

"No," Kate muttered, with a sigh. "Yet this guy has been beaten to a pulp. So, it's really just … sadistic," she added. "And there appears to be an escalation in our killer's behavior. We need to find him and find him fast, before the next businessman goes missing."

Reese hesitated, and Kate filled in the silence. "I know, … and, chances are, we're already too late."

KATE SAT DOWN on a bench off to the side in the hospital hallway and started making notes. They had to find the vehicle, the gray van, which wasn't much of a description, but it was something they couldn't afford to let up on. They also couldn't afford to forget the fact that they were close to the US border. As much as they didn't want to consider that this killer was border hopping, leaving his victims up here in Canada, still it was a possibility and could be exactly what was happening.

The cab though, for Sonny Hilton, that was something she was anxious to run down. She hadn't even finished her notes when Rodney called.

"Got an update on the taxi," he began. "It was a Yellow Cab, and the taxi company told me that Sonny wasn't there for pickup."

"Wasn't there for pickup?" she repeated. "How did that happen?"

"When he didn't show, the cabbie called the number that put in the request and were told something like it was a mistake, like he had another ride, something like that. The cabbie didn't have any details, was very busy, and headed off to the next pickup."

"But that makes no sense," Kate noted, frustrated as hell. "Why would Sonny have canceled the cab?"

"We're assuming he canceled it," Rodney pointed out, sounding dispirited too. "It could have just as easily been the killer."

"Good God," Kate noted. "That would imply our killer knew the cab was ordered and may have had some insight into Sonny's travel arrangements."

"That's what it would look like," Rodney agreed. "And it is an interesting consideration, but for somebody to have canceled the cab ..."

"We need to contact the place where Sonny worked," she said.

"I've already tried to call them, and they're looking for a manager to call me back."

"Of course they are," she grumbled in exasperation. "Guess what? They don't get to wait for a manager. They'll get me." She checked her watch. "I can be there in a few minutes."

"I don't know about that," Rodney stated, "given the traffic."

"I won't give them too much time to come up with some other story."

"Do you think they had something to do with it?" he asked.

"I have no idea, but I won't let the opportunity to sort it out just slide, all because they're waiting for a chance to talk to a manager and to get their stories straight," Kate declared. "Let's just hope, for their sake, there's a manager when I walk in."

With the address written down, she headed for her vehicle. As soon as she found the building in question, she stepped inside, only to find the office was upstairs. It was a company that dealt in medical devices, and, noting that, she headed up there. As soon as she stepped inside the main entrance, the receptionist looked up and frowned at her. Kate frowned right back.

She held out her badge. "I have a few questions." The woman looked at the badge with almost a recoiling effect.

"We did say that we were waiting for a manager."

"That's nice," Kate muttered, "but one of your sales people is in the hospital in very bad shape, and we need to know why the cab that was supposed to take him to the airport was canceled."

She looked at her. "I don't know that answer."

"So, you don't, but somebody here should," Kate stated, staring her down. "I want to speak to that person, and I want to speak to them now."

The woman shook her head. "I can only tell you that no manager is here."

"I don't care if no manager is here or not," Kate snapped, her tone hard, her voice getting louder. "Do you have a CEO? Do you have a director? Do you have anybody here?" She stared at the woman with an implacable expression, trying to convey that she wasn't leaving until she talked to somebody.

Hearing a cough, she looked up to see a man standing nearby, wringing his hands. "There really isn't anybody here at the moment," he said apologetically.

"That's nice," she quipped, turning to look at him. "But this place must have somebody from middle management around."

"A lot of them work from home right now," he explained. "So, nobody is necessarily here, at least not physically."

"In that case I'll talk to you, and you can provide me with their contact information, and, while I'm standing here in your office, I will contact them myself."

His eyebrows shot up, and he looked over at the receptionist, who just looked relieved that he was there. "Come into my office," he said, then led Kate to a small room just down the hallway.

As she stepped in, she looked around and asked, "Who is the CEO, and who would have been Sonny's boss?"

"I would have been Sonny's boss," he replied, his tone careful. "I am Tom Barnes. Are we speaking in past tense?"

"No," Kate replied, "but Sonny won't be showing up for work anytime soon."

He swallowed hard and nodded. "Did I understand that he's been beaten up?"

"First, let's talk about why the cab was canceled that was supposed to take him to the airport."

"It was a mix-up," he said. "I would normally have taken him to the airport myself because I live in that direction, but his flights were booked early enough that I couldn't get off work, due to meetings, so he booked the cab. Then my meetings were canceled," Tom explained, "so I was supposed to take him."

"And then what happened?"

"I told him to go outside and wait, but then I ended up on a phone call. When I went back outside to take him to the airport, he wasn't there."

"And?"

"I sent him a text, asking if he was on his way to the airport. I didn't get an answer, but I presumed that's where he was." Tom frowned and added, "He gets testy if things don't go as planned, and this is not the first time he would have walked out and not responded. I just figured that he grabbed a cab anyway."

"So, he would have taken a cab?"

"Yeah, and he would have just grabbed a cab close by. He wouldn't have ordered it. It would have just been any cab that he could have hailed as he stood outside."

She got up and looked out the window to the streets below.

"Cab companies troll this area on a regular basis," he

stated. "Lots of businesses are around here."

"And I would have thought most businesses would have phoned in for cabs."

"Yes, we do, and on a regular basis," he agreed. "But sometimes ... Sonny can be one of the more ..."

"Difficult people to work with?"

He winced. "I don't want to speak ill of him."

"I don't care if you speak ill of him or not. I need to know who he is, what he's like, and how he got himself into this situation."

"All I can tell you is that I expected to take him to the airport, but, when I went outside, he wasn't there, and we never heard from him again."

"And that didn't cause you enough concern to follow up or to put out a report on him?"

"No," he admitted, "but, now that you say it that way, I feel as if I've completely missed something."

"Would he have been expected to check in with you upon arrival at his new location?"

"No. He traveled all the time, coming and going from deals constantly, and we have no company protocol for that."

"And how was he regarded by others in the office?"

He stared at her. "He wasn't here all that much, what with the travel, but, as far as I know, everybody got along with him. Honestly, he wasn't here enough to *not* get along with him."

She stared at him. "Meaning?"

"Just that he traveled all the time. He would come in, settle up his paperwork from the last trip, pick up his travel papers, and be on his way out again. So, as much as we expected him to be here, doing what he would be doing, we're also not surprised when he's not. For all we know, his flight got changed. Instead of going east, he's turned around and gone west, and then there's the whole travel-delay scenario."

"Who okays his flight plans?"

"Me, to a certain extent, and then my boss, the director of the company."

"Okay, then I need to talk to him."

He stared at her for a moment and shook his head. "That'll be a little difficult."

"Why is that?"

"Because he's in Thailand," he explained.

"He works in Thailand, or he's there on a holiday?"

"He works remotely, from Thailand."

"Then a phone call would do, wouldn't it?" she asked, her tone calm.

He frowned at her and asked, "Seriously?"

"Yes, seriously," she stated. "I need to know everybody here, where they were, and whether anybody saw Sonny get into a cab or some other vehicle or not."

He frowned and said, "I can ask around."

"No," she corrected. "*I* will ask around. How many people do you have in the office right now?"

He looked at her and shrugged. "I don't know."

"Aren't you supposed to know?" she asked in frustration. "I'm not sure how this place is supposed to run, but surely you must have some idea of who comes into work on a daily basis and who doesn't."

"A lot of our people are traveling. A lot of our people work from home," Tom replied, clearly frustrated now. "So, I have seen probably four or five people this morning, I'm not sure I've seen more than that."

She stared at him. "Okay, I want to know how many

were here on the day Sonny left."

He walked out to the receptionist, who was trying hard to ignore them. "Analise, do you have any idea who was working in the office on the day Sonny left?"

The perky blonde turned to him. "I have no idea," she said, tucking back her hair.

"Do you not have a sign-in system?" Kate asked. "I understand it's not school, but do you not have some way of tracking who is here and who is not? How else do you keep track of who's working?"

"Because they're all online," she said, "and they're in meetings a lot."

"Okay, so I still need to know," Kate began again, taking a deep breath, "who might have been here and who might have seen Sonny get into a vehicle."

Just then another man walked into the lobby, a big smile on his face, until he took one look at Kate and frowned. She asked Tom, "Who is that?"

The man's eyebrows shot up. "I work here, at least I think I work here," he noted, turning to look at Tom.

"You do," Tom confirmed, raising a hand to calm down the man, who looked as if he was stumped, and he no longer wore the big smile. "Sorry, this is an unusual situation, but Sonny, who was on his way to Toronto ..." Tom glanced at Kate, then went on. "Sonny is in the hospital after being badly beaten up. This detective is here looking into it."

The man frowned as he stared at her. "Do you have your badge?" She pulled out her badge, and, his voice suddenly hoarse, he muttered, "That says homicide."

"Yes, it does," she stated, without further clarification.

"He's that bad?"

She stared at him. "Who are you? And where were you

two days ago when Sonny was leaving the office?"

"I'm Julian. I would give him a ride to the airport if Tom couldn't," he shared. "Sonny told me that he was fine and that he would just grab a cab, then muttered something like he shouldn't have canceled it in the first place."

She nodded. "And do you have a cab company that he would have called?"

"No," he replied, looking at her. "You can track that from the credit card, can't you?"

"Maybe," she noted, "unless Sonny decided to pay cash and would have turned in some receipt later." She turned and looked at Tom. "You have a company account, I presume."

"Yes, yes, of course," Tom stated.

"So, Sonny would have used the company account then, wouldn't he?"

He looked at her and jerked. "Oh, yes, absolutely. Let me go to my computer, and I'll bring it up." He walked back over to his computer, while she stood and studied the new arrival, Julian.

"Did you see Sonny get into a vehicle, cab or otherwise?" Kate asked Julian.

"No, I didn't," he said, frowning. "This is really serious, isn't it?"

"Yes, it is," she confirmed.

"Oh my God, what about poor Anna?"

"She's at the hospital with him right now," Kate shared, studying Julian intently. "Do you know anything about their relationship?"

"No, I sure don't," he stated. "I stay away from all kinds of drama at the office."

"And do you know if there was any drama at the office?"

She eyed him shrewdly.

"I don't know," he said, with a smile. "Believe me, that's not something I ever want to get into." He turned to Analise, the receptionist. "Analise would know about Sonny's personal life."

She winced and shook her head. "I don't know." Then she looked around at the nearby cubicles. "Maybe Angela knows something."

"And who is Angela?" Kate asked.

"I can call her for you," Analise offered.

Kate nodded, and, within a few minutes, another woman came to the front desk. She was well dressed, pretty, and very well put together.

Angela looked over at the receptionist, then at Kate. "What's going on?" she asked.

Kate held up her badge.

"Oh, good God," Angela muttered. "What are the cops here for now?" She shot a look at Analise, clearly unhappy to be called down into the fray.

Kate stated, "I believe you know Sonny."

"Yes, of course. I work with him. We all do."

"Do you know the status of his relationship with his wife?"

She stared at them blankly. "Why would you ask me that?"

"It's a question I'm asking a lot of people," Kate replied. "No need to worry or to speculate, just be honest. Would you know the status of his marital relationship?"

"No," Angela replied, frowning.

Kate stared at her. "Do you want to have this conversation in private?" she suggested, and the other woman flushed bright red.

"Is there a reason why I should? What is this all about?"

"He was beaten extremely badly and is in the hospital," Kate shared. "Frankly, it's not looking good."

The color drained from Angela's face. "Good God." She put a hand on her chest. "And what about Anna?" She turned and looked at the others.

"Anna is at the hospital with him right now," Kate replied, searching for a clue as to Angela's state of mind in the moment. "So, what is the status of your relationship with Sonny?"

She flushed again. "We work together. We're colleagues. That's it."

But Kate and everybody else in the office could tell it was a lie. Kate sighed. "Angela, if that's a lie," she began, staring at her intently, "I will find out, and I will be really pissed off when I do. I don't need anybody wasting my time right now. And then there's the question of whether Anna will find out too."

"Why would she need to find out anything?" Angela asked in horror.

Kate stared at her. "I imagine she'll have questions and would want to know what happened in the last few hours before Sonny caught his flight."

"He was at work," Angela said. "What else could you possibly think?"

Kate continued to stare at her, seeing the telltale signs. "Look. This isn't a conversation that needs to feed the office gossips," Kate muttered. "You can come with me to my office."

Angela snapped, "Do I need a lawyer?"

"I don't know," Kate replied. "Do you?"

Angela glared at her, then shrugged and led the way to

her own office.

As they stepped into Angela's office, Kate asked, "Did you have an affair with Sonny?"

Her shoulders slumped, Angela nodded. "Yes, I did," she muttered, "but I don't know how relevant that is."

"You don't seem particularly put out that he's in the hospital."

"If his wife's there, it's not like I get any rights to see him, do I?"

"No, and that's one of the things I'm interested in seeing, who will show up and who won't."

"You can't think I had something to do with it?" Angela asked in a shocked voice.

"I don't know whether you did or not," Kate noted. "What I do know is that I have something to solve, and I will not stop until I've turned over all the rocks, and all the people who put the rocks on top of crap like this."

Angela flushed and glared at her resentfully. "You didn't have to make it public."

"Really? It's funny because, when I asked who else might have some idea about the status of Sonny's marriage, your name came right up."

She frowned and stared in the general direction of the front lobby. "Good God, do you think they know?"

"Oh, that's a given," Kate declared. "That's an absolute given."

Angela raised a hand to her face. "I, ... I ..."

"You what?" Kate asked, staring at her intently. "You didn't know, you didn't expect, you didn't think anybody would ever find out?"

She glared at her. "None of that is any of your business."

"It's *all* my business, and, if he dies, I'll tear apart *all* your lives," she stated. "So, you might want to keep that in mind the next time you have an office affair with a married man." And, with that, Kate got up and walked out.

As she headed out to the main room, she stopped at the lobby area, and Tom came out to talk to her. She saw that his face was flushed too.

"I don't have any sign of a credit card charge," he shared, "and nothing here says that he took a cab."

She grimaced. "If he didn't take a cab, ... would anybody else here have driven him?"

"I would have said that …" He looked back toward Angela's office, where she stood at her open doorway.

"I didn't take him to the airport," she snapped.

"When did you last see him?" Kate asked Angela.

"Before he left," she replied stiffly. "We were discussing work."

Kate rolled her eyes at that.

Angela glared at her. "You don't know anything."

"No, I don't," Kate admitted, "but what I do know is I've got a very badly injured man and a devastated wife, who hasn't yet found out the entirety of how bad this will be for her."

Angela turned and slammed the door to her office.

Kate faced Tom. "I'll need to know if a charge comes up over the next few days. Sometimes it can take a day or two."

"You're right. I should have thought of that." He frowned. "I don't know who else might have taken him. Usually I do the airport trips just because I live near there. Julian does too, but mostly it's just me."

She nodded. "I hear you, but any number of issues could be going on here." The big one that wouldn't leave her thoughts was the idea that this killer could be trapping his victims by posing as a cabbie, then locking them in the vehicle so they couldn't get out. She added, "I need a list of everybody who works here, and I will be in touch."

"Can we contact his wife?" Tom asked.

"Can you?" she asked. "I don't know, but I'm sure Anna would appreciate it if somebody did. You would think that somebody cared, and not just ..." Then she stopped and shook her head. "This job never ceases to amaze me." And, with that, she turned and walked out.

She wanted to say so much more, but, as she'd discovered long ago, her morals and ethics apparently didn't match up with a lot of the world's. Now there would be one very devastated wife trying to figure out what had happened to her world, only to potentially find out what her husband had been up to beforehand.

With a sad sigh, she got into her vehicle and headed back to the office.

Later that evening, she walked into Simon's apartment building, tired and frustrated, but also incredibly sad.

Harry took one look at her and frowned.

"I'm fine," she muttered, with a wave of her hand. "Just a crap day."

"Oh my," Harry murmured. "You have way too many of those."

"Isn't that the truth?"

* * *

SIMON HAD A hard time determining his mood. As soon as he realized Kate was on her way up, he walked outside on the balcony and turned on the grill, wondering at the domestic inclination of wanting to cook a meal tonight. And yet he felt just something about time going by too quickly, life happening when you weren't looking, and any other clichéd comments that one could think of.

When she walked into his place, and he saw the fatigue on her shoulders, he nodded. "It's just that kind of a day, isn't it?"

"It's definitely that kind of a day," she noted. "I shouldn't be surprised, since I've seen it over and over, but it's still frustrating that people screw around with other people's lives, and they just don't care. They're not even worried about getting caught, beyond the humiliation of people finding out what they're up to," she muttered.

"Oh, it sounds as if you had an afternoon."

"Not in a good way," she declared, shaking her head. "Just people being people." She explained about the man in the hospital and the affair he was having with somebody at work and the wife not knowing. "She's there at the hospital, breaking her heart over Sonny, who is fighting for his life. Yet he had an affair with Angela, and Anna, the wife, has no idea."

"Or maybe she does," he pointed out. "Have you talked to her?"

"I've talked to her, but not about that," Kate clarified. "It's just one of those things, but I'll get there."

"And do you have to tell her?"

"Is it a kindness to tell her?" she asked, looking at him. "Is it mean to tell her? In a way, I need to know. Did she arrange to have Sonny beaten like this because she knew of his infidelity?"

"Oh, right," Simon muttered. "That would be shitty, wouldn't it?"

"It would be shitty, but an awful lot of women are out there who would say it was totally justified."

He nodded. "What was your take on her?"

"Exhausted, worn out, absolutely stunned at the change in her life," Kate shared. "I don't think she knows, but I'll have to find out." She shook her head at that thought.

"And his prognosis?"

"Not good," she noted. "Obviously there's always hope, but I don't think the doctors are looking at a significant recovery. He's had brain surgery, and still, there is a good chance that he will have brain deficits if he survives. And I don't know that they're looking much beyond that."

"That's crappy," Simon whispered.

"He seemed somewhat cognizant when I spoke to him in the warehouse, and it sounds terrible, but it was probably one of his last-ditch efforts to get help."

"And fear being the strong motivator that the guy who did this to Sonny was coming back."

"I haven't talked to the coroner yet, but I'm wondering if maybe this guy serves up his punishments, then leaves them there to die. And then comes back to gloat. Or, if something else entirely is going on, I have no clue at all."

"Right," Simon noted, "and has it got anything to do with the fighting?"

"I have no idea," she admitted, turning to him. "That's another completely different issue that I haven't gotten an answer for. It would suck if it did because that's just unbelievable, but it would also suck if it didn't because that would mean we have two completely different murders to follow up on. So, one is neither better nor worse than the other. They're just both terrible options."

Simon didn't say anything for a moment and kept fussing with the grill. "I'll put on the steaks, or do you want to shower first?"

"Yes," she said, her eyes lighting up at the idea of a steak. "What got into you that you're all of a sudden looking to cook?" Then she saw the expression on his face and nodded. "Arnie, right?"

"Arnie and Elsie of all things," he shared, with a laugh. "Never had a pet, but, boy, did that man love his."

She nodded. "I was thinking about that today myself. I never had a pet either."

He frowned at her. "Not even when you were little?"

"Not that I remember," she stated. "If a hamster or whatever showed up, honest to God, my mother would have just flushed it down the toilet." He winced at that, and she nodded. "And it's not as if she would have ever done right by it."

"Sometimes people just suck, don't they?"

"Yeah, they sure do," she murmured. "I'll go have a quick shower and see if I can shift my mood."

"I'll work on shifting mine while I'm outside dealing with the steaks."

"Anything to go with the steaks is a good start," she said hopefully.

He laughed. "There's potatoes, and I have a few prawns here."

"Ooh, now you're talking," she replied in delight. She turned and raced inside.

He had to laugh. In her case, the way to her heart was definitely through her stomach. He'd never met anybody who loved food quite as much as she did, yet would be completely disinterested if it interfered with her work. She was all about work, that one. And maybe it was a good thing, considering the work she did.

Still muddling through his thoughts on Arnie, Simon

put some seasoning on the steaks, checked that the temperature was good, and tossed them on. He glanced at his watch, knowing that he only had about four minutes a side on the steaks, which meant that he'd probably jumped the gun a little. On the other hand, since steak was on the menu tonight, Kate would likely be superfast with her shower.

By the time he had them plated and a meal served, she was grabbing cutlery out of the drawer and coming to sit beside him.

"Too bad we can't sit outside," he said, with a smile, "but it's way too cold."

"I agree," she murmured. "I was thinking about the *Running Mate* today too."

He nodded. "Yeah, I'll have to take a look to see what needs to be done since Arnie was there."

"Did he have any problem leaving?" she asked curiously.

"No, he was more than ready to go. I even offered him another night to get himself together, but he literally had just been trying to give Elsie time to complete her life," he explained. "It was such an odd feeling to realize that he was serious about it too."

"And what about his life?"

"He told me that he's done, that he'll be gone soon, and that gave me the weirdest feeling too."

"That he knew he would be gone soon, or that he didn't care and was happy about it?"

"All of it," he said, looking at her. "I can't say that life is always glorious, but I haven't come to the point where I want to sit here and be complacent about it being over either." She just nodded. He looked at her and added, "I know that you did come to that place at one time."

"Sure," she admitted. "I think we all get close to that at

times, but that doesn't mean we do something about it, and I'm not sure that very many of us who get there are truly serious. It becomes something you always think about and can't get out of your head, but … it's just an option, not a good one, but it's an option."

"And Arnie asked about that too. Is there an option for that for humans?"

"You mean, is there medically assisted suicide, if that's even what it's called?" she asked. "Yes, … there is. Generally it's reserved for serious cases, debilitating diseases with no cure, lots of pain, increasing costs, that sort of thing. So, at the end, it's easier on everyone."

"I would like to think something is out there," he noted. "I think about what Arnie's facing, and he has zero resources, and I don't even have a place to put him," he noted, looking at her in a weird helpless way. "And it occurred to me that I have all these buildings, and I'm doing all these rehabs." Then he fell silent, shaking his head.

She looked over at him intently. "Maybe it's a good time for you to reconsider what you're doing with them all," she suggested. "I don't know what they're slated for. I presume rentals or commercial or whatever." She shrugged. "I don't know what it is you're trying to do, besides buy the world, I gather."

He snorted. "I am so not trying to do that."

"Good," she replied, "I would think it would be rather expensive."

He gave her a droll look. "You think?"

She smiled. "So, maybe this is just, I don't want to say a wake-up call, but maybe it's a call for you to consider what you want to do with these buildings, or at least one or two of them," she offered. "I know a lot of them have to pay for themselves, but do they all?" she asked, looking at him. "Is there room in any of them for somebody like Arnie?" she asked.

"How would I even find other *Arnie*s, who are potentially honest? But I don't even know that he is. I don't know if he's ... It's a stupid idea," he decided, shaking his head.

"No," she countered, "it isn't. This has certainly brought up a need within the system, and maybe it's more along the lines of needing somewhere for pets that have no other place to go."

"That's an option too," he agreed, with a nod. "It's just something that struck me."

"And that's okay too," she said. "Sometimes we have things that happen in our lives that get our attention. We think that we're immune to a lot of things, and then we find out that not only are we not immune but we really aren't even aware of half of what's going on around us. Look at Sonny's wife today. I'm pretty sure she has no idea that her husband was having an affair, but I'll have to figure it out, just in case she's behind any of this."

"And you don't seem to think there's any chance for him to survive?"

"I got the impression that the docs believe Sonny has significant brain damage, but, last I knew, they hadn't made any final determinations. They were keeping him in a medically induced coma when I was there, but I don't know about now."

"Ouch. I wonder if she's ..." He shook his head and added, "I'm already wondering if she's considering organ donation."

"I would say of course not because, at the moment, she's not even considering that he won't make it. She still has hope."

"That's true. Why wouldn't she? Plus, she's probably still just adjusting to the fact that he's in there."

She smiled. "I do think that she genuinely loves him. At least at the moment. She's also dealing with a degree of shock."

"I understand," Simon said, "and you want him to be loved. You want somebody to care. It's like that body that we found, the skeleton."

"I know, but really who doesn't report a body like that?"

"Oh, I did ask Arnie about that."

"*Uh-oh*," she muttered, as she cut into her steak, then popped a bite into her mouth and chewed, now with pure joy on her face as she closed her eyes and moaned.

He chuckled. "That look on your face is one of my favorites."

"Sorry," she muttered. "It's as if I haven't eaten for weeks, and then you give me something delectable like this?" As soon as she swallowed, she focused on him and continued. "Okay, so go on. What about Arnie?"

"He had heard lot of rumors that the place was haunted, and he'd even heard a body was up there somewhere, but he'd only ever heard it from the street talk."

She nodded. "And nobody was willing to contact the police or to do anything about having somebody officially find the body?" she murmured.

"I still don't understand why it was as ..." He chuckled nervously. "It wasn't stinking."

"Not right now, no," she stated, "but it was past that point. I would think almost no flesh was on it anymore. It was dried out and on the top floor in a building with no insulation. The heat over the last few years has been absolutely stifling, so I imagine it probably stank at the beginning, and that might have been enough to keep people away, but now he's mine," she declared.

He looked at her, one eyebrow raised. "You don't get all the bodies though, right?"

"No, but believe me, that one will be mine."

"So, he was murdered?" he asked hesitantly.

"Yes, I would imagine so. The one blow to the back of the head? That was the final blow—or would be my guess. But I could be wrong, and, without any soft tissues left to look at, I would imagine it would be hard to determine if he had been brutally beaten first. But there was definitely a major blow to the head."

"Which would line up with your other cases."

"Yes," she confirmed.

"Before you ask, … and I know you aren't asking and haven't asked, but I want you to know that I haven't had any contact with anybody else."

She laughed. "Haven't you had contact with enough spirits already?"

"Yes, I really have," he agreed, turning to her. "I was just thinking that I don't want to be the middleman for people, spirits, to contact me and say, *Hey, by the way, my body is over here.* Like hell freaking no. … That would just suck."

"And yet it's happened a couple times."

"Well"—he frowned—"the one recent guy was alive."

"Yes, maybe, and maybe not—because it's the same building."

"Oh shit." He stared at her. "You're right. I assumed it was him."

She smiled and nodded. "But, because we found the other body, the skeleton, it's probably a really good chance that was the same one who was talking to you."

"Do you think he knew about the other one?"

"No, I don't think so. He probably thought you were coming in his direction and then got completely sidelined, and he's wondering what happened." She laughed. "I don't know how much knowledge they have about any of this," she admitted, smiling at him. "Maybe nothing."

"Maybe," he murmured. "It does seem it's never-ending though."

"It does."

With that on his mind, they finished their meal in silence.

CHAPTER 10

KATE WOKE TO a phone call blaring by her ear. As she sat up in bed and carried her phone out to the living room, she realized that it was seven o'clock in the morning.

"This is Anna," the quavering voice said.

Kate racked her sleep-deprived brain, trying to figure out who Anna was. "Hello, Anna," she replied cautiously. "What can I do for you?"

"They say he's brain dead," she muttered, sobbing, "and they just suggested that I might want to pull the plug sooner than later and decide about organ donation."

Kate winced, making the connection now. "I'm so sorry," she muttered. "I did understand that the damage was severe."

"Very," she added, sobbing harder now. "Did you find out who did this?"

"Not yet," she replied. "I do need to ask some more questions."

"Ask away," she whispered.

"I'm not quite mentally there," Kate shared, with half a thread of humor in her tone. "I haven't even had coffee yet."

"Maybe you could come to the hospital, and we can get this over with," Anna suggested hopefully.

Sensing something in the back of the woman's tone— like Anna wanted a heart-to-heart talk—Kate agreed. She might find out more about Anna's marriage without having to ask her directly. "I'll be down there in about twenty minutes."

Anna ended the call.

Kate stared down at the phone, wondering who on earth would consider her to be marriage counselor material. But she dressed quickly, and, as she was about to walk out the door, Simon came out in his pajamas, a questioning look on his face. "The man Rodney and I found in rough shape, Sonny? … I guess the docs have decided that he's brain dead and that his wife should consider organ donation."

He blinked several times. "Already?"

"I know. It does seem fast, but I guess the doctors were pretty sure yesterday. They did everything they could, but now it's literally only the machines keeping him alive."

"I don't think she has to make that decision immediately, though," Simon noted.

"I'm not sure it was a matter of making the decision, as much as she's now feeling incapable of coping," Kate noted.

"Right." Then he frowned. "She called you?"

"Yes," she muttered, with a note of humor. "I was just thinking I'm the last person anybody would normally call to help grieve the loss of a husband."

He nodded slowly. "Unless she has something to say."

"And that's what I'm hoping," she pointed out, as she headed to the door. "I don't know if I'm about to hear a confession, or will just have an absolutely distraught woman crying on my shoulder."

"Either way," he noted, "look after yourself."

And, with that, she raced outside. The traffic was light but still intense for Vancouver, and, by the time she made it to the hospital, thirty minutes had passed. She walked into

Sonny's hospital room to see Anna curled up in a tiny ball on the visitor's chair.

When Anna looked up and saw Kate, the poor wife burst into tears and raced toward her. Kate didn't know what to do except open her arms. Anna crashed into them, sobbing terribly. Kate held her for a long moment as she looked over at the man in the bed. "I'm sorry. I'm so very sorry," Kate muttered.

"I just realized how much of my life centered around him, and now he won't wake up again," she wailed, as she stepped back, looking up at Kate in sorrow. "I can't even begin to imagine what comes next."

"First off, you don't have to make a decision about life support right now," Kate began.

"And I probably rushed that. I don't even know that I exactly heard what they were saying. Yet, when they mentioned how I might consider organ donation, my mind went blank. We had always talked about that as being something we intended on doing," she murmured. She brushed back the tears from her eyes. "I'm just exhausted, and I seem to go from one crisis to another, and I really don't know quite where I'm at."

"Of course," Kate agreed. "You get this devastating news, and it's just so hard."

"It is hard," she declared, and then she sighed. "Could you check with the doctors to see if that's really what they're telling me?"

"Of course," She stepped out and walked down to the medical station and asked for the doctor attending her victim. As it was, a voice behind her stated that he was the attending physician. She turned, and there was the same man she'd spoken to yesterday.

He nodded. "Sonny had a series of ministrokes during the night," he explained, "and, unfortunately in this case, there's no chance of recovery."

"Ah," Kate muttered. "I'm really sorry to hear that."

"So are we," he murmured.

"Did you mention something about life support to Anna Hilton? She's very confused as to what stage this is at."

He winced. "I don't know that I did, but I wouldn't be surprised if somebody somewhere along the line asked if she had considered whether organ donation was something she was interested in," he replied, his face emotionless. "Obviously nobody wants to push her into something at this point, but he is 100 percent brain dead. We take him off that machine, and he's gone."

"But while he's on the machine he is alive, correct?"

He gave her a ghost of a smile. "Depends what you mean by *alive*, and that's one of those legal issues that is never clear," he pointed out. "Will Sonny ever talk, walk, or think again? No, the damage to the brain is too severe."

She nodded. "Okay. Anna just seems very confused at the moment."

"A lot happened overnight," he noted, "and I don't think she even understands all of it."

He explained a little bit more, and Kate got more or less what she needed to know. Then she asked, "How long is ideal for organ donation?"

"The sooner, the better," he declared bluntly. "The machines are keeping him alive, but, in terms of actual prime organs, the clock is running."

"He's also been badly beaten. Do we even understand what organs are good enough to transplant?"

"That's a good question," he noted. "I would need to

bring in the transplant team to address that. Why? You don't think somebody beat him up for that purpose, do you?"

Her eyebrows shot up as she looked at him. "No, I hadn't considered such a thing, and I really hope I never need to."

"Me too," the doctor replied, with feeling. "There's enough pain in the work we do, especially when these devastating cases come in. I would hate to think that somebody was doing this deliberately."

"Me too," she murmured. She headed back toward Anna. As she got to Sonny's room, she found Anna sitting at her husband's side, tears in her eyes.

Anna looked up at Kate and asked, "What did they say?"

"He had a series of strokes during the night."

"They took him out of here," she noted, her tears pouring. "He was gone for hours, and then, when they brought him back, nobody really told me anything."

"I am sure you are frustrated, but they were able to do some tests this morning."

"I guess it's just over. Is that what they told you?" she asked, tears welling up in her eyes. "Is he brain dead? Gone?"

"He had a series of strokes on top of the severe injuries he'd already sustained. That compromised any remaining hope," Kate murmured. Hoping that she got the phraseology correct, but knowing that this woman wouldn't be concerned about terminology, she cut to the chase. "So, the sad fact of the matter is, in this case, he will not be coming back."

Anna nodded, tears still in her eyes. "I guess when I couldn't get anybody to really say anything and saw those pitying glances in my direction, I knew." She took a deep breath. "Do you know what happens now?"

"I guess it depends on what you want to happen. Organ donation is potentially still a possibility," she added, "and I say *potentially* because he's been so badly beaten that we don't know which of his organs can be transplanted. That will have to be assessed right away."

"God," she whispered, as she looked down at her husband. "Can you even imagine thinking that this would be the way you would go?"

"And you didn't talk to him at all once he'd left that morning?"

"No, I never did. He's always so busy at work and doesn't like being disturbed."

Kate nodded. "And do you know if he had any …"

"Any what?" Anna asked, turning to her. Then she frowned. "Oh, enemies? You mean, anybody who hated him at work?"

"Has that been a problem?"

"Actually that's quite possible. He was the star salesman. He always earned top commissions and everything. He made a lot of money. I would have happily taken less money and had him home more."

"Of course," Kate replied. "Did you ever have any marital problems? Was there any chance that he might have had … you know?" She hesitated again.

The woman turned and looked at her. "You must really hate your job."

"There are times," Kate admitted, as she walked closer. "I have to ask these kinds of questions, so I find it best to just get it over with."

"So, you're wondering if he ever had affairs? I know of one that he had, but it was a few years ago, and he promised me at the time that it was the only one. … I didn't ask after that. I didn't really want to know and wasn't sure I could handle the truth."

"Of course," Kate said.

At that, Anna frowned at Kate. "But what you're trying *not* to tell me is that there was someone, wasn't there?"

Kate hesitated, then nodded. "Yes, at work."

"Christ, no wonder he didn't want me phoning in."

"You forgave him after his one indiscretion?"

"Yes," she said, "though the people I knew back then did tell me to leave him and that it wouldn't be a one-time thing. One of my friends suggested that getting caught once would just make him sneakier, so he wouldn't get caught a second time. … I guess that's what he did." She stared down at her husband, then leaned in close and spoke to him. "And what good did it do you, Sonny? All that traveling, all that being away? Even if it wasn't with me, what good did it do you?"

Standing up, she turned back to Kate, shaking her head. "I told him to change jobs, that he didn't have to work so hard. But he always said that he had to, that the company wasn't doing very well, that the company depended on him to get through this next period. I don't even know if that was true or a lie."

Kate shrugged. "I didn't speak to anybody about that at the company, but it seemed to be doing well enough, except for an awful lot of empty desks, what with people supposedly working from home."

Anna looked over at her. "Sometimes there was an opportunity to work from home, but, after COVID, everybody was ordered back," she stated. "At some point, they had a lot of layoffs. And maybe he didn't need to work that hard. I don't know. But I know that he was always there, always trying hard to be the best. He ..." She winced and added, "He was very competitive."

"Of course," Kate agreed. "Top salesmen tend to be that way."

"Right," Anna muttered. "Even if they don't have to be, it just seems to be built into their nature. And it sucks for the rest of us because we aren't that way at all."

At that, Kate asked her, "Did you use to work for the same company?"

"No, not this company, but we worked at the same place years ago," she shared. "That's one of the reasons why I didn't leave him when he had an affair because he did the same with me."

"Meaning?" Kate asked.

"Meaning, he was married before." Anna crossed her arms over her chest. "We had an affair at work, but he left his wife for me, and she really struggled with it. She became suicidal afterward. I never really understood, but I guess I get a chance to experience that now, won't I?" She shook her head.

"I regretted everything at the time," Anna admitted, "but I really loved him. And, of course, now I realize that he really didn't change at all. He just went underground, exactly as they told me that he would."

"I'm sorry," Kate whispered.

Anna looked at her. "As I said, you must really hate your job."

"Sometimes it's pretty rough," Kate admitted, with a pensive smile. "Sometimes people lie, cheat, steal, or worse, and I have to somehow sort through the mess of whatever they're trying to hide to see if it's really criminal or just shitty behavior."

Anna snorted. "Apparently my husband was topping the shitty behavior list."

"He was, indeed."

She frowned. "It wasn't that Angela, was it?"

Kate looked at her and asked curiously, "You've met her?"

"I met a lot of people. It was at a summer barbecue party, and I felt this odd vibe between the two of them." And she groaned. "I didn't even see it then, probably because I really didn't want to. God, I'm such a fool."

"I don't know about being a fool, or what you may have gone through before this with him or without him," Kate clarified, "but I do believe it was Angela, yes."

"It would be," Anna snapped, staring off in the distance. She turned back to her husband. "Then this is the way you go out? Nice move, Sonny." Anna turned back to Kate. "And you still have no idea who beat him up?"

"No," Kate shared. "I have no idea at this point. According to the office, he called a cab, but, so far, they don't see a charge on the company credit card for the cab."

Anna frowned. "What does that mean?"

"It could just mean that the credit card charge hasn't been posted to the bank account yet," she explained. "That happens sometimes."

"Yeah, it does. I've always handled a lot of our finances."

"And will you be okay? Financially?"

"I'll be okay," Anna replied, "but, if you have any other bombshells to drop, I would just as soon not hear them."

"Of course," Kate said. "That's understandable."

And then Anna groaned and shook her head. "No, as much as I might want to bury my head in the sand, I need to know the worst of it, so I can figure out where I stand and eventually pick up and move on. I don't think I will ever get married again though." She shook her head and then chuckled. "I don't think men are meant to be monogamous." She looked over at Kate. "Are you married?"

"No," Kate said.

"Any committed relationship?"

Kate hesitated and then nodded. "Yeah, I guess you could say that."

She laughed. "It doesn't sound very committed."

"It's plenty committed, just new."

"Ah, young love. That's the nicest stage of all."

Kate didn't want to discuss her relationship in the least and quickly changed the subject. "Do you think anybody at work would have had enough hate for your husband to do this?"

Anna gasped. "God, I hope not. … That's just too horrible to even contemplate. But maybe I'm the last person you should ask, since apparently I didn't know nearly enough about Sonny, though I thought I knew him inside and out." Then she looked over at Sonny and asked Kate, "Would you mind? …. I just want to be alone for a bit."

"Okay, and if you want to talk about what decision to make, you can always give me a call."

"Thank you," she muttered. "I guess the decision has already been made. If he is brain dead and if somebody else can use his organs, then that makes sense to me," she murmured.

Kate added, "I don't want the news that I just brought you to be a compelling force."

"No, it shouldn't be, and it isn't. But maybe in a way it is. I don't want to sit here, spend my life pining away for him, when I now know he never missed me at all." She shook her head. "Damn, when life throws you lemons ..."

Kate nodded and slipped out the door. The last thing she wanted was to get into a deep philosophical discussion about monogamy and faithfulness. As soon as she could, she pulled out from the hospital and headed to the office.

CHAPTER 11

"HEY, WHERE ARE you coming from?" Rodney asked, giving her a quick look, and then did a double-take. "You don't look so great."

"Thanks," she muttered, "nice to know."

He winced. "I didn't mean it that way."

She laughed. "No, but you're right. I don't look great. I just came from the hospital."

He stopped in the act of pouring coffee. "Oh. What's the news?"

"Sonny? Our victim from the warehouse had a series of mini-strokes during the night. He's now officially determined to be brain dead and is on life support. Discussions are happening about pulling the plug, since at least some of his organs could be viable for donation."

"Jesus Christ." Rodney stared at her. "That went fast."

"Yes, it did," she agreed, "though, all along the doctors were clear, at least with me, that the head injury might not be something he would survive, at least not in a functional sense. Then last night he took a bad turn with the strokes and all, and that was the final straw for his brain. It was just far too damaged, and there was no way to save him from that," she murmured.

"Jesus. How's his wife?"

"Maybe a little bit better, maybe a little bit worse. There

is something to be said for having clarity about his condition, even though it's bad."

"So, does she know … about the—"

"Yeah, I didn't get very far, and she guessed as much. I was trying to be gentle about it."

He snorted. "Really no way to be gentle about an affair."

"And she also guessed who it was," Kate noted. "So I don't know how that'll go over. And this wasn't the first time apparently. Oh, and he was also married before, and that time Anna was the side piece. He ended up leaving his wife for her."

"Jesus Christ," Rodney repeated, staring at her in shock.

"So, Anna's doing a lot of thinking about life at the moment, maybe even karma," she added, with a brief glance in his direction.

"Yeah, you're not kidding," he muttered. "That's always a hard one."

"Which is why I don't understand why people do this shit. Why can't they stick to one at a time? If they don't want to be married any more, then go through the divorce process and get out of it. At some point in time, you just need to stop screwing around on the side. I just don't get it." Kate frowned at him and asked, "Is that fresh coffee?"

"It is. I just made it."

She hopped up, walked over, and stated, "So, now the Sonny case is ours."

"Absolutely," he murmured, "and now we really get to look into the details of his life."

"Exactly," she said. "First and foremost, did a cab charge go onto the company's credit card, and, if not, is there one on somebody else's?"

"Meaning?" Rodney asked.

"What if Sonny didn't happen to have the company credit card on him? What if he accidentally forgot his card this time?"

"Oh, you're right. That could happen."

"All kinds of things could happen. We also need to know if any security is around the building. This all happened very quickly, and, when we consider everything that's gone on, as a timeline, this is even uglier."

"True," Rodney agreed. "Let me see if there's security around the company building."

"Were you ever able to contact the owner of the warehouse building?" she asked, as she ambled over to her desk.

"It's for sale, and the owners live in Germany. I spoke to their real estate agent, but they haven't had anything to do with it yet. It'll be listed here soon," he added.

"Right, they need somebody like Simon to buy it and to turn it into some good thing."

"He's certainly someone who has that kind of money."

"I have no clue what Simon has for money," she stated flatly. "That's not a discussion I care to have with him. For all I know, he can go buy Mars."

Rodney snorted. "Why the hell would you want that planet?"

"I don't want any planet or anything else," she stated, with a smile.

Rodney shook his head. "You've got one of the richest men around hanging all over you," he pointed out, "and you really don't care?"

"No, I really don't," she declared. "It's not my money. It's his." He stared at her, and she stared right back.

"You really mean that, don't you?" he asked. "You know how unusual that makes you?"

"No, it doesn't make me unusual at all," she snapped. "It just makes me, … well, … *me*."

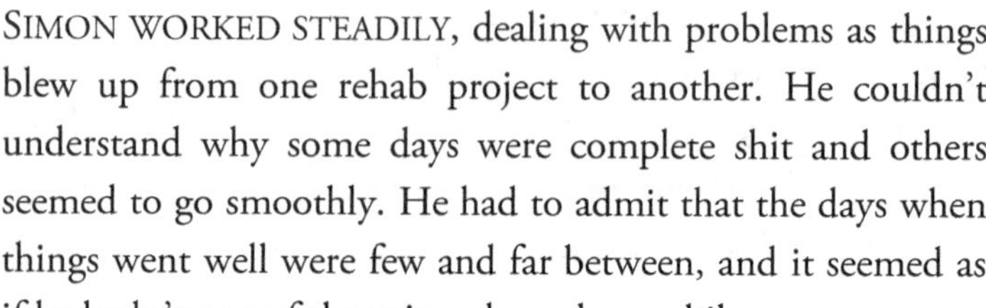

SIMON WORKED STEADILY, dealing with problems as things blew up from one rehab project to another. He couldn't understand why some days were complete shit and others seemed to go smoothly. He had to admit that the days when things went well were few and far between, and it seemed as if he hadn't one of those in a damn long while.

As he finally left the one rehab project and walked to another, he stopped to look at the skyline, his attention drawn to the warehouse where they had found the skeleton of that poor dead man. He realized he would always look at this building with that same sadness. "Somebody really needs to do something with it," he muttered.

Then he snorted because Kate would be all over him if she heard that. He could almost hear her saying, *Well, … do it then.* It's not as if he was built of money, but, if he shuffled things around, he could probably finance it. That was if it was even for sale and if he even gave a crap.

Honestly, he did give a crap. He just didn't know what to do about it.

Ariel, his stalking Realtor, who kept inserting herself in his business, called him a few hours later. "We need paperwork."

"Hello to you too."

"I need the paperwork cleared."

She was not messing around, and her tone was all-business, with none of her usual chatter and flirtation. "You were supposed to get it to me," Simon noted.

"I did," she snapped, "and you didn't sign it."

Frowning, he quickly looked through his emails and stated, "I don't have any of it."

"What?"

"I don't have it," he repeated flatly. "So, if you want me to sign docs, then you need to get me the paperwork."

"It's coming your way *again*," she said in a huff and ended the call.

He wasn't sure if she was just busy or if it really was something that had gone off the rails, but he hadn't even given that project any thought. When the documents came through a few minutes later, he forwarded them to his lawyer, asking for a reading, ASAP. He couldn't possibly ever move without getting a feasibility study.

Allen contacted him and asked, "These are on the Queensborough, yes?"

"Yes," Simon confirmed. "The Realtor seemed to think that I had the paperwork already and resent them just now, so I want to confirm they're on the up-and-up."

"I'll go through them. When do you want them?"

"Now," he replied succinctly.

His lawyer laughed. "Of course you do," he muttered. "Let me make some coffee, and I'll sit down and read through it." With that, he ended the call.

Simon realized coffee was something he rather desperately needed right now too.

He headed to his favorite coffee shop, frowning as he realized it was hard to even imagine it as a *favorite* anymore—not after he'd already had something to do with discovering that a customer here ended up being a serial killer. Still, he stepped up and ordered coffee and a muffin. Just as he went to sit down with it, his phone rang again. He looked down to see it was his lawyer. Allen Moore.

"It's all good," he declared. "Sign away, as long as you're okay with the price." They went over what the conditions were again. Then Simon quickly signed the doc and sent it off to the Realtor.

Ariel contacted him about an hour later and stated, "Okay, it's a done deal."

"Good. I need to start running some numbers through on future plans for this one."

"Yeah, it's a hell of a property."

"Location-wise it's a hell of a property," he corrected. "Building-wise, it's a piece of shit."

She snorted. "Yeah, but you apparently do those."

"I do," he confirmed, "and most people won't touch them."

"I never understood why you do them and other people won't."

"It's a cost issue," he explained. "You have to figure out if you can swing it and still be standing at the end of the day. By the way, do you know anything about a warehouse?" Then he gave her the address.

"Oh, shit," she muttered. "That's the one where a skeleton was just found."

"Yeah, not only that body," Simon clarified, "but a man was found beaten up in there the previous day as well."

"Good God, seriously?" she asked.

"Yes."

"Wow, I hope he's okay. That's a really rough area of town."

He refrained from giving her any answer. "I just wondered about the building."

After a moment of silence, she asked quite playfully, "As in?"

"As in, I just wondered what the deal is with the building," he clarified. "I'm sure you could find out."

"Do you want to purchase it?" she asked.

"I don't know," he replied, frustrated. "Let's just say that I've got a lot of things on my mind. I really don't need another one, especially considering what I just bought, but I am curious about that property."

"Fine," she said, all flirtatiousness gone. "I think it came up in a discussion at the office the other day. I'll check it out and see what the deal is."

"Good," he replied and rang off. He knew it was a foolish thing to even consider. Beyond foolish. The last thing he needed. But then again came that little voice in the back of his head. *But sometimes you have to do what you have to do.*

"But I don't," he snapped.

Wincing as he realized he'd brought some attention to himself, he hoped they would think he was talking on Bluetooth or something. Realizing he was always one step away from looking like he'd completely lost his marbles, he picked up his coffee and started to walk. The last thing he really needed was another project.

The hotel that he'd just purchased was cheap enough, and it could sit for a while. He could even just unload it, if he dropped it, cleaned it up, and set it up as a new building site. However, he would make a ton of money if he set it up for business. It would probably take forty million to do it properly. Swearing at that, not sure where he's going with that thought, still not really having any choice but to consider it, he walked on. This was where his business sense went out the window, and it became an issue of the heart.

He found himself walking right toward the warehouse he'd just asked Ariel to look up. As he stood here, she called him.

"So, turns out it will be sold, and I happen to know the Realtor with the listing," Ariel began, back to her same old flirtatious tone. "It's apparently going for sale this next week—or at least it would have, until this mess happened."

"Right. … So what price are they looking at? Do you know?"

She shared the asking price that had his eyebrows raising. "Really?" he asked, with a dry laugh. "It's derelict, haunted, and all kinds of other things."

"Including prime real estate."

"But we both know it needs a crap load of work. Nope, not for me," he said, his tone calm. "That one's full of bad woo-woo vibes." Ariel went silent, and he laughed. "I know. I never say that," he admitted, "but it is what it is. This one's got a really bad feel to it, and it needs to be dropped. I would need a far-more-reasonable price if I were to get into it."

"Are you thinking that you're the one to drop it?" she asked him cautiously.

"I don't know. If the sellers are set on that price, no way," he declared, "definitely not. And, once people find out that not only one but two murdered people were dumped there, that won't go over well."

"No, they'll do a quick sale and try to keep that out of it, if they can. You're right. Once news like that gets out, it just becomes too much of a headache."

"It already is," Simon noted, "and, as we both know from experience, all the locals avoid it, and everybody else will too."

"Yet not you," she stated, with a note of amusement. "You're walking right toward it."

"Maybe not," he said, "definitely not at that price."

He ended the call and stood here, looking up at the old

building, and whispered, "Sorry, sweetheart. Some projects are definitely way too expensive for even me to take on. And now that I have another one ready to drop, I don't think anything good can be in the works for you." It was almost as if she understood, and he felt a true sense of sorrow. He frowned.

"Look, if this is something I'm supposed to take on," he added, "somebody needs to show me that it's worth my time and effort. Otherwise, hell no," he muttered. "If it was supercheap, then maybe I could try, but only if it comes at a bargain-basement price."

And, sure enough, Ariel called him back ten minutes later.

"So, how badly do you want that property?" she asked.

"Why?" he asked.

"Because the owners have found out about the two murders, and they don't want anything to do with it. Apparently they're quite religious, and this is triggering all kinds of bad vibes for them. Maybe that bad woo-woo you were talking about. I think they would agree with you."

"I don't know," Simon replied. "Depends on what they're looking for as a sales price."

She laughed. "The price that they were originally asking for was decent," she began, "but the price they've dropped it to now is shocking. If I had the money, I would be all over it myself."

"Sure," Simon noted, "but you still haven't told me what the new asking price is." As soon as she stated the new figure, he was excited as hell. "That's less than half of what they were asking."

"I know, and believe me that my Realtor friend is beside herself."

"Sure, less than half the commission for her."

Ariel snorted. "When we do these kinds of deals, it's not even about the commission. As you very well know, it's all about repeat customers."

"People like me," he stated in a wry tone.

"Yes," she agreed cheerfully. "People like you also pay my mortgage. On the other hand, people like me keep you in these buildings that you want to sign up for."

"Not all that sure I want to sign up for this one though, but at that price—"

"I know, and I think that's why they're doing it," Ariel exclaimed. "It might go out to the market differently, but right now, at this moment, if you make an offer, it's a done deal."

He frowned at that. "I have to talk to my banker and my lawyer, you know, to see if I can finance it."

"You do you," she said. "I'm just telling you that, if you want this one, you've got to strike while the iron is hot. The more time that passes, … I don't know why but …"

"But what?"

"The owner, Elsie, she's not well. She's saying sell it right now because she thinks it might be connected to her health issues."

"What?" he asked, his mind still reeling from the name. "Did you say her name was Elsie?"

"Yes, that's her name."

"And why did she think that?"

"I guess she has a few regrets for things she might have done when she was younger. Now she's thinking that she's being punished and that this building might have something to do with it."

"I don't suppose she murdered any of the men found in

her warehouse, did she?"

At that, Ariel snorted. "Yeah, no, I don't think so. But that doesn't mean she wasn't a beautiful woman in her day and might need to be clearing her conscience sometime soon."

"These things just boggle the mind," he muttered. "I'll call you back." With that, he ended the call, phoned his lawyer, and barked, "Take a look at this property." He gave him the address.

"Another one?" Allen asked. "You want to confirm you're not spreading yourself too thin."

"I know," he replied. "Otherwise I'll be out in a damn casino, gambling for money again."

Allen paused, and then he started to laugh. "I forgot that's how you got started. You had the darndest luck. Anyway, I'll take a look at it, if you're serious about this one."

"Oh, I am," Simon declared.

"What's so special about it?"

"Well, for one, it's where my partner found the man who was beaten up in there. Two, we found another body when we did the full search of the warehouse, and three," he added, "the owner's name is Elsie."

"And?" Allen asked. "I get the first two, but what's that name got to do with anything?"

"I don't expect you to understand that one." Simon sighed. "Just take a look at it." His next call was to the banker. David was not happy at all, but who gave a crap what he thought? It didn't take long before Simon had the purchase cleared, even if he had to start moving some money around.

"It's always good to do business with you," David said in

a casual tone.

As soon as Simon got off the phone, he called Allen back and told him to look at this sale now.

Allen replied, "I'll get right on it. You have a good feeling about this one?"

"Maybe," Simon noted. "I just want to confirm I don't overstretch my boundaries here."

"Are you concerned about it?" Allen asked in alarm, and he chastised himself for having asked it in the first place.

"No, I'm not concerned about it," Simon stated. "I'm just being sensible."

"Sensible is good, at least in my books," Allen said, with a snort. "So, I'm all for it. Let me know if you want to write up something formal on this one."

"Will do," Simon said. "Read it over and let me know what you think."

When Allen got back to him, he muttered, "That's a hell of a price. I'm not sure you can lose on this one."

"Oh, I can lose," Simon admitted. "Yet, even if I completely destroy the warehouse, which in this case might be the best thing, it's still prime real estate."

"It is, and it's a hell of an opportunity at that price."

"I know," Simon said. "So, are we all right on your part?"

"Yes, definitely a green light on this one," he confirmed, his tone cordial. "And, damn, I'm envious on this one, you're just full of luck."

"Maybe, but that doesn't mean I'll offer full price either."

After a moment's pause, Allen laughed. "That's a valid point. Why would you? If that's the price they're giving, that's just a starting point."

"I agree," Simon confirmed, "but I also can't go too low and have them turn around and list it."

"Right, it's a fine line," Allen noted. "Good luck."

When Allen ended the call, Simon quickly phoned Ariel. "Write up an offer," he said.

"Really?" she asked in delight.

"Yes," he replied, but he named a figure substantially lower.

Cautiously, she added, "I'm not sure they'll go for that, not after making such a drop already. They may not accept your offer."

"And it might come up, but, right now, as you said, the iron is hot, though I don't really want to take advantage, not too much."

"Really?" she questioned in a droll tone. "But you're right," she conceded. "It's business. Let me write it up."

She sent the paperwork within an hour, while he was still at his next coffee shop, sitting here, munching away on a sandwich. He quickly signed the offer and sent it back.

As he did, he looked over in the direction of the warehouse. It still called to him. "This one's for you, Elsie. I've got no idea what I'll do with it," he admitted, "but surely we can do something to help people in your situation."

Of course, Elsie wasn't among the people in the situation as described, but the problem bothering her needed to be dealt with. As soon as he sent off the signed paperwork, he got a call from one of his foremen.

As they talked through a couple things, the foreman added, "It might be time to start looking at another project, as this one's definitely on track. We won't be finished today or tomorrow, but it is coming along nicely."

"I am thinking about another one," Simon declared.

"I've just picked up one property, and I'm looking at a second right now."

His foreman snorted. "Well, good. Tell me about it."

"Not much to tell yet, these just happened," he noted.

"Any thoughts on what you'll do?"

"Not yet."

Completing the call, he turned his attention back to his lunch.

Before he was even done eating, Ariel called again.

She shared, "The buyers are not saying no, but they're asking if you can come up."

"And how much do they want me to come up?" he asked.

She hesitated and finally said, "Honestly, not very much."

"Give me the figure, so we'll negotiate and then counter."

"They don't want to counter unless they can talk to you about it. They want to know why you want the building."

"I'm not sure why I want the building," he stated, "but I feel something about it."

"I tried to explain to them a little bit about what you do, and the client was of the opinion that this building needed to be dropped."

"And maybe she's right. I don't know yet," he replied. "After my partner found the one man beaten but alive one day, followed by our finding the skeleton of a man the next, I'm feeling fairly protective about it."

"Good. Let me talk to them about it again. Stay tuned." She called him back a few minutes later. "They didn't realize that you were there when the body was found."

"Yes, and I was there at the time with my partner when

they found the second one."

There was silence at first. Then she muttered, "Jesus, that's just creepy. You know that building should be dropped."

"And I might just do it," he stated, calm and collected. "However, I won't make that decision right now."

"No, of course not," she muttered.

After they ended the call, he got up and checked out the choices of ice cream here. It was way too cold for it, but it was looking mighty tempting.

While he hemmed and hawed, Ariel called back and said, "She'll split the difference, if you want it."

He thought about the split-the-difference part because that would be a good chunk of change. "Fine," he said. "Have them send a counter, and I'll go from there."

"Will you accept the counter?"

"I don't know," he snapped irritably. "I'll figure that out when I see it."

She moaned. "You are so frustrating."

"I may be frustrating, but I'm also the one who's making the offer," he pointed out in a droll tone.

"Yes, you are, but it's also a hell of a deal."

"So, either get it done or don't," he snapped once more. He ended the call, only to realize another customer was staring at him. "Sorry," he muttered, shaking his head with a shrug. "*Realtor.*"

The guy just laughed. "They're all sharks," he declared. "Make sure you don't let them walk all over you."

That seemed to start a general conversation in the entire coffee shop. By the time he was outside and on his way, everybody had given him all kinds of advice. He just smiled, knowing that was the last thing he really needed. Yet he appreciated the sentiments.

Realtors did get a bad reputation, and maybe they deserved it. Maybe they didn't. He certainly painted all of them with the same brush, but he was struggling to handle the one he was dealing with right now.

As soon as he made it over to the second rehab project, his foreman looked over at him and smiled.

"So, how's it going?" the foreman asked Simon.

"It's going," he muttered, watching him closely. "More to the point, how are you doing here?"

"We're doing better," he stated. "We won't make up for lost time, but things are definitely holding."

"Good," Simon replied.

"And did you get that new property, so we've got another job to do?"

"We do have another job to do, but we both know how long it takes to get that shit done."

"Right. As soon as you have another project on the go, then I don't need to be looking for work."

Simon rolled his eyes. "As if I haven't kept you in work for these last what, ten years by accident?"

"Nope," he agreed, followed by a loud guffaw. "And generally, at this point in time, I would know that you have another project in the wings. Just checking in."

"I bought one building, and I'm looking at a second. I wasn't planning on the second one, but that's the way it goes sometimes."

"Wow, that will tie up a lot of cash," he noted, his eyes narrowed. "Normally you only do two at a time."

"I might sit on one for a bit," he shared. "I'm not sure yet, but I'll also drop it."

"Wow, that would be two you would drop," he noted.

"This one just might need it."

"The only time it might need it is if it's got bad mojo." Then he stopped and looked over at him, and a look flashed in his gaze. "Oh, man, you didn't."

Simon looked at him and shrugged. "Not yet I didn't."

"The only way I'm working on that one," he declared, "is if you literally take the stuffing out of it and take it right down to the ground."

"And I might have to. In this case, it might even be part of the agreement," he added, with an eye roll.

"Really, the owners don't want you to fix it all up?"

"No, something to do with these last murders and the fact that the owner is having some health issues again," he shared.

"It seems as if we've got people who have been hanging on to these properties for a long time," he suggested, "looking to maximize the eventual sale."

"Sure, but, if they'd sold them earlier, people could have done something with them, but now they're so derelict that they're not worth saving."

"And they're all emotionally attached," he noted, with a sigh.

"Right, emotionally attached and yet financially on a pull string." While he stood there, his phone buzzed. He looked down and muttered, "Here's a counteroffer right now."

"What'll this one cost you?"

He looked over at him and shrugged. "Enough, but believe me that it's a deal. Otherwise I wouldn't be taking it."

"It has to be," he stated. "In all seriousness, that one could be bad news."

"It could be, but I think dropping her and starting something fresh and new would be good for her."

His foreman smiled. "I do like the fact that, to you, they're not just dead properties."

"No, they aren't. Yet I still have to cover costs. If it even gets to the break-even point, I can live with that."

"I'm not sure how you do it, but somehow you seem to manage." He shook his head and quipped, "Go on. Buy yourself the next universe."

He laughed and added, "Now you sound like Kate."

"How is she doing?" he asked, eyeing him quizzically.

"Busy, dealing with the two bodies found in that one property."

"Oh, and that's why they're selling right now," he noted, his eyes squinting. "Talk about bad publicity. That's a bargain-basement deal now."

"It is, which is also why the iron is hot," he said, with a laugh. He looked down at his phone and opened the text message with the counteroffer and smiled. "She did counter, but she didn't counter as much as she said."

Ariel called him back and said, "I'm really surprised at this too. I think she really just wants to get rid of it."

"I would believe that except they didn't accept the original offer."

"No, but this is not much of an argument."

"Agreed," he said, as he looked at it and realized it was just about perfect. He quickly signed it and sent it back to her. "Done deal. I signed the paperwork."

"Nice doing business with you," Ariel declared, with almost a cackle in her tone.

He smiled. "Yeah, that's two in a couple days."

"Yep," she confirmed, "but I've been working on the other one for a very long time."

"You have, and now you can get off my back. I won't need anything else for quite a while."

"Unless another deal comes along."

He frowned. "Okay, unless another deal comes along."

She laughed and rang off.

With a smile, he looked over at his foreman and nodded. "Okay, two buildings, and you've got enough work to keep you going for the next ten years."

His foreman laughed, raised a hand, and nodded. "Damn good thing you've got money. Everybody else in this business is going broke. I don't know if you heard, but old man Horseman, his son has just declared bankruptcy."

Simon frowned at him and asked, "Seriously?"

He nodded. "Yeah, high cost of labor and all the rest," he said.

"Yeah, but they're not keeping a close enough eye on the bottom line," Simon declared. "As long as I don't get called in to deal with that one, we're good."

"Do you think you would?"

"No, I don't think so." He rubbed his chin. "I don't know too many people in that family."

"Good, because, once a rich big-business family goes down, the in-fighting starts to get really good."

"Yeah, that depends on whether you like fighting or not," Simon noted, with a headshake. "Me? I would just as soon stay away from it all."

"That's because you've got nobody to fight it out with," his foreman pointed out, with a snort. "If it was me, my brother would be all over it. He would sue me for mismanaging the company, and it wouldn't end there."

"Some families are like that," Simon agreed. "We've seen good families go under for no good reason."

"Yeah, we sure have. It's sad."

"Sad, yet just be grateful it's not you." He gave him a smile and turned to leave. "Now I have to deal with the reality of these new acquisitions. I'll talk to you later." And, with a bit of a spring in his step, Simon turned and headed down the street. And his feet took him right back to the warehouse he'd just bought.

He smiled up at her. "It's okay, sweetheart. I'm not sure what we'll do with you, but you'll be fine from here on out." And, with a warm heart, he turned to walk away. He had gone all of five steps when something inside him called out.

Not so fast.

He stopped and slowly looked around, but nobody was nearby. Frowning, he called out loud, "Who was that?"

Me, said the voice in his head. *You don't think this will be the end of it, do you?*

"I hope so, unless you've got something to say otherwise."

Oh, I've got something to say otherwise, the voice snapped. *You still haven't found me.*

Those words put ice down his back. He was frozen for a few moments, until the voice snapped at him again.

Find me.

"Are you in that same building?"

I'm in that same building, and nobody even gives a crap.

"Maybe you need to tell me where and what's going on."

I can't. I just know I'm here, and I can't leave until you find me.

"Well, crap," Simon muttered, as he stared at the building.

Yeah, you're not kidding. Nowwww or neverrrr.

CHAPTER 12

KATE WENT THROUGH the most recent vehicle reports that Reese had just dropped off on her desk. Reese watched as Kate matched them up to the statements from the onlookers. Apparently multiple delivery vans worked in the area. Most were white, but a couple were dark blue, and another one was black and was fairly well-known. She was running through the reports, looking for the one her witnesses had described, hoping that it was at least local and not something they would have to cross the line to even get information on it. She stopped, tapping the page. "Now we have an interesting one here," she muttered.

Standing beside her, Reese nodded. "That's the one I was thinking of too. I've been trying to call the owner, but I haven't gotten anywhere."

"Any idea what it's used for?" Kate asked.

"It's registered as a delivery business, but further research shows that it's a single person, and it looks as if he made a niche for himself, simply by providing delivery service in that corner of the world," she shared. "I've left a couple messages, but he hasn't gotten back to me yet."

"Of course not." Kate frowned. "I wonder if we can get any idea where else he might be. And I need better photos."

"Why?" Reese asked, already headed to her computer, yet turning back to her. "Will you go after him?"

"I'll go talk to him for sure," Kate stated, looking over at her. "He could be the delivery vehicle that was seen near the warehouse property."

"Which would make sense if he was delivering stuff."

Kate gave her a wry smile. "Not to that building. It's a derelict warehouse. Nobody lives there, and nothing productive is happening in that place."

Reese frowned and nodded. "Something's probably close by."

"Maybe, but he's definitely somebody I want to talk to."

"All I've got is a P.O. box." Then she stopped and checked her phone. "Nope, nothing's registered to the business at all. That's not right. He needs to have a physical address."

"Find me his physical address, and I'll hit it up this afternoon. Also more pictures of the vehicle, if you have anything for it."

"I can get you something like it, but it won't be exact."

"I'll take whatever you've got."

Reese waved and took off.

With that, Kate got up and headed over to the coffeepot.

Meanwhile, Rodney walked in and asked her, "Hey, are we getting anywhere?"

"Somewhere," she replied, nodding at him. "I'm still waiting for the coroner over the last body, the skeleton."

"Chances are, they'll have to bring in a specialist for that one."

"I know," she muttered, "and I'm waiting for Reese to get me more pictures of dark vans, but we may have a line on the delivery vehicle seen in the area."

"Oh, good," Rodney said. Then he eyed her intently. "Are you planning on going out this afternoon?"

"Yes, I am," she declared, with a nod. "I don't know how many more people we have missing or in this nightmare that we've got going on, but I do need to figure out as much as we can before somebody else gets taken."

At that, her phone rang. She looked down and frowned, as it was not a local number. She answered it to find a Burnaby detective contacting her. "Hey. What can I do for you?"

"I was talking to an associate over in Coquitlam district," he began, a hardness in his tone. "Something about you wondering if you have similar cases. I haven't put this into the database yet, and it's just happened in the last couple days, but we have a case of what was a missing person who now appears to be the homicide of somebody who's been very badly beaten."

"Where did you find the body?" she asked curiously.

"That's the weird thing. It was found in the back of a truck in a junkyard."

"Good God. Seriously?"

"Yes."

"How long was he missing?"

"Only a couple days," he replied. "Which matches what you're looking at, right?"

"Yes. So, tell me, Detective …"

"Detective Mark Zimmer. Call me Mark."

"Okay, so, Mark, was he by any chance a mild-mannered businessman type?"

"Yes." He hesitated and then added, "Also he was having an affair. I don't know if that's pertinent or not."

She sucked in her breath as she thought about it. "That would be a very interesting comparison to make, not that we'll necessarily know for everybody. However, we do have one of the two men recently identified, and—from what we know so far—my victim also had an affair."

"Interesting," he murmured. "I can send you this report, if you give me your contact information." He went on, with a hint of sharpness in his tone. "I really don't want to see this case get slid under the carpet. I don't know the family, but it could be anybody."

"I hear you," she replied. "That's part of the problem in these cases. Since the killer could be anybody, unfortunately it seems to be lining up to be a challenge."

"If this is a stranger abduction, they're way harder to sort out, as it's all about opportunity," he added.

"True, so was your guy about to head out and do any traveling?"

"He was, indeed. He was going on a trip, but, in this case, it was holiday."

She pondered that for a moment, comparing it to the Sonny Hilton case. "Any idea if he took a cab?"

"He did," he noted curiously. "Why? Do you have something like that going on?"

"One of them," she shared cautiously. "One for certain. We have less information on the other victims, and we're not sure yet on the circumstances surrounding those."

"Did you get a hold of the cabbie?"

"So far we don't even have documentation of a charge for a cab."

Silence came on the other end. "I'll follow up on that lead right now." And he ended the call.

She felt the excitement building inside her. Something was here. Definitely something was here. And just as she was about to pour a cup of coffee, Reese stopped by with several pictures and more information. Kate nodded, thanking her, and shared, "It looks as if Coquitlam and Burnaby may have another connected case as well."

Her eyebrows shot up. "It didn't show up in the search."

"It just happened," she pointed out. "I just got off the phone with Detective Mark Zimmer in Burnaby. ... So check on that too if you can. He apparently heard that we might have a serial killer case in the works here. He's checking up on the cab information on his case right now."

Her phone rang again, and it was the detective.

"We find no charge for the cab," he stated, "so that could very well be what we're looking at."

"It could be," she agreed, looking at Reese, who stood beside her. "In which case that'll be a whole lot harder to sort out."

"And we can't exactly put out a warning, telling everybody not to use a cab, or to confirm they know the cabbie, because that just won't happen."

"It could be worse," she muttered. "Thankfully we don't have much of an Uber presence here yet. That would be way worse."

"It would give people another alternative right now, though," he pointed out.

"True enough," she agreed. "Send me the file, and I'll run some comparisons here." With that, she ended the call and looked over at Reese. "That will come over to you."

"Good, because we need any new related cases."

"This is a recent one. ... He went missing *a couple days ago*. I don't know for sure that it means two days ago to Zimmer. I'll check it out. Really though, what we're looking at is who went missing before this guy. Before the ones we have here. Who is victim zero?" she stated, her frustration oozing. "If we figure that out, we'll have a much better idea what we're looking at."

"Oh, you already have a good idea what we're looking at," Reese declared, shaking her head as she walked away. "What we have here is another asshole, this one preying on businessmen who are not in very good shape, and somehow a beating is a big part of it."

Thinking about that, Kate walked slowly back to her desk. Then suddenly she felt this urge to check up on Simon, realizing something was off with him right now. She picked up the phone and tried calling him. No answer. She ended the call, then dialed again, and still got no answer. Feeling a sense of urgency, she looked over at Rodney. "I have to go downtown to check up on Simon." When he frowned at her, she shrugged. "I can't reach him, and I'm getting a really ugly feeling."

Rodney got up. "I'll come with you."

She frowned. "I don't think that's necessary."

"You don't know about that for sure," he clarified, grabbing his jacket. "For all you know, our serial killer has picked him out. He is a businessman, after all."

She studied him and nodded slowly. "Yet he doesn't fit the physical description."

"No, but maybe this guy thinks he's up for a bigger challenge now."

"Jesus," she muttered. "You think that's what it is?"

"I don't know what this is," Rodney admitted, "but what I do know is that we've got a killer here creating challenges, and people are failing to rise to his challenge because it's pretty heavily weighted to the killer's side. So, what happens when he decides he's good enough to move on?"

"He'll go for another businessman, and somebody who's

in a lot better shape but not great shape," she pointed out. "So, I think, at the moment, Simon is safe."

He frowned, then muttered, "If you think so."

"I do, but, Jesus, thanks for putting that thought in my head. I'll handle this one myself." She waved goodbye and dialed Simon one more time. When she still got no answer, she raced outside and called his foreman. When the foreman confirmed that Simon had left a few hours earlier, she knew exactly where he would be. But just to double-check, she called the doorman at his penthouse, only to be told he wasn't home.

With that cleared, she headed downtown, to the same warehouse building where the bodies had been found. She didn't know why this warehouse was so important, but it was where they had found two people so far. Chances are, it still called out to him for some reason. When she finally got there, she parked off to the side and called him again, still getting nothing. When she headed to the main entrance of the warehouse, she heard Simon calling out to her.

She turned, the relief evident on her face.

He looked at her. "I wasn't expecting to see you here."

She frowned as she eyed him intently. "Are you okay?"

He nodded. "I'm okay," he replied, an odd look on his face. "Is there a reason why I wouldn't be?"

"You haven't been answering your phone for one thing," she stated angrily. "Then I got this horrible feeling."

His eyebrows shot up, and he nodded. "Did you pick up on something about forty minutes ago? If so, it would be fair enough."

"It was about forty minutes," she agreed, as she checked her watch, "but it takes time in traffic to get here."

"It does," he noted, as he gave her half a smile. "So, either you're really getting in sync with me or you're getting psychic yourself."

"No fucking way," she exclaimed, staring at him in horror. "And joking or not, why would you even say such a thing?"

He burst out laughing. "It can't be that bad."

"Oh, yes, … it can be," she declared, frowning at him. "So, what's the deal then? Are you fine?" She pushed back her hair and glared at him. "I tore out of my office and came racing down here."

"Yeah, but why here?" he asked, studying her with interest.

She turned around and frowned. "Because," she relented, "because this building calls to you in some way, and whatever is calling out to you, it felt wrong."

"I don't know about wrong," he clarified, "but definitely that same voice is talking to me. He called himself Jay, and I had thought it was his body that we found, but he says it's not."

She stared at him in shock, too stunned to say anything right away. She swallowed. "Please don't tell me that you think another body is on this property?"

"But I *do* think there's another body," he stated, "or at least Jay thinks he's in here … somewhere."

"And do you have a name other than Jay? That nickname could work for all kinds of given names, even last names. Any clue as to who he is?"

Simon shook his head. "No, I don't have anything on him. I just know that, because of him, I came here and found Arnie and Elsie, you found Sonny, and then we found the skeleton," he pointed out.

She looked up at the building. "And have you just been

inside?" she turned, frowning at him.

"Yes. I wasn't sure if it was cleared from the police or not, but, as the new owner," he declared, with a wry look at her, "I figured I should probably go in and take a look. I was just taking a look around the perimeter when you arrived."

She stared at him for a long moment and then sighed. "You bought the building?" He nodded. She didn't even know what to think about that. "Why this one? I thought you worked with buildings that needed saving."

"I do," he confirmed, "but I feel this building is crying out to be demolished."

"Demolished?" she repeated, her eyebrows shooting up. "I didn't think that was something you did."

"Neither did I," he admitted. "But I've got to tell you, this one's different."

"Oh, I hear you, but there's always been derelict buildings with bodies found in them," she noted, "whether it's drug addicts or something else entirely."

"I know," he muttered, "but what can I tell you?" He shrugged. "I just needed to buy it."

"I won't question your financial decisions," she said, holding up a hand. "That's definitely an area of expertise I do not have, but this person, this voice—"

"I know," he replied. "You don't like the voice."

"What's to like about the voice?" she asked. "And the fact is, it has already brought you here to find Arnie, and Rodney and me to find a man who was very badly injured, and then to someone else's skeleton, who was here for a very long time."

"I know," he agreed, "and I don't know what to tell you, but Jay says that wasn't him."

"And is he expecting you to find him?"

He winced and nodded. "I would say that's a given."

"That's nice," she muttered, glaring at him. "What if you can't?"

"I don't know," he admitted, shaking his head. "I haven't got to that part yet."

She noticed the plans that he had in his hands. "What are those?"

He unrolled the papers. "These are the plans for this building, per City Hall," he shared. "One of my men pulled them for me."

She frowned and asked him, "You're looking for Jay, aren't you?"

"I don't know what else I'm supposed to do," he bit off. "If another body is here, I feel as if I need to find it, and if there isn't? … Well, maybe Jay will leave me alone … and in peace."

She bit her lip as she studied him. "Okay," she conceded finally. "Did you see anywhere in this mausoleum of a property where a body could be hidden?"

He hesitated and then shrugged. "Not today, no, but I did just get the plans."

"Okay." She brushed the hair off her face. "In that case, where do we start?"

———— ❧ ————

SIMON LOOKED OVER at Kate, the woman who continuously surprised him in a never-ending way. From being terrified, to being supportive, and then sometimes back to being terrified, she always stood by him, even if it made her uncomfortable.

"You don't have to go with me," he offered.

She raised her eyebrows. "If another body is in here, I

need to know, and I need to know if it's connected to my current cases." He shook his head. She frowned. "That was pretty fast."

"I see that," he muttered, staring off in the distance, "but I don't know why."

"And, if you don't know why, you also may not know the answer."

He smiled. "You could be right. I'm not saying that I know everything, and I sure as hell don't know anything when it comes to this," he muttered. "I'm just trying to follow the bread crumbs."

She nodded ever so slowly. "In that case, where are these breadcrumbs leading you right now?"

"You don't have to stay with me, you know?" he repeated. "This search could be completely fruitless." But she stayed, just staring at him intently. He frowned. "Is there some other reason you're here?"

"Sure," she replied, with a negligent shrug. "To confirm you're okay."

Something bloomed deep inside him, and he realized she had literally just dropped everything to confirm he was okay. "You know, some people would say that puts us in a very unique relationship."

Her eyebrows shot up. "I don't know anybody who would disagree with you in terms of our being a unique couple," she noted. "However, I do not make a habit of discussing our relationship with anybody, and I generally refrain from getting into it. All questions regarding my relationship will get an answer leading the conversation in a completely different direction."

His lips twitched. "Particularly when it comes to me and my weird habits."

"Everybody always wants answers on various things with our cases," she explained, "but we don't get answers that way. If they come, then I will put them to good use. If they don't come, I won't sit here and cry about it," she declared in a defiant way.

He looked at her and nodded. "I can live with that."

Her shoulders sagged, as if she thought he might have had a problem with it.

"You know, Kate, I'm totally okay to accept you as you are."

"Good," she replied, "and I'm working on accepting you as you are."

He burst out laughing at that because he knew it to be true. Kate was nothing if not absolutely honest, sometimes to a fault. But he could always count on what she told him would be the truth as she knew it. "I can live with that too," he added comfortably. "So, shall we go explore?"

"But it's just an open cavernous room here, with stairs on the side, and floor after floor of open warehouse," she noted, not sure where to start. "What is it you're looking for?"

He pointed at the docs in his hand. "That's why I had the building plans brought in."

"Okay, meaning?"

"Meaning, this building has to have utility rooms, furnace rooms, electrical panels, all of that," he noted. "So somewhere—"

"Oh, right," she interrupted, as she looked around, frowning at the huge cavernous walls. "We never saw anything like that, did we?"

"No," he agreed, "but generally they're down, not up."

Immediately her gaze dropped. "Is there a basement,

another floor below this?"

"There should be at least some kind of an electrical room," he stated, skimming the drawings. "This warehouse is a huge building, and there's got to be accessible power somewhere."

"Good enough." She waved him forward. "Lead on."

"I haven't figured out where we can get to it yet."

"No elevators," she muttered, as she glanced around, "so check for stairs."

"Not seeing any stairs that go down."

She frowned. "Outside access?"

"Now that makes sense. They would still be stairs, but likely hidden somehow. But the only way to hide stairs would be with a storefront or something, as the stairs would be unsightly. Which is why it'll be ..." He paused, looking at her, one eyebrow raised.

"At the back of the building," she pointed out, "where nobody will see it, and they can keep all the ugly stuff hidden."

He laughed. "You know, a good electrician takes pride in making sure there is no *ugly stuff*, as you put it."

She rolled her eyes. "Maybe, but the truth of the matter is, that stuff can get pretty ugly looking very quickly."

"It sure can," he acknowledged with a smile, then led the way to the back of the building. It was still a hugely open and spacious warehouse. Yet, with the busted-out windows and open ceiling in various places, where some of the metals had been ripped off, and nothing but garbage strewn around on the floors, it had such a desolate, empty look.

"I really am not against you dropping this one," she added. When he looked at her, she shrugged. "It's been a grave for somebody for at least two years."

"I suspect it's been a grave far longer than that."

She frowned. "Do you think that's what's going on with the current voice?"

"Yes, whatever *this* is," he noted. "I don't understand why everything keeps changing, but I am sensing something is here."

"Maybe it's …"

He frowned at her. "What?" he asked, hating the challenge in his voice.

"Maybe it's partly because you're changing."

He stopped, then stared at her, one eyebrow up.

She shrugged. "You're not the same person you were when I first met you. I'm not the same person I was when I first met you. And every day, in all kinds of ways, we both change a little bit, a lot really, but it's almost as if we're one percent different, every day maybe, just because we're moving forward all the time."

"I kind of like that thought," he shared, a smile touching his lips. "Not everybody wants to consider themselves stuck and stagnant."

"I'm sure a lot of people are stuck and stagnant, depending on where they're at in life," she noted, "but a lot of people aren't. A lot of people are moving forward, growing, changing all the time. And, if your abilities grow and change with you, then it all makes sense."

"I don't really want to be a megaphone for all the people stuck on this side because they can't leave their bodies behind."

"But the real question is, why can't he? What is stopping him?"

"I don't know," Simon admitted, with a shrug. "That's a question I can't understand myself."

"Too bad your grandmother isn't around."

"Don't think I haven't thought of that more than a few times recently," he muttered, glancing back at her. "She's definitely somebody I now wish I had paid more attention to."

"Which is also why she's probably up there laughing her fool head off at you," she added, with a smirk.

"I would like to think that maybe she's up there having a holiday from all the strife, pain, and suffering that people put her through down here." As they walked, he thought about that. "Her life wasn't easy at all. People judged her, some feared her, and yet, when it came to her, she helped everyone she could."

"Of course."

"If she had answers, they wanted them, but they hated the fact that they had to come to her to get them. Then, as soon as she would give them whatever answers she had available, they would misjudge what she said, particularly if it was something they didn't want to hear."

"Did she talk about it?"

"Rarely. She didn't like talking about it much," he noted, with a headshake. "There was always a sense that she would help anybody, but just because she offered help didn't mean that everybody would take it."

"Of course not. People don't always want to take advice, but they're happy enough to dish it out," she pointed out, looking over at him. "But taking it? Now that's a whole different story. ... How's Danny working out?" she asked abruptly.

He smiled. "He's doing just fine."

"You're sure? Every now and then I think about him and worry if he's got his depression and suicide tendencies under control and realize I haven't even asked about him in a while."

"He's doing fine," Simon repeated, a smile on his face. "He's still going to therapy, and he still shows up for work every day, which is huge for him."

"I'll take that," she said, with a smile. "We all need to have something that works for us in our lives."

"He's also become pretty close with Joe."

Joe was one of his foremen and was always on Danny's ass. Danny had been very depressed when they met him after he became involved as a witness in one of Kate's cases. He had been in a bad way, to the point of being suicidal, so Simon gave him a try as a laborer on one of his rehab jobs. Joe took Danny under his wing, and, since then, things had improved a lot for Danny. "So, how's that working out for Joe?"

"Fine." Simon chuckled. "Joe's got half-a-dozen kids," he shared, with a laugh, "and has supervised men of all ages and in all kinds of situations for many years. He's more or less managed to work Danny right into the crew, as well as his family."

"That's really good of him."

"He would say it's just who he is. And he does it so naturally that calling it a good deed would be a judgment."

She laughed. "And again, here we are, talking semantics. What seems to be a good thing to me just seems to be a natural thing to him. It's neither good nor bad, but, because I know I'm not geared for doing it," she admitted, "to me it seems to be a really good thing."

"Exactly." He smiled, as he walked with her around the warehouse. Then he pointed at the very back of the building.

"That's not a door," she said.

"No, it's not, but it looks as if they tried to board it up to stop people from getting at it."

"So, it just looks ..." She stopped and noted bits of plywood were lying around, some of it on the ground, some of it above. None of it looked useful. And none of it seemed to be trying to hide anything. "I'm surprised the plywood is even here, what with the cost of wood right now."

"Particularly dry plywood like this," he noted, with a bright smile.

"Yeah, it's probably worth even more money," she muttered. "It seems as if lumber twists so badly."

"That's why plywood is better than straight lumber, depending on the application. You can still get good kiln-dried wood. You just have to pay more for it."

"Paying more for it," she said, with a roll of her eyes, "is one thing, but paying outrageous amounts? ... That's a different story. But that's what you pay, isn't it?"

"Not on purpose, but sometimes I have to," he conceded. "It's not as if it's a choice when I need the wood and have projects to be done. Sometimes you pay a little more, especially if it's holding up the crew."

"And is that *little more* here and there where you end up running into problems with buildings?"

"Only if it really impacts the bottom line," he noted. "However, the bottom line suffers most of all when delays get us off schedule. One thing I can't have is a crew sitting idle, just waiting for materials. So, all too often, it just makes more sense to get materials to keep the crews moving, despite a higher cost."

He pulled work gloves from his pockets and started removing the still upright pieces of plywood. It didn't take very much to rip it off the wall.

She frowned at him. "Is it supposed to be that easy to take off?"

"Nope," he confirmed, "but time, weather, and vandalism loosens the screws that we use and the materials they go into."

"At least it was screws, not nails." He laughed at her comment. As he separated the lumber from the wall, she saw the stairs they needed to access the basement. Even with her help it took twenty minutes to expose an area big enough for them to get through. Going down there, he now saw the bits and pieces of an electrical box nearby.

"I guess I didn't really even think about it, but there has to be a ton of plumbing involved too, right?"

"Yeah, and all of that should be somewhere in here as well."

"And yet—" She shook her head.

"It's old, and lots of it is just damaged."

As she stepped in farther, she looked around, turned on the flashlight on her phone and muttered, "This is what I would have expected."

"Every building has a place like this," Simon said comfortably, as he moved forward.

"But when we did the search of the building, we didn't find this. No one came this way."

"You and I didn't search the outside of this warehouse because we found the body inside," Simon explained, "and I don't think any of the officers who did the rest of the search would have noticed and pulled away all this lumber. The building hasn't been condemned, but I'm pretty sure that's coming."

"Particularly after this, but then what would you do?"

"Drop it," he said. "I would drop it and would clear out

the space and would start fresh. More to the point, if we found another body, we'll have to."

"Jesus," she muttered, as she made her way forward. "I guess it is a perfect disposal spot."

"Not necessarily," he countered. "It depends on how it came about."

As they continued on deeper into this area, she noted, "It would also be nice if this had nothing to do with my current cases."

"I don't know that it does," Simon replied. "Not sure why, but I have the impression that this is old."

"It may be old," she agreed, "but that doesn't make it *not connected.*"

He faced her and nodded. "I hate to think that it is though because, if it's that old, Jay would have been here for a very long time."

"Which is what we're here to find out," Kate declared. As they stepped forward a few more feet, she looked around and noted, "There is a dusty, musty smell."

Simon explained, "Old buildings do have a tendency to smell like this."

"I'll take your word for it," she muttered. "Old buildings are your specialty, not mine."

"Maybe, I don't know. I seem to have gotten my hands into it a bit more than I had expected."

"As in too much more?"

"No," he said, with a headshake. "Just more than I had planned on."

"Of course. You bought this one."

"And another one," he admitted. When she frowned at him, he just shrugged and carried on.

"I have faith in you," she added, as she walked beside

him.

He stopped to smile at her. "That's just one of the weird things I like about you."

She looked at him. "*Weird?* Am I supposed to call you a damn fool instead?"

He laughed. "Lots of people would. Most would probably be afraid that the takeouts would stop or the boat would be sold."

She winced at that. "If it does, it does," she muttered, with a shrug. "I must say though, that I have thoroughly enjoyed the *Running Mate*, but, if you need the cash, then you need the cash. That's just simple economics."

He burst out laughing. "No worries. We don't have to sell the *Running Mate*."

"Oh good," she said, with a huge smile. "That makes me feel better."

"I was joking with my banker," he added, as he led the way forward, "and told him that I would have to go back out gambling again."

"I would just as soon you didn't do that," she shared.

"If you go into international waters, it's not illegal."

"Maybe not," she acknowledged, "but it sounds dodgy as hell."

"Maybe so, but it works." He said it in such a cheerful tone that he knew she wouldn't know whether he was joking or not. He was dead serious, but she wouldn't know that.

He walked forward and came through to where a lot of the utilities were located. "So, this is more or less what I expected to see here," he declared, shining a flashlight over the corners.

"Sure, but is there a body? That's what we came for," she muttered.

He looked at her and nodded. "And, of course, the voice in my head is silent."

"Right," she muttered, with a scoff. "That seems to be pretty typical, doesn't it? *Find my body, find my body. Oh, you're looking? I'll just leave you to it.*"

He burst out laughing and then reached over to pull away some moldy fiberglass and some other old material. Both just crumbled away. And there in front of them was another hole in the wall. "What the hell is this?" Simon asked, as he peered into it. He looked back at her and announced, "Another part of a basement is down here."

"*Great,*" she muttered.

"You stay here. It's not very safe in this area."

"If it's not safe, the whole building should come down."

"It should," he agreed, suddenly frowning, "but what I don't know is exactly what's back there." He pulled apart another area, letting them see what passed for a small room, not easily accessible, but somehow it was big enough for the two of them to stand in.

She looked around and shared, "This has a horror movie feel to it."

"It sure does," Simon agreed. Then he tapped her on the shoulder and pointed. There against the far wall was another body, and, this time, it was clearly old enough that there was no doubt it had been here for decades. It was just a skeleton against the wall.

"Hell," she grumbled, as she stared at it, her hands on her hips. "I wonder how long this one's been here."

"A long time," Simon stated. "I just asked Jay if this was him."

"Any answers?"

"I'm getting silence."

"Oh no, no, no, no," she cried out. "There can't be another one."

"I don't know," he declared, shaking his head, "but we'll have to tear apart this room to find out."

CHAPTER 13

THE DAY THAT had started so promising had ended with her spending hours at the warehouse, as a new forensics team came in with tools. They slowly and carefully pulled apart more walls, finding an even bigger area where this one body had been stashed. And with it a second one.. How many more could there be?

Even the pathologist looked at it and shuddered. "This has been here a long time," the female pathologist declared. "No doubt he was murdered."

"How bad?" Kate asked.

"Bad. ... A bullet hole in the skull."

"Right, well, that's pretty definitive." She shook her head. "So, it's not connected to my cases then." The coroner, not Dr. Smidge this time, stared at Kate, who shrugged. "I have an open case with multiple bodies from this place," she shared, "but one of them is current, and he was a beating victim."

"Is he alive?"

"On life support but potentially not much longer," she noted, glancing at her watch. "I haven't had a chance to check in with the hospital yet."

"I doubt it's connected then, unless the killer or your beating victim has long ties to this building."

"Now that could be an interesting line to tug." Kate

quickly sent an email to Reese, looking for her to do just that.

"It could very well be your killer," Simon stated, looking at her. "He might have a tie to this place."

"Maybe," she muttered, "shitty deal though."

"I don't know," he replied. "Depends on the people involved."

"Speaking of which, what about the person you bought this from?"

"I don't know much but her name," he replied. "I presume you can contact her or her realtor and get whatever information they have. The owner's name is all I can give you, but at least it's something."

"If they even know anything," the coroner noted, as she turned to look at him. "It seems as if people just buy, then turn around and get rid of things. I don't know that they keep any history on these buildings."

"I do," he stated, turning to her. "I'm a developer, and I tend to hang on to everything."

"These owners might for tax purposes, I suppose, but past that? … I don't know." She looked over at him. "You would know that better than me."

He nodded, then faced Kate. "I would like to see what turns up and even contact the previous owner and see what she's willing to say."

Kate studied him. "Remember that you got it cheap?"

He nodded. "Yeah?"

"Maybe there's a reason it was such a bargain."

His eyebrows shot up as he understood what she was saying, and he nodded. "Definitely the building is unsafe though," he noted. "Yet the city hasn't shut it down yet. Be very careful, you guys. I have extra insurance on it, but I don't want any accidents happening."

"We'll be out of here as soon as we can," the coroner replied. "I'll need to bring in an anthropologist for these bones." She called for a member of her team, and he came quickly. She gave him instructions on what was needed.

"I am on it," Bailey stated, turning to look at Kate and Simon, sharing his name with them, should they need anything further.

"Good enough," Kate said. "It would be nice to have details on these older deaths, but I'm not exactly sure how many details will be available."

"Not much," the female coroner declared cheerfully. "Yet we'll do what we can." And, with that, the bodies, four now, were loaded and taken to her vehicle, and she drove away.

It was now three in the morning.

Kate looked over at Simon. "It almost seems as if there's no hope of any sleep for us."

"Oh, no, no, no," he argued. "You need at least a couple hours."

"I've been sending emails off to Rodney and Reese for them to get started in the morning," she shared, "but I do need to crash, at least for a little bit."

"Let's go," he said. As they walked back outside again, he stopped.

"What's the matter?" she asked. Then she saw the look on his face. "Oh, no, no, no. Don't tell me that Jay says it's not his body."

Simon winced and nodded. "Yep, Jay's back. And that's exactly what he's saying. It's not him."

"And?"

"And I'm not allowed to leave until we find him."

"Oh, crap," she groaned, throwing back her hair. "Honestly, I think you need to tell him that you'll be back. You might need equipment."

"I don't think I need equipment, but we'll definitely have to get to the bottom of this," Simon declared, his tone bitter. "I just get the feeling that a couple more could be in here."

"A couple more? You're kidding, right?" she asked, turning to look at him.

"Sorry, not kidding," he muttered, staring at her.

"A couple more, Jesus," she repeated. She turned, came closer to Simon, and added in a hushed tone, "Nobody will appreciate getting called back here."

"But the forensics team is still here."

Just then one of the techs called her over. As she joined him, he pointed at another in-between area. "Found another one," he stated.

From the other side came another yell. "And we've got still another one here."

She looked over at Simon and whispered, "I really hope you drop this place. This is now a grave for I don't know how many souls."

He nodded. "And you won't get any sleep after all, will you?"

"I will in a bit, but not right now." She turned to him. "Go on. You don't need to stay just because I get no sleep."

He smiled at her. "I'm the owner of the building, so I'll stay," he decided comfortably.

She looked at him and shrugged. "Your funeral." Immediately she scowled. "Dear God, let me retract that."

He snorted. "I'll go buy coffee and get some food in here," he suggested, turning to look at the team. "They'll be here for a while."

"They sure will," she muttered, as she looked around, then nodded. "Not a one of them will say no to food and coffee." Several of them turned and looked at her hopefully. She nodded. "We'll grab something. It just depends on what we can get at this hour."

"I'll take fast food," suggested the forensics tech in front of her. "This will be an even bigger job now."

CHAPTER 14

B Y THE TIME Kate walked back into the office—after grabbing a short nap—Lilliana eyed her expectantly.

Nodding at Kate, she said, "Just heard the news. That was a hell of a deal."

"Yeah, you're not kidding," Kate muttered.

"How do you think Simon feels, having just bought the building?" Lilliana asked.

Kate winced. "Not my skin in the game, so I'm not sure."

"I hope he didn't pay very much for it," Lilliana said, with a smirk.

"Yeah, he's probably thinking about that right now too," Kate added, with a smile. "Yet he planned on dropping it already, and, since it will undoubtedly be condemned as soon as the city ordinance guys get there, that's a good thing."

"Yeah, you're not kidding," Lilliana noted. "What did you find?"

"So, current count is two recent floaters, one skeleton in the warehouse from a year or so ago, now four very old skeletons in a secret basement room of the same warehouse, and a sickly homeless man—which was an exception—plus our beating victim. And that's not counting the four dead bodies in other precincts that seem to have been beaten to death as well. What we don't know," Kate added, "is whether there is any connection between the newly dead and the long-ago dead."

"Of course," Rodney noted, as he walked back over to his desk, a cup of coffee in his hand. He looked at her, held up the cup, and said, "A fresh pot is in there."

"You know that does sound good, yet I lived on coffee all night."

"Were you there all night?" he asked.

"Most of it," she said, waving a tired hand at him. "We found one long-lost skeleton in the boarded-up basement. Then, just as we were about to leave, forensics found two more, so that meant pulling an all-nighter."

"Of course," he muttered, "so you probably didn't get a chance to question our van delivery guy."

"No, but I will be going back there today."

"I'm coming with you," he added. "That building is now one hell of a dumping site."

"I know, and I'm sure the city will be there as well. It's just one of those lovely little sites that needs to be dealt with," she noted, "the sooner, the better."

He nodded. "We can go now, if you don't want to settle in over a cup of coffee."

"Let's have a short meeting," she suggested, "and I'll bring you up to date on what we found, and then we can head back." And heading back put her right at the same warehouse, but thankfully forensics was gone by then. It was almost noon. She and Rodney went inside the main warehouse and took another look around, specifically searching for boarded-up doorways inside the building. As she looked out the window, she noted that most of the crowd had dissipated as well.

"That's a good thing," Rodney noted, pointing outside.

"It is. At the same time, it feels pretty rough to know these bodies were discarded here all that time."

"And was ... Simon behind all that?"

"Simon is the reason we kept looking," she admitted. "Obviously, when the building finally comes down, the bodies would have been found, but it's better that it can be dealt with now."

"Yeah, that's a good thing."

"It's still hard to think that so many people were left in that situation. Some of them have probably been there for years, decades even. I don't know yet, but we'll hear soon, I hope."

"Where were these bodies at?" Rodney asked.

"They were jammed in the basement, along with the utilities," she explained, "or behind them. Another room was just behind where the utilities were. The door to access the basement was outside, all boarded-up. Simon will try to talk to one of the previous owners and see if they give up any information. Then I'll have to contact them myself, of course."

Rodney looked around the interior again. "Just another desolate empty warehouse, like people just picked up and left. Half the stuff here is from the last company, and half the stuff is just garbage from vagabonds over the years."

"Exactly," she agreed. "Simon has the plans that were on file at City Hall. He had them delivered so he could take another look, and, since he is the new owner, it made perfect sense for him to do that. That provides good cover, considering why he probably really contacted them."

"You mean, why he pushed it?"

"Yes," she stated. "What I still don't know is whether

that voice in his head has gone quiet because, if it has, then hopefully we've found all the bodies."

"Or at least found *him*, the body of the voice," Rodney pointed out. "I have to admit, since meeting Simon, I've had to rethink my views on life and death a bit."

"I think we all have," she noted, "including Simon."

"And that's the part that just blows me away, that he really had no clue about any of this psychic stuff."

"Just what he knew of his grandmother," she noted, turning to look at him, "but he swore he would never get into that."

"Yeah, and look how well that's gone for him," Rodney quipped, followed by laughter.

"I have no idea what's going on in that mind of his half the time. And you're not kidding. Simon is definitely not impressed with it these days."

They walked outside to the back of the building now, and she showed him where everything had been boarded up. Then she brought him to the hidden basement area.

He stepped inside to the small extra room where the final two skeletons were found. Rodney shook his head. "Jesus, it's like it could have been created just for this."

"That was my thought," she shared, as she looked around. "Hence the need to talk to the previous owners."

"But how long were they the owners? This could have been built over decades ago."

"We have the history of the building, and the main warehouse has been around for about one hundred years," she shared. "So we know the bodies were left here after that."

"True," he murmured, "but maybe not by much. It was pretty rough in those days. Nobody necessarily reported anybody missing."

"Even if they did," she noted, "it doesn't mean that they were ever found or that files were ever opened. It was definitely the wild, wild west back then."

"It's scary to even think that something like that can happen."

"And yet it happened all the damn time. We can only work with the tools available to us, and think about what they had back then."

"I know." He shook his head, as he stepped back out again. "And now it's all on Simon's plate."

"It is and it isn't. He plans to drop it, and we're expecting the city to come through now and officially condemn the place."

"How come it wasn't done before?"

"I guess it was, and then the owners paid some fees or something to get it back to a status where they could fix it up, but then they didn't do it. Meanwhile, that city inspector must have retired, died, decided it wasn't his problem. I don't exactly know," she said. "Or who knows? Maybe a lot of money changed hands, if that's even a thing."

"Of course it's a thing," Rodney confirmed, rolling his eyes, "but now it's almost as if maybe they had a personal reason for it."

"That is definitely a concern, but we don't have anything to connect that to our recent beating victims."

"Right, and the one guy found alive upstairs?"

"I don't know about Sonny. I haven't got back to him yet," she said, turning to look at her partner. "I'm not sure he's connected to anything here either. It's not as if he was in here in the basement, with all these other skeletons."

"Right." Rodney frowned at her. "Damn, this is a hell of a thing to be caught up in."

"It sure is, and it makes you wonder how many other places in this city are empty like this and filled with bodies. One hundred years isn't even old in this city."

"No. Not for a building like this."

She shook her head. "God only knows how many other things are going on around this warehouse. But it was just left to decay, and that's probably one of the biggest problems with it."

He nodded. By the time they had a thorough idea what they were looking at, Rodney suggested, "I would say we should take another look around, but I don't even know what else we could possibly find."

"We'll have to take another look around for sure," she stated, with a nod in his direction, "because, every time we come here, we keep finding more victims."

"What about the old guy you talked to? Arnie, wasn't that his name?"

"Yeah," she said. "What about him?"

"Was he old enough to know anything about this building?"

"Old enough perhaps," she replied, "but I don't know whether he's always been here or came from somewhere else. I've been meaning to check on him anyway, so it's worth a shot."

"Is he likely to be around here?"

"He should be around this part of town, I would think, but I don't know exactly where. So we'll probably have to look around." But, as she stepped outside, she saw Arnie and several of his cronies staring up at the building.

When he saw her, he frowned.

"Or not." She laughed and waved at him. "Hey, Arnie. How are you doing?"

"I'm doing okay," he stated. "So much better since Simon took care of Elsie."

"Simon is a good guy," she noted.

"And you"—he looked at her—"are you?"

"I would like to think we're the good guys, but maybe not always," she admitted, giving him a smile. "I don't know if you've heard …"

"Oh, I heard," he stated abruptly.

She nodded. "But they're old murders, not recent at all."

He relaxed at that. "As in *old*, old?"

"As in ninety, maybe one hundred years ago. We don't know exactly yet."

"Oh, wow," he muttered, staring at her.

"It looks as if they may have been walled in, down in the basement," she muttered, "but we don't really have any detailed information yet."

"Right." Arnie shook his head. "That really sucks."

"It certainly did for them. Listen, Arnie. Have you seen that dark van at all?"

"No," he replied, "but it does come around here on a regular basis."

"Right." She looked over at his friends, identified herself, and said, "Still looking for this van." When she held up the grainy photo, they just shrugged and didn't say anything.

"You think it's connected then?" Arnie asked, staring at her worriedly.

"No, not necessarily, but, until I can talk to the owner, I can't write him off, can I?"

"Right, right, right," he muttered, as if that made sense.

She nodded to his friends and turned to walk away. "Take care of yourself, Arnie."

"Hang on a minute." He drew closer. "Make sure you

tell Simon I really appreciate it," Arnie whispered. "Elsie meant everything to me."

"I know she did." Kate smiled. "I think that's one of the reasons he ended up buying this old wreck of a property."

"He bought it?" he asked, staring at her in shock. "This mess?"

She nodded.

"But why? It's nothing."

"Simon felt a connection in some way."

"Oh, I don't know about that," Arnie murmured, looking up at the desolate building in wonder. "Nothing is here."

Kate laughed. "But the owner's name ... was Elsie."

He stopped, and tears came to his eyes. "Now *that* I can understand." And coughing a bit to clear the raw emotion choking him, he headed back to his friends.

Rodney, still at her side, just stared. "Seriously?" he asked her.

"Oh, it was definitely part of it," she stated. "Simon doesn't do anything for no reason, but he does listen to his inner voice a lot."

"But you don't just buy a piece-of-crap building because the owner has the same name as a dog," Rodney stated in amazement.

"No, of course not," she agreed, "and, if the numbers hadn't worked, it wouldn't have worked at all." But inside she just smiled because, of course, it was Simon. If he could make the numbers work and still fit it into what he wanted to do, then that's what he did. Especially if there was a tug on his heart. That's how he rolled. ... Hell, that's how everybody rolled.

As they walked to one of the main streets and took a look around the area, she turned to Rodney and asked, "Do you want a coffee?"

"Absolutely," he declared, a smile on his face. "You must really need some since you didn't have any at the office."

"No doubt, but that's okay. A couple coffee shops are right around the corner." As she reached the corner, she pointed. "That one over there is decent, and this one is where we got our coffees earlier."

"Oh, so you've got them all scoped out then, do you?"

"Not me, Simon. He works in this part of town a lot," she shared, with a laugh. "Trust me that he knows them all."

Rodney laughed at that. They picked up a coffee and kept walking. As she went to take a seat on a bench, she froze.

Rodney looked at her. "What's the matter?" he asked.

"What's that up ahead of us?"

He turned and looked. "What? Are you talking about the van?"

"Yeah. What color is it?" she asked, already off at a good clip.

"Oh, shit," he muttered and took off walking. It was all he could do to keep up with her.

As she came around the side of the van to see the driver, he was ticking off deliveries on a big chart he had in his hand. "Hey," she greeted him and held up her badge.

He looked at her. "Hey. What can I do for you, Detective?"

"So, are you Oscar?"

"That I am. My name is right here," he said, as he flashed her a smile and pointed to his name tag on his shirt. "If you need a package delivered, I am your man."

"You're around here all the time," she asked, "in this area?"

"Yeah, I sure am," he confirmed. "This is a route I carved out for myself quite a while back. I'm not one of the big name-brand guys, just a little guy trying to make a living, but my customers can count on me, even if it's late in the day. I'm here to confirm stuff gets from point A to point B."

She nodded. Pointing in the general direction, she asked him about the warehouse building they had just left. "Do you ever go over there?"

"Oh, there ain't no building there. Well, … there is a building," he clarified, then shivered. "But that's just a bad scary-ass building," he added, shaking his head. "I even heard they found more bodies in it. I'm not surprised, as that place is freaking spooky."

"And do you do deliveries around there?"

"If anything is open around there, it's certainly within my route," he clarified, eyeing her curiously. "Why you asking?"

"Just curious," she replied, "since your van was seen in that area."

"Sure," he said, his smile odd. "My van would be seen in all kinds of areas. As I mentioned before, it's all part of my route."

"Okay. Are you the only one who drives it?"

"Yeah, I sure am. Why?"

She hesitated. "Because it's been suggested that it might have been used in a crime."

Eyes wide, he frowned at her. "What?"

She nodded.

"No way," he declared, eyeing her as if she were a viper. "I spent most of my lifetime building up this business, so no way in hell I would do something so stupid. If I was in trouble, nobody would trust me with their stuff, so I would be done. And really done since deliveries are my only source of income."

She nodded, as he stammered on and on.

"Why the hell would I do that?" he asked, staring at her. "But I can tell you one thing. I've worked hard and earned respect from my clients. Do you know what that means for a guy like me? No way I would do anything to jeopardize my business."

"Understood," she said. "Do you ever see any other vans like this?"

He shook his head. "That's why I chose this one, so people know it's me. Everybody else has white delivery vans."

"Why this color?"

"I just needed to be different, to be unique, so I was easily identified," he explained, scratching his head. "You can look at my schedules. I don't care. I've got nothing to hide."

"I appreciate that," she said, and then gave him a searching look. "So, I'm going to ask this question again."

"Which one?" he asked, obviously still very confused.

"Does anybody else ever drive your van?"

He shook his head again. "It's the only wheels I've got."

She nodded. "And where do you live?"

"Downtown," he replied, naming a street in an area she was familiar with. "I've been there for a long time. I don't make much money," he said, staring at her. "I make about a dozen deliveries a day, but that's all. This is hardly a business that'll make me rich, and, when I die, won't be anybody to take it over because there won't be anything left. Hell, I've had to fight to stay in business as it is because of the big delivery companies. We get all the big guys in here too, and there's no room for us. Sometimes I'm not even sure I'll be in business much longer," he shared, frustration evident in his tone, "but I still am because I've worked with these people for a very long time. I'm small enough to provide good service to my customers and can get things moved pretty quickly, when they're in a pinch."

"So, you do courier runs as well?"

"Sure, I do anything and everything," he said, then frowned. "Anything that's legal. I'll deliver most anything, but again, I'm not risking my business moving something illegal."

She smiled at that. "I'm glad to hear that, and it's a smart choice. So, you've never lent your vehicle to anybody, never? It's just not something that you do?"

"Hell no," Oscar stammered. "Again, it's the only set of wheels I've got, so I can't *not* have it when I could get a call for a job anytime. I even take it to the shop on weekends, when I don't do deliveries. It was in the shop here just a few days ago, on the weekend. That's the only time I can get work done on her, without risking losing business."

"What shop did you take it to?" she asked, something twigging in the back of her head.

"The one down by my place," he said, naming a big mechanics franchise. "Then I pulled her back out, and I'm on the road again. I take her in for regular maintenance all the time."

"And you didn't notice anything different when you picked it up?"

"No, of course not," he said. "It was clean. Every once in a while, they do that, if they have time, not that they have very much time anymore, but it was cleaned this time. I sure as hell appreciated that. I can be bad about that," he admitted, looking around as if that were a crime. "You know, leaving coffee cups, food wrappers, and garbage inside. I'm really bad at that," he repeated. Then he frowned. "That's not a crime though."

She smiled at him, aware that he was confused and a little nervous. "No, no, it's not a crime, and I get it. I get busy, and my vehicle suffers too."

"Right," he agreed, smiling nervously. "We're out here working, so it's not as if we have time for anything else."

And she believed him. But he had given her one little lead, and she would take it. Thanking him for his time, she took his contact information, then turned to Rodney. "Let's go."

Just as she was about to walk away, Kate turned back to Oscar. "Where do you keep your vehicle parked at nighttime?"

He shrugged and said, "In the garage at the back of my place. ... I've had a few break-ins but nothing major. I don't keep much in my vehicle, and I don't keep it locked."

"Why not?" she asked, narrowing her eyes at him.

"Because if it's locked, and they're looking for a few bucks, they'll just break my damn windows. It was happening so often that the insurance was threatening to not cover me anymore," he shared, anger in his tone. "I ain't got nothing to hide. You want to take a look at it?"

"Please, if you don't mind, I want to," she replied.

He shrugged, walked around to the back, then popped it open for her. As she walked around, Rodney asked, "Where do you get it serviced, which one of those centers?"

"The one off House Street, in the back. They are usually pretty accommodating for me."

She took a look inside the van, but outside of parcels and a clean deck at the bottom, there really wasn't a whole lot here to see.

When she got into his van, he popped his head around, looking worried.

"I'm just looking to see what's behind the parcels," she explained.

He shrugged. "More parcels, that's what I do."

"Right," she agreed, as she hopped out and looked at the vehicle, then nodded, trying to maintain a casual tone. "You ever do any fighting?"

"Fighting?" he repeated, looking at her. He held up his hands, revealing damaged fingers. "Nope, God no. Ever since I got these so busted up in an ugly fight ten years ago, I avoid as much physical contact as I can. I'm not made for it."

She just nodded as she looked at his fingers. "Are they painful?"

"Only when it rains," he muttered, glaring down at his fingers. "But, for the most part, I'm good with it."

"Got any family?" she asked casually.

He looked at her, his gaze narrowing. "You can't really still be thinking I've been doing something wrong?"

"I don't know what to think at the moment," she admitted, keeping her tone cool. "But we obviously have a situation, and I feel the need to ask questions."

He groaned. "Yeah, so, for family, I've got a brother, and he's ..." Oscar sighed. "He's in a home. It's one of the reasons I'll probably never retire. He'll always need some help."

"What happened to him?"

"He used to be a boxer, and he got the shit kicked out of him. My brother was up against one of those fighters who was nice enough, but, when you get them in a ring, they take out their temper on you. Anyway, he took a real beating, and that ended up causing permanent brain damage," he explained. "So, he's mostly a man-child when he's having a good day and a vegetable when he's not," he shared, glaring at her. "Not everybody has nice sweet lives, you know?"

"I do know," she declared, "and I do understand. I'm not trying to make your life difficult, yet I have a job to do."

And, with that, whatever defensiveness or stubbornness he'd had in him faded away, and he nodded. "Look. Just ask your questions. I really don't care. The only thing I care about is making sure you don't hold me up. I can't get off schedule. If I can't get my parcels delivered on time, things can get ugly, and I can't afford to work for free."

"Do you often offer your services for free?"

"Not on purpose, but, if I screw up somewhere along the line, then I don't have a choice. I generally offer them a free pick-up, free delivery, or something," he said, with a wave of his hand.

She nodded and he continued.

"You've got to keep your customers happy. Otherwise they'll go to the big companies. They don't treat the packages with any more kindness, but they can do it for less because of the volume. They don't pay their drivers that well either, otherwise I might have picked up a job with them myself. Honestly, a couple midsize companies local to the area are always telling me that, anytime I want a job, I've got one."

"Why don't you?"

"I really like the freedom of my own schedule," he replied. "Then, if I need to check on Oliver, or if I need to run errands or pick up something for me along my route, I can. It's not as if I get a chance to do much of anything anyway, but still. Here I am, talking about the joy of having your own business, but honest to God? ... It's shit work, and it's not really any easier than if I had a nine-to-five. Matter of fact, it's a whole lot worse since you've got all the accounting to do and the taxes, insurance, and other expenses that come around and hit you." With a morose expression, he looked at her. "Can I go now? I really don't want to be late for this next job."

"You can go," she said, "and thank you for your time."

And, with that, he hopped in his van and took off down the road.

Kate stood here for a long moment, long enough that Rodney nudged her.

"You good?" he asked her.

"I don't know," she muttered. "Something very important was in all that."

He raised an eyebrow, staring at her, then looked back down the road where Oscar had disappeared. "And what part of all that did you think was so important?"

"I'm not sure yet," she said, still standing here, "but there was something—a nugget of gold in that conversation. I just need to sort it all out."

"Let me know when you do," Rodney said, shaking his head. "I sure didn't hear it."

"I did, but I'm just not sure what the important part was."

Rodney snorted. "While you're thinking about that, I suggest we follow up on the other things we have to follow up on. Then we can go from there."

"Absolutely. Let's also get Reese to double-check his brother, that he's really in a home and that his condition is exactly what Oscar says it is."

Rodney whistled. "Oh, now that would make sense."

"It would," she agreed, "and let's see if Oscar has any

other family members. We also need to go to the shop that works on his vehicle, and we need to double-check his house."

"His house?" Rodney asked, frowning at her, as he was texting Reese.

"Yeah, because, if he keeps the van in the garage and doesn't lock the van or the garage, who's to say somebody isn't taking his van out for a spin once he's in for the night?"

Rodney nodded. "That could be way too possible. Unless he went out to the garage to check, he would never know. And probably the only thing he would maybe need his van for after work would be to visit his brother, wherever that is."

She nodded.

"Unless his brother is at the one place downtown," he noted, "and that would be in walking distance."

"And that's entirely possible. So, let's get to the bottom of a few of these threads," she said, "and then we'll know a little more about whether Oscar's telling the truth."

"But you liked him, didn't you?"

"I liked him, and I believe he's telling the truth, but somewhere in that story of his is a nugget we need to mine somehow. I think if we do, it'll pull apart this entire thing."

"Sure," he muttered, staring at her in confusion, "but you have failed to tell me what the nugget is."

She turned to him and chuckled. "That's because I haven't figured it out yet."

And, with that, she walked back to the car.

SIMON TOSSED HIMSELF on his bed, trying to catch an early afternoon nap. Kate might have had enough sleep, but he sure hadn't. As he closed his eyes for the umpteenth time, trying to get back to sleep, a voice whispered through this mind. It was that same thready voice, one that he easily recognized by now.

"Dammit," he muttered, until he realized what the voice was saying. It was faint, but it was definitely a *thank you*. He opened his eyes. "So, we found you then, Jay?"

Yes. And now I can rest.

It was a whisper, and indeed the voice was thready, and it was fading, as if coming from far, far away. "Are you leaving now?"

Yes, I don't need to be here anymore.

"You didn't need to be here this whole time either," Simon pointed out. "We would have found you when I took down the warehouse."

Maybe, but maybe you would have waited twenty years. I don't have that time to wait.

Not understanding that, Simon decided to ask him about something else. "Do you know who did this to you?"

No, but …

After that, Simon heard Jay speaking, but his words were jumbled. Then suddenly it cleared up again.

Some people from back then that were … just not the people who you want to meet.

"I gathered that already," Simon noted. "So, if you don't have anything to offer in terms of information about who killed you, I can't do anything about getting you some justice for what they did to you."

They're almost gone anyway. They'll have to face judgment themselves. And, with that, Jay's voice faded off into the distance.

No matter how much Simon tried to call out to him, Jay

had gone quiet. Simon was grateful, but Jay's warning was a hell of a note to leave with Simon, one that wouldn't help him get back to sleep. With a whole lot more effort, he finally collapsed back into sleep, only to find himself in yet another empty warehouse.

Aware that he was dreaming, yet caught up in the lucidity of it, he walked around, trying to find the exit, so he could get back out of it. It wasn't the same warehouse he had just been in, but it was another one down there somewhere. And with almost no ability to define what or where it was, he got more and more frustrated.

Just as he went to dive back out and to tell the dream to take a hike, he heard a man groaning. Swearing to himself, he turned to see two men in a boxing ring. It was an odd layout, but, somewhere in the background, another man was yelling, "Fight, damn it. Fight, you moron."

Just as Simon understood what was going on, he turned and caught sight of the man's face in the ring and swore, waking up. He reached for his phone and called Kate. "Where's Rodney?" he asked, panic in his tone.

"Rodney, why? He's here at the office, with me."

"Oh, Christ," Simon muttered.

"Why? What's going on?"

"Can you talk somewhat privately?"

"Yep, I'm getting up right now," she said. "What's the matter?"

He quickly explained about the dream.

"Rodney? Are you sure it was Rodney?"

"Yeah, it was Rodney," Simon confirmed, "and this guy was just yelling at him to fight, and every time he wouldn't, he got socked again."

"Jesus, Simon," she whispered, then walked over to the

nearest interrogation room. "But that would be a complete change in MO because he's not a businessman."

"I know," Simon agreed, frustration in his tone. "The only thing I can think of is that maybe he was seen, so maybe now he's being targeted as the next victim. I don't know how or when or what, but you'll have to keep an eye on him. All I can tell you is what I saw."

"Well, shit," she muttered. "And now the only thing I can do is tell him what you saw."

"And tell him to be very careful."

"Yeah, and I'll be honest," she added, not sure if she should tell him. "He's the one who thought that you might become the next victim."

Simon went silent for a moment. "Why?"

"You *are* a businessman."

"Yes," he replied, "but I'm not exactly at the same fitness level as your victims."

"Right, and I mentioned that to him, but Rodney's point was that maybe our killer decides he has beaten up enough losers and is ready for somebody who can really give him a challenge."

"Well, shit," Simon muttered. "That's a lovely thought, isn't it?"

"No, it really isn't," she argued, "but I understand what he's saying."

"*Great,* so, in that case, both of us need to be careful."

"Yeah, but wouldn't it be nice if he came after me?" she suggested, her tone hard.

Simon swore at that. "No, that would really not be nice at all," he snapped. "Believe me that I'm just damn happy it wasn't you in that vision."

She snorted. "It needs to be one of us, and damn soon,"

she declared, "because I'm getting tired of this asshole." And, with that, she ended the call.

He lay back down, thinking about what she'd said about him being a businessman, wondering how this guy found his victims. He knew Kate was struggling with that as well. Was it just random? Was it pickups waiting for a cab? Or was it somebody heading to the airport?

He rarely took a cab, but, every once in a while, he did. And maybe that's what this was. Maybe it was literally a case of somebody who just needed to find a random businessman who the killer thought would be an easy target. And that just really pissed off Simon.

Unable to go back to sleep now, he headed outside for some fresh air. Then he decided to walk down to the *Running Mate*. At least she should bring him a bit of solace. After spending a wonderful hour on the *Running Mate*, he decided it was definitely time to get something done. As he stepped out, wondering where he should go first, a cab pulled up to the wharf.

It didn't appear to be looking for him, but something was off about it. He watched it for a long moment. It wandered around, as if looking for customers, which wasn't all that unusual, except a big cab company probably wouldn't have a cab running around on their own. But lots of these guys had their own schedules and didn't necessarily work through a dispatcher.

As he continued to watch the cab, it went down the dock and then came back up again. With no one asking for a cab ride, the driver took off. It just made Simon wonder if that's how Sonny Hilton had gotten picked up. Would it have been some cabbie literally working that area? Or would the killer have gone to them at random? But random wouldn't guarantee a fare, that's the thing. If the cab driver was looking specifically for somebody—an out-of-shape businessman—would that have been the best option? And, if not, where could he guarantee a ride for a businessman? Downtown would definitely have the businessmen, but Simon wasn't sure that would give this cab driver what he wanted out of this.

Still pondering, he caught the aquabus across and headed over to his first jobsite. As he walked inside, his foreman Joe looked at him and sighed.

"Hey, rough day for you, *huh*?"

"Yeah, you're not kidding," Simon replied. "How's everything going here?"

It took him three hours to sort through some of the issues that had popped up, but it was a good thing he had stopped in. By the time they had finished, he decided he would take a quick trip across town and check in on the other project. As he got there, his other foreman looked at him intently.

"Kind of late for you today."

"Maybe, I spent some time at the other site."

"As long as it's not my job, it's all good."

"And is it all good at your jobsite too?"

He shrugged. "We had a couple issues this morning," he noted, "but I think we're back on track now."

As they went over the details, Simon nodded.

"Have we gotten an architect in on any of these jobs yet?" the foreman asked.

Simon snorted. "No, I have yet to book one."

"This job is coming along pretty decently," he shared. "So, you'll need something in the works for … probably April to June, somewhere in there."

"Which means, I need to get my ass in gear."

He nodded. "Yeah, … that's what I'm trying to say." His foreman smiled. "Just a friendly reminder is all."

"Ah, got it," Simon said, with an eye roll.

After that he picked up another cup of coffee, then wandered over to the warehouse building, wondering just what he did want to do with it. Now that he knew one of the four skeletons in the boarded-up basement belonged to Jay, and thus had been found, Simon was free and clear to walk on by.

As he did, he saw the dark van that Kate was looking for. He took a photo of it and sent it to Kate.

She called him. "We talked to him this morning," she said.

"Him?" he asked. "A woman is driving it now."

"What?" she asked, startled, then froze. "No, no."

"Why not though?" he asked. "Why couldn't a woman have done this?"

"Because of moving the bodies," she pointed out. "That's a whole lot of physical strength."

"But you could."

"I could," she said in confusion, "but these men would overpower her."

"Not if she's any good at boxing or any kind of a fighter. It would also explain why she isn't picking on people who she couldn't necessarily beat."

"You have certainly given me something to think about," she muttered, followed by a hard groan. "Let me think about it. In the meantime, don't approach the van, please."

"No, I won't." But he was already walking toward it.

She called out, "Damn it, Simon."

Frowning, he looked around. "How the hell can you see me?"

"I can't see you, but I know you."

He laughed. "She's parked up ahead, standing outside the van, right in front of me. She's getting a delivery or two out of the back of the van."

"Can you tell me what she looks like?"

"She's about five six, solid muscle from the looks of her. Fit, and she's wearing yoga pants and running shoes. She's got a T-shirt on, and she's moving at a pretty good pace."

"Interesting," Kate muttered. "Now that is somebody I want to talk to. Also, can you grab me the license plate off that van?"

"Oh, you're thinking it's a completely different van?"

"I don't know," she said in exasperation, "but, while it's there, you might as well get confirmation of that."

He walked around and snapped a photo of the license plate and sent it to Kate.

Almost immediately, the woman in question came around and glared at him. "What are you doing?" she cried out. "Get away from my vehicle."

"Sorry," Simon said, holding up his hand. "I just was interested."

"In what?" she asked suspiciously, as she came around and faced him. "Nothing to be interested in here. It's just a delivery van."

"Do you work this route all the time?"

"Not all the time, but some of the time. It depends on my uncle."

"Your uncle?"

"Yeah, it's his vehicle. He got up this morning and had an emergency. It happens once in a blue moon, but today is it," she explained, glaring at him. "So, whatever. I'm here to help him out, and I'm already way slower than he is, so out of my way, please." And, with that, she hopped into the van and took off.

He called Kate back, "She says that she's covering for her uncle, who had something come up today."

"Bingo," Kate declared. "Damn, I was hoping it wasn't him."

"Doesn't mean it is him," Simon pointed out. "She could literally just be filling in for him."

"Yeah, but why?"

"I don't know."

"Did you—" Then she stopped, and Simon heard Rodney in the background. "Oh, now I know why," she shared with Simon. "His brother took an ugly turn last night."

"There you go. That would explain why he's not on the job today."

"Yeah, it would. I'll go to the home and contact him."

"Oh, he'll love that."

"No, he probably won't, but I don't think he's guilty in the first place. I'll hound him because he's connected to some of this, somehow. I just haven't figured it out yet."

"The psychic in me would tell you to sit down and to let it all roll through your head."

"Yeah, sure," she muttered. "And the Simon I know would tell me to just work away at it until I got the answers I so desperately need."

"Maybe," he conceded, "although I'm trying to work smarter these days."

She laughed. "Let me know how that works out for you." She then ended the call.

He really was trying to work smarter these days, and, with so many projects on the go, and more projects to come, he knew that he had to. The dark van had taken the corner up in front of him. He walked that way and took that corner too. Sure enough, she was there delivering something else, and then hopped in the van and took off down a few blocks, then hopped out again.

She appeared to be doing exactly what she said she was, which would fit in with what Kate had mentioned, so she was golden. He just didn't know if anything was weird about all this or if they were once again barking up the wrong tree. And so much of the work of a detective was going after one thread, then another and another, until they've barked up all the wrong trees, and only one thread was left. As he thought about it, he realized that, from Kate's perspective, this was about the only thread they had left.

Unable to stop himself, he kept walking behind the woman in the van for the next hour, watching as she climbed out, delivered parcels, climbed in again, and carried on. Sometimes she brought out more parcels and scanned them before she drove on. As a matter of fact, she seemed very competent.

When she saw him again, she frowned at him, then stopped and opened her window. "Are you following me?"

He shook his head, not coming any closer to her. "For somebody who is filling in, you seem to be very competent."

"Of course I'm competent," she stated arrogantly. "Why wouldn't I be? It's a job I used to do before. The company was bigger at one time, when his brother worked with him."

"Is that your father?"

"Yeah, my father."

"And he can't do the job?"

"No, not anymore," she said.

"How is your father?"

She frowned at him and asked, "What do you know about him?"

"Not a whole lot, but if he's not here ..."

"Yeah, and he'll never be here. He's not much more than a vegetable most of the time, so what can I say?"

"Ouch. I'm sorry to hear that."

She nodded. "And what the hell? I don't even know why I'm telling you this."

He smiled. "A lot of people say things like that to me. *I don't know why I'm talking to you,* or *I don't even know who you are.*"

"Yeah, that's about right," she muttered, scowling now. "Anyway, it's got nothing to do with you, and we're doing just fine on our own. We've been doing this for a long time. It's called family, and family pitches in. Maybe you should try it sometime."

"I would, but I don't have any."

She stopped and groaned. "Jesus. I'm sorry. I'm just feeling rushed, and I'm not being very polite."

"It doesn't matter."

"It does, and, if you ever need anybody to deliver parcels," she suggested, with a smile on her face now, "customer service is the end-all and be-all."

"Do you have your own business, when not helping out your uncle?"

"Yes," she replied, as she studied him hopefully.

"I don't know that I use couriers that much though," he admitted.

"We deliver anything and everything," she declared, still with a smile. "And sometimes it's pretty unconventional."

"Right, do you always know what you're delivering?" he asked, as another glimmer of recognition hit.

"No, but we don't do anything illegal, obviously. It's way too easy to get caught these days. So, I don't, but I've known a few guys who do.”

“Really?” he asked.

She frowned. “Is that what you’re looking for? Somebody to do illegal stuff?” She slowly pulled back from him, even while still seated in the safety of her van.

“No, I’m not,” he clarified, “but a vehicle like yours was seen in this area, where a man was dropped off who had been badly injured.”

She shook her head. “It wouldn’t be our vehicle,” she declared. “No way something like that would happen.”

“Why is that?” Simon asked.

She laughed. “Because we’re family. And I get it. You probably don’t know what that means, but, in our case, we’re there for each other when we need to be.”

She had said it with such confidence, as if it was something she was well accustomed to. “So, when you’re not driving the van for your uncle, what are you doing?”

She looked at him, surprised, and replied, “My brother and I, we run Tambo’s Gym, right around the corner. We own it, but you know the guys don’t think that a woman can own a gym. So, on the front, it looks as if it’s my brother’s, but, in reality, I own it.”

“And your brother, what does he do?”

“Oh, he’s big and physically fit and runs it with me,” she said, with a shrug.”

Again, he’s family.”

“Meaning that you gave him a job, even if he’s not somebody you normally would have hired,” he guessed.

She stared at him. “That wasn’t nice,” she declared, shooting him a look. “I don’t know who you are, but you’re getting awfully personal.”

“Got it. Sorry about that.” He could see that she was

already easing up, if only ever so slightly.

Just then her phone rang. She looked down and groaned. "That's my brother calling, which means I need to get back to work."

"Got it," he said, a smile on his face. "Sorry for taking so much of your time."

She answered the call loud enough for Simon to hear. "Hey, Tambo. What's going on? … Yeah, I know. I know. I was just talking to somebody."

Simon couldn't hear any more of her side of the conversation, as she drove off.

She stopped a little way up ahead, still talking to her brother presumably, as she ran a parcel inside, and came out still talking on het phone. Simon watched from a distance, and, by the time he finally lost track of her, he'd already sent Kate as much information as he could.

Kate called him a few minutes later. "They run a gym?" she asked.

"Yes, I guess she's the brains, and her brother is the face, just because she doesn't feel as if women will inspire that same confidence in their clients."

"They don't," Kate confirmed. "It doesn't matter what business you're in. When it's something like this, a male-dominated sport, it's always a good idea to have a man at the forefront."

"Maybe," Simon conceded, "but it's stupid."

She laughed. "That's what you say, but a lot of people would agree with her. Anyway, what is the name of this gym?" He gave it to her. She added, "I'm heading in that direction anyway, so I think maybe I should pop in at Tambo's."

"Good, I'll meet you there." Then came silence from

Kate's end. "I'm heading down there myself," Simon shared.

"And I need you to stay out of this," Kate stated, her tone sharpening. "I already asked you not to contact her."

"But, if I hadn't," Simon reminded Kate, his tone turning silky, "you wouldn't have known what you know now."

"Maybe not, but we would have followed up."

"Sure, but when?" he asked, sadness in his tone. "And I have a vested interest, since there's been one hell of a lot of bodies found on my new property. And I sure don't need any more people haunting me."

She groaned. "I get that. I do." Then she sighed. "You have an interest for a lot of other reasons, but I don't want you getting into anything that'll compromise the case. I'll get down there to sort this out in a few minutes." And she ended the call.

CHAPTER 15

RODNEY FROWNED AT her. "Really? Simon saw me in a vision? In a boxing match?" Definitely a little bit of nervousness filled his tone.

"Yes, and, as much as I don't want to believe him, he has been right time and time again, so be careful."

"So, you're benching me?"

"Yes. I'm heading down to talk to this woman, seen driving Oscar's gray van, making deliveries on his behalf."

"That's fine and dandy, but I'm coming along. We need to talk to the woman's father, her brother, and now Oscar again, as he failed to tell you about the niece driving his van. This seems like a big mess and about to get bigger. No way you're going alone."

"Fine," she snapped. "This is our first actual lead, and, with all the fighting involved—"

"Boxing isn't fighting," Rodney declared.

"Maybe not," she admitted, "but you don't know that they don't do other forms there too."

"Sure, but boxing's still not fighting."

"I hear you. I just don't know what you want me to say."

"And what about the theory that our serial killer could be a woman?"

"I've been pondering that," she shared, picking up her jacket, motioning for them to head on out. "The only way

it's a woman is if she's got help. Dennison, Sonny, John? …
None of them were lightweight, by any means."

"That's true," he admitted, frowning. "Hell, I'm not
even sure *I* could have lifted Dennison." He held open the
front door for her.

She nodded. "Exactly. Or maybe they were made to
walk on their own, but what about the floaters?"

"I guess she could have taken them to the docks at
nighttime and dumped them, and that vehicle would
definitely give some cover for it, but not easily."

"I was thinking about that too," she added. "She and her
helper would still have to pick them up and get them into
the water … unless they were rolled," she noted, frowning.
"They could have found a corner behind a warehouse,
something that ends up right on the water's edge." She
walked to her car, slipping into the driver's seat, as Rodney
took the passenger seat.

"True," he agreed, staring at her with a spark of interest.
"As delivery drivers, they would certainly have known about
those places."

"Maybe," she conceded. "I'll say maybe for now, since
it's obviously not something we have as a solid tip."

"No, but …"

"I know." Kate knew he was referring to Simon, and she
got that. "What about the other related bodies though?" she
asked, staring at him. "What about the ones in Burnaby and
the two other areas?"

Rodney nodded. "That could just be smart on his or her
part to dump them at various places."

"I was considering that as well," she muttered.

"It's never easy, is it?"

"No, it sure isn't. These guys always use some trick that

we never really find out about until right at the end. What I don't want is any more victims," she stated, looking at him, as they drove downtown.

"I agree, and I don't want to be a victim either," he stated.

She nodded, looking back at the road. "Then be smart and don't get into any cabs, walk with any strangers, or go to the spooky warehouse, or now this gym alone."

"And what if it's not a stranger?" he asked, looking at her.

"Clearly I didn't think that through," she muttered. "Just be careful, will you?" With that, she pulled up in front of the care home that they had on record for Oliver. She looked at it and frowned. "Wow, it's a full-care facility."

"That makes sense though, right? He's got brain damage and is far from fully functional."

"You're right," she said, "and this place is very expensive, even if they are subsidized."

"I think *expensive* is the answer for all this stuff," he muttered. "We might have free medical, but it always comes with a price."

She didn't say anything as they hopped out of her vehicle and walked into the facility, asking to see the man in question.

The woman at the front desk replied, "He's got visitors right now."

"I need to see him right away," Kate stated.

"I am sorry, but, if you aren't on the visitors' list, I simply can't," she noted apologetically. "No way I can let you in to see him."

Kate just nodded, then pulled out her badge. "How about now?"

The woman flushed. "Again I can't. I have no such authority."

Kate asked, "Who is his doctor?"

At that, the woman pulled up his computer records and shared, "Dr. Markin Roy. He does happen to be here right now."

"Good."

"Do you want to call him for us?" Rodney asked, charm in his tone.

Happy to do something constructive, she picked up her phone. When a man ambled toward them a little bit later, he was talking on his phone. He ended the call as he turned his attention to Kate and seemed surprised when she pulled out her badge. "What can I help you with, Detective?"

"You have a patient, Oliver Hardy."

"Yes," the doctor confirmed. "He's been here for a number of years."

"I understand that, in order to see him, we would need to be on the approved visitor list."

"Yes, that is a standard practice for any center of this nature," he stated, with a smile. "May I ask what the purpose of a visit would be? Why do you want to see him?"

"I need to confirm the condition he's in," Kate explained, "and I want more information on what happened to him."

"I can certainly help you with both of those things. Follow me, and we'll go to my office and go over his stats first." As they settled into his office, he brought up the online case files and motioned for them to sit down. "He was in some fight—boxing, as I understand it—going on maybe ten years ago," he shared, checking his computer screen.

"He took one-too-many blows directed at his head, and

unfortunately he suffered a stroke. That was followed by a series of other strokes. When all was said and done, we had significant brain damage, and, over the years, that has not improved."

"So, he isn't exactly there anymore?" Kate asked.

"Yes and no."

"You want to be more specific?"

"He's generally nonresponsive, though he eats when we put a spoon against his mouth, but he's not at all capable of caring for himself. He's been here ever since his accident."

"So, this is a full-care facility."

"Yes," he said.

"So, for our own peace of mind and to confirm that this is exactly what it is, we want to see him."

He stared at her. "I'm not lying, Detective."

"I'm not suggesting that you are, and frankly it doesn't matter if I think you're lying or not," she spelled out. "All I'm requesting is the opportunity to see him. I won't talk to him or in any way upset him. Looking through a glass door would be fine. I'm just doing my job."

Surprised at the request, he nodded. "You have a very suspicious mind."

"I have my reasons," she declared, still with a smile. "So, let's just leave it at that."

He got up, apparently perturbed at her request, but walked them down the hallway to a room where several people sat in wheelchairs. They were seated around a TV, but they didn't appear to even be looking at it—or anything else for that matter. She winced as a caricature came to mind. This sad scene looked like somebody attempting to have a life, yet it really was no life at all. It was just a façade.

The doctor pointed to a middle-aged man off to the

side. "That's him there."

She looked at the man and asked the doc, "So you are confirming for me that this is Oliver Hardy?"

"Yes," he replied.

She nodded. She walked closer, even walked around the man, but he showed absolutely no sign of recognition that anybody was even there in front of him. As she walked back over to the doctor, she asked, "His brother, Oscar, he comes to visit Oliver a lot, doesn't he?"

"Oh, yes. Oliver's brother is very involved in Oliver's life. I know it's been very hard for him, but he comes regularly," the doctor shared. "Oliver had a bad day yesterday, so Oscar was here this morning."

"Yes, I understand that," Kate confirmed. As they walked back to the main entrance, she raised an eyebrow to Rodney to see if he wanted to add anything. Rodney just shook his head. She thanked the doctor. "We appreciate your assistance." And with that she walked outside, knowing that both the receptionist and the doctor were staring behind her.

As they got back to the car, Rodney noted, "You really do have a suspicious nature, don't you?"

"Yes," she declared, "and it's twigging pretty strongly."

He nodded. "A *twig* is one thing," he pointed out, "but finding the proof—"

"I know. … It's a completely different story," she muttered.

"One of the first things we need to do is grab that vehicle," Rodney suggested. "And I suppose you've sent out calls for it already?"

"Yeah," she said, "based on suspicion of its being involved in a crime. I want it at forensics, and I want it there now."

"But if it isn't them, Oscar could very well lose his business."

"No," she corrected, shaking her head. "We would give him a chance to rent a vehicle for tomorrow's deliveries," she explained.

"That would cause quite a load of chaos."

She nodded. "It sure will, but they should be grateful that I'm doing that much."

Oscar was anything but grateful, when they told him what they were doing and shared their idea that would allow him to operate his business. Yet it clearly wasn't enough.

"I'll sue you for this," he exclaimed.

"You can try," Kate replied, "but you better hope I don't find what I suspect I'll find."

He stared at her and shook his head. "I don't know what you're looking for, but I didn't have anything to do with anything."

Such a note of helplessness filled his tone that she felt bad for him. "I hear you, and I believe you. However, still your vehicle could have very likely been used to perpetrate a crime," she explained. "And you failed to tell me that your niece sometimes used your van and made your deliveries, In fact you failed to even mention you had a niece and a nephew. Up until I heard about that, I believed what you told me, Oscar."

He shook his head. "You were asking me question after question. I told you about my brother. I was getting to my niece and nephew. Besides, you would have found out he had children if you checked into Oliver's background. And my niece helps me out in emergencies. It's not that she's my partner or my employee. She's family. She helps out when needed."

Kate typed into her phone some notes of Oliver's explanations. Then she looked up at him and added, "Now I'm telling you once again, you can take the parcels. We'll have to look at them first, of course, but you can rent a vehicle right now and go on about your day as usual. Be prepared for the same tomorrow."

He swore. "I need my van, not some rental, so my customers know it is me. My van is with my niece, Tamzen. She hasn't brought it back yet."

Kate nodded. "I know that. We saw her downtown."

"You haven't talked to her, have you?" he asked, staring at her in horror. "She really wouldn't understand."

"There's nothing to understand," Kate told him. "All we're doing is checking your van. We're doing our job."

"*Right*," he muttered, hanging his head. "She's a good girl, a hard worker. So is her brother. Damn it, we don't need this shit." Still grumbling, he got on his phone and had a vehicle rented within a few minutes.

Kate added, "Now, when she comes back with the van, I want you to remove only the parcels and what you need to run your business, and I'll need the keys to the van."

"I still don't know what you're looking for," he muttered.

"And I won't tell you, as it's part of my ongoing investigation," she declared. "I'm really hoping we don't find anything."

He stared at her for a long moment. "You really mean that, don't you?"

"Yes, ... I do," she stated, "because, if I do find something, it'll be hell for you, even though it would also be good for my case."

Confused, he turned at the sound of a vehicle, and, sure

enough, his niece drove up.

She hopped out, "All done, Uncle," she announced, "and I'm heading off to the gym now." She waved at him and at Kate and Rodney—not understanding who they were—then took off on foot down the street.

"And she's going to the gym, why?" Kate asked Oscar.

"She's the owner. My nephew often steps in and works there with her, but she's the owner." He spoke with a touch of pride in his voice.

"Good for her," Kate noted. "I'm sure that can't be easy in a man's world."

"Christ, no." Oscar snorted. "They made her life hell for quite a while, until her brother basically became the face of the gym. So, she runs the business side, works out, keeps a few female clients," he explained, with a shrug. "I keep hoping that will change, for her sake, you know? Yet not so far. For whatever reason, that business is very male-oriented."

Kate nodded. "I'm sorry for her sake that she can't be open and honest about her involvement."

"Yeah, me too," he agreed, "but the world sucks, and you can't do anything about it sometimes." He opened up the back of the van, quickly brought out the few parcels inside, scanned them in, and pointed. "Okay, it's all yours."

Kate faced Oscar. "You look like you lost your best friend."

Oscar shook his head. "Every time I finally get a leg up in life, it seems something kicks me back down, and it's never the same anymore." With his hands on his hips, he added, "I didn't do anything. I really need you to believe me."

"I do believe you," she replied, looking at him with a smile. "But that doesn't mean somebody else didn't do something wrong, while using your vehicle."

He froze and stared at her. "God, I hope not. It's the only asset I own free and clear. The bank owns the house, and every month I have to contribute to my brother's care. There's nobody else to help."

"What about his kids?"

"They do help," he added, "at least Tamzen does, as much as she can."

"It's her father, right?"

"Stepfather actually."

Kate got curious and asked for more details.

"The kids' biological father died when they were young. The kids' mother remarried, so Oliver is the only father those kids remember," Oscar offered, with a smile. "Then even he was technically taken from them about ten years ago, when he suffered a traumatic brain injury. Yet we've always been close, and she does help some, but it's not her problem anymore. The trouble is, it's never anybody's problem," Oscar muttered in frustration. "It's just me and Oliver, since our parents are long gone. Oliver has been … He was always full of life until …."

"And Tamzen's mother?"

"Ah, well, … that woman could spend money like no tomorrow. She flat-out told me that she hasn't got any to spare for Oliver's care, and I believe her because she probably spent it on her twenty-seventh latest designer purse," he noted in disgust. "Paying the bills or helping somebody else is just not her style."

"Even though it's her husband?"

"Oliver *was* her husband," he clarified, as he shook his head. "They were going through a divorce at the time, right before his brain injury. She got the house out of the divorce because he had just beaten the crap out of her," Oscar admitted, with a groan. "So, he essentially had no assets when he went into the home, which is why he gets government assistance. If it wasn't for that, he would have to live somewhere else. At least with him there, I can visit him on a regular basis."

"You'll probably hear that we did stop in there earlier."

He looked at her in surprise. "How was he?"

"Honestly, he didn't appear to be noticing much around him."

Oscar gave a sad sigh. "That's pretty much the way he's been for years."

"Do you know who he was fighting at the time?"

"Rod Sullivan," he stated. "Now that's somebody I could really get behind giving a good beating," he muttered, with a hard laugh. "Yet it's just not my thing, and I don't even think he's alive anymore. I heard some jealous husband shot him. That's just who he was. I know it's not nice to say anything bad about the dead, but that man was hell on wheels when he got into the ring. He was generally a good sport—until he got in the ring. Then he didn't have any mercy for anybody."

"You knew him?" Kate asked. "Personally?"

Oscar shrugged. "I remember him beating up some guy at one point in time, just a kid, telling him to stop bawling and to smarten up. The kid died," he stated. "That was pretty sad."

"Did you see it?"

"No, I didn't, but I sure heard about it," he declared, as he shook his head. "He bragged about it, how some punk kid tried to rob him, so he taught him a lesson. Knowing Rod, he probably stepped into the middle of something or just started the fight. He loved to pick a fight. If he could deliver a killing blow? … Believe me that he would do just that. He called it self-defense, even though he would have taunted the guy to fight him."

Once the tow truck arrived and took away the vehicle, Oscar watched, tears in his eyes. He looked back at her. "I don't know what you think you're after," he muttered, "but I really hope you're wrong." And, with that, he turned and stormed inside his house.

She looked over at Rodney. "I don't think he's having a good day."

"No, I don't think so either," he agreed, "and I sure hope you're right."

"Me too," she muttered. "You know that somebody will be on my case if I'm not."

"You mean, outside of the expense for forensics to scour his van?"

"Yeah, that too, thanks for reminding me." Then she announced, "I'm heading to the gym."

"And I'm coming with you," Rodney replied, jumping to his feet. "You're not leaving me anywhere now."

She laughed. "Seriously?"

"Yeah, I'm not kidding," he stated, looking around the block. "Simon's shit always comes true, and you know that." She stared at him, and he shrugged. "You know he's right. He's just way too accurate, and I'm not taking any chances."

"Sometimes it seems you think he's not accurate enough."

"Maybe," he muttered. "However, the only time I ever want to be in a ring and fighting, I want to be in a whole different fitness category than I am right now. Believe me that I was already thinking about this case and what that'll mean to somebody like me."

"Let's just hope that our killer is stuck on businessmen only because *that* you are not."

"Oh, that's right," he said, brightening up. "Thanks. I'm still coming with you."

She laughed. "Come on, slugger. Let's get to it."

***

SIMON DIDN'T WANT to wait for Kate but knew that she would be busy doing her thing. Yet his mind was a little too distracted to do very much on his own. Still he had shit to do. As he walked away, trying to get some of the stuff off his plate, Bartlett's lawyer contacted him.

"Hey," he greeted Simon. "I just wanted you to know that we're pretty well into the homestretch of this trial."

"I hope so," Simon muttered, "but, then again, you're pretty fast."

"The court case is making it a little easier to get some cooperation."

"Yeah, I would think so," Simon replied, "not to mention that I imagine she's screaming for her money."

Baxter's wife was the one Simon had to watch out for. She was out for his blood—literally shooting at him, hence the trial—all because he had backed Bartlett rather than her. Thus Simon ended up with control of Bartlett's estate and his company, after Bartlett had died.

"Money we're trying hard not to give her since she's the one responsible for her husband's death. She sure as hell shouldn't benefit from murder."

"Exactly."

"There're also the other kids."

"Of course," Simon muttered, "but you don't need me

for any of that, do you?"

"No, I just wanted to say thank you for helping us get this far."

"Good enough. I'm just damn sorry Bartlett ended up being killed over this."

"Yeah, … you and me both," he agreed. "That's when you wonder about getting married at all. I was married years ago and was thinking I might jump back into that whole dating game, but now I need to rethink it."

Simon chuckled. "I don't think women are all quite so crazy as she is. But, if you find one who's a spoiled shopaholic, like Bartlett's wife," he suggested, "you should know better and run."

"Yeah, I wonder whether we ever really know better, or we think it's not so bad, or that we'll fix it, change it, whatever," he added, with a snort.

"I don't know," Simon countered. "You need to find somebody whose values align with yours, someone willing to give when giving is the thing to do."

"Yeah, I haven't found that person yet," the attorney shared, with a chuckle. "I hope for your sake that you have."

And, with that, he rang off, leaving Simon smiling and staring up at the building he'd just bought, the second one today of all things. The more he thought about this warehouse, the more he realized that maybe he would do something with a social benefit here.

He just wasn't sure how he would make any money on that. The existing warehouse needed to come down first of all, and he would deal with coming up with a plan for the site later. However, until the cops released this crime scene—and the city issued a formal condemnation of this warehouse—he wouldn't demo anything just yet.

The city inspector had already shown up to condemn it, as expected, and, when Simon had told him that the police weren't done with it yet, the inspector rolled his eyes.

"That's great. No point in my condemning a building that I can't keep them out of."

"Let them at least get their forensics done," Simon suggested. "We've found several murder victims in here."

"Well, shit," he muttered, his eyes wide. "This building has been a pain in the ass for a long time. We've had no end of complaints."

"And yet it should never have been taken off the condemned list before, so why was it?"

"No clue, but I presumed that somebody was getting a little helping hand of sorts, which allowed them to be more cooperative."

"I tried to get a hold of the previous owners," Simon noted, "but they aren't being cooperative at all."

"No, they're the ones who managed to get it off the condemned list," he stated, "so I'm not at all surprised."

"Still, at least some of these crimes were probably before their time."

The inspector looked around, then added, "I think her father owned it before, and he was connected to the mob." He laughed at that. "Or at least that was the rumor."

Simon tried to get more information by continuing their chitchat, but, when nothing more was forthcoming, he went to the city and pulled out the archives for the building. He already had the blueprints for the warehouse itself, but still another huge file was involved. Having the bulk of it printed off cost him a bundle, but he wanted a printed version and an emailed version. Then he headed home to get comfortable and to study it. It wasn't very long before he saw some of the connections that had kept the building in the same state that it was in now.

Swearing to himself, he contacted his stalking Realtor. "This previous owner of the building, Elsie, and the one before that, what do you know about them?"

Ariel's voice was distracted. "Very little, why?"

"Is this a bad time?" he asked.

"No, just running through paperwork," she said, with a scoff. "It's been a busy few days for me."

"A good busy?"

"Yes," she declared, with a laugh.

"Good to know."

"Now, what about the previous owner?" she asked.

"I have put in several phone calls to them," he began. Ariel waited patiently for more. "You do realize that her father had mob connections?"

"Mob connections? What the hell? This is Canada."

He laughed. "You really think the mob didn't have their fingers in everything?"

"Maybe," she muttered, still sounding a little distracted, and that bugged him too. "What difference does it make?"

"There's a good chance her father built that hidden room in the basement, where the dead bodies were found."

Silence came on the other end. "Good God," she replied. "You do know how to ruin a day, don't you?"

"No, not really," he countered, with a chuckle, at least happy that Ariel was paying attention to this conversation now. "I'm still trying to get a hold of Elsie, and she's not responding."

"She's not responding to me either, but, as I told you, she's older and has some health issues. And there's the time change. Make sure you're not calling Germany in the middle of the night."

"I understand," he said, "but I still want any information we can get from her on her father to close this. And, if she has any information, now might be a really good time to clear her soul."

"Jesus," Ariel muttered. "Fine, I'll try again. I'm not sure what time it is in Germany but I'll give it another shot." She ended the call.

Simon smiled because, even though it wasn't her job, he'd bought several buildings from her and had made her hundreds of thousands of dollars—if not millions by now—so that tended to make Ariel more helpful.

She called him back almost immediately. "I talked to her husband, and he agreed it would be a good idea, but he doesn't know if he can convince her to do it or not. I did explain that, with the sale and all these dead bodies, it would be a good time to come clean, before they went to meet their maker. He went very quiet, then said he would see and ended the call."

"So, it does sound as if maybe Elsie knew something."

"I don't know whether she knew, but maybe she suspected, or was trying to protect the family name. I don't know. Regardless, it explains why she was eager to sell the building so quickly."

"And I'm happy to buy it," Simon added.

"That's what I told her husband, that you weren't looking to get out of the deal, but you did want any information you could get so family members of these dead people could get some closure, and so all these nightmares from generations gone by could be put to rest. I don't know that I succeeded to convince him of anything though."

Simon laughed. "It's pretty hard to be delicate about

bodies in the closet, especially if Elsie knew. Worse yet, if she actively worked to keep the sordid secrets of the building from being discovered. *So, yeah, lady, we need the information now, … before you die.*"

Ariel winced. "God, that sounds terrible when you put it that way."

"It probably is terrible," he acknowledged, "but, if that's what she's done, I—"

"I know. I get it, but I don't think she's too concerned about facing charges for it."

"No, of course not, and all the more reason to come clean, so everyone can get whatever closure is possible."

"Hang on. I've got another call coming in." She ended the call with Simon.

He sat and waited a little bit for her return call. When his phone rang a little bit later, an old crotchety voice came through.

The woman announced, "You're on Speaker."

"Okay," Simon replied. "Who am I speaking with?"

"Elsie Monroe. That's my warehouse you just bought," she added.

Simon started to record the conversation. "Thank you for talking with me," he began. "I don't know what you've been told, but we've found several bodies in that building."

The silence on the other end lasted for a few moments. "That would have to do with my father," she admitted, with a heavy sigh. "He placed such a burden on me all these years. I swear that's partly the reason I'm in the condition I am now."

"Guilt?" he asked.

"Not for me, for him. He died of a heart attack, left me the building and a letter," she shared. "I can send you a copy of the letter, but it's not to be made public."

"Maybe not," Simon replied, "but you have to understand there's a hell of a police investigation into this."

"And maybe that's fine too." She coughed, a loud rasping cough that made him wince. Finally it stopped, and she continued, "I know that he shouldn't have done what he did, and he shouldn't have left me to deal with the mess afterward."

"And what did you do with the mess?"

"Nothing," she declared. "I was stunned by the contents of that letter and didn't want to believe it. He ran things as if it were his personal right to decide who would live and who would die, depending on what they could do for him," she grumbled, sadness filling her tone. "He was a horrible father, a horrible husband, and he terrorized the neighborhood. However, he's also been gone thirty years, even after living well into his eighties. Times were different back then."

"Maybe, but murder is still murder."

"You're right," she agreed, "and, if you're finding bodies in the warehouse now, they have to be old. Like *old*, old."

"I would think so," Simon noted somberly. "Basically skeletons, at least some of them, but we're still trying to identify them, and that won't be easy."

"Right, but the families do need to know," she conceded. "I think it's in the letter. I'll have my husband send you a copy."

"The sooner, the better," Simon said. "Take a picture and email it to me, until I get the original."

"My grandson is here, so I might give him instructions on how to handle it."

"Have him email it to me as well," Simon repeated. "The sooner this is dealt with, the better."

"From my point of view, I would prefer it happened after I'm done and gone," Elsie shared. "I didn't know what to do about it, or even where to begin, so maybe I'm just as guilty for doing nothing," she murmured. "Yet it all happened so long ago."

"I understand that. I do, but, for the people who just found all this and are dealing with the horror of these murders, it's like it happened yesterday."

"I'm sorry for that," she muttered. "Nobody should have to deal with it."

"And yet they did, and we still are," he stated.

"What will you do with the building?"

"At this point, I'm pretty sure it will be condemned again, as soon as the police are done."

"Yes. … I wanted to sell it, but I never quite could. When it was condemned, I would have to drop it, but then the bodies would show up. So, I paid money and did everything I could to keep it from being condemned, causing me more headaches. I'm grateful that it's your headache now," she admitted, with a sullen chuckle.

"It is not only my headache but also still a headache for the families who don't have any answers too."

With a sigh, she muttered, "I'll send the letter, but not until I'm dead." And she ended the call, leaving Simon to stare down at his phone.

Before she cut him off, Simon wanted to say something colorful, like, *Thanks for nothing, and I hope you die soon, you selfish old bat.* While he would likely never say such a thing to anyone, a part of him wanted her to kick off soon, just so he wouldn't have to worry and wait even longer for answers.

He swore. He should probably contact Kate about it. But given the day and everything else she had on her plate, he would hold off until she came home. It might stop her from still being pissed off at him, … maybe. He laughed at that, checked the clock. When she showed up, she would be hungry and tired, particularly after very little sleep last night.

He sent her a quick text. **Pasta for dinner?** He got a thumbs-up and laughed. If he'd asked her how she was doing or anything else, he probably wouldn't have gotten a response, but bring up food, and she was right there. With that, he happily placed an order from Mama's, for the special of the day, then sat down to wait until Kate came home, happy that, for once, the voices in his head were silent.

If he was lucky, they would stay that way.

CHAPTER 16

KATE AND RODNEY approached the gym. As they walked in through the front double doors, such an unmistakable smell filled the place, identifying the business here and the purpose of the building. Although it was relatively clean smelling, it was still undeniable.

"It's quite clean, and it looks good," Rodney muttered.

"What, are you in the market for a gym?"

He shrugged. "Kinda."

"This one isn't exactly close to home though, is it?"

"No, and that would be a problem. I'm trying to spend more downtime, not more traveling time. We do enough of that at work as it is."

"We sure do," she agreed, with a smirk.

A man approached and asked if he could help them.

She smiled at him and pulled out her badge.

His eyebrows shot up. "Wow, I hope there's no problem."

"I hope so too," she replied. "And who are you?"

He frowned. "I'm Tambo. This is my gym."

She studied him intently. He was a well-built hunk of a man, with some hints of boyishness still evident in his face. "But not quite, right? Isn't it really your sister's?"

He flushed at that and then nodded. "Technically, yes," he said, with a stiffness to his tone that indicated he didn't like that distinction being raised.

"But you're the face of it," she said, with a nod. "Is your sister here?"

"Not at the moment, but she should be here soon. Why?" he asked, his tone instantly suspicious.

She raised one eyebrow at him. "Because we want to talk to her, and talk to you too."

He shrugged. "I don't have a problem answering questions. I just don't know what we could possibly be in trouble for."

"Who said you're in trouble?" she asked. She sized him up, realizing that he was probably exactly where he should be, in the gym, since he didn't have the look of somebody capable of running a business. "Do you like the business part of it?" she asked him.

"No," he stated emphatically, "definitely not my thing. I'm much happier out on the floor."

"Of course," she said. "Room for everybody in this world."

"I was accepted into the university," he shared. "Yet, when I got there, I knew it wasn't my thing."

Such a studied nonchalance filled his tone that she looked at him inquiringly. "That's okay too," she replied, "I never went either, but, as I already said, there's room for all of us out here."

He flushed and didn't say anything more, yet he obviously had a chip on his shoulder over something.

"Your uncle," she began, staring at him, "the one who runs a delivery service …"

"What about him?" he asked.

"Do you ever borrow the vehicle?"

"That old black van of his?" He laughed. "Not if I can

help it. It's a mess."

"I'm sure it is. Any idea how long he's had it?"

"No clue. Shouldn't you be asking him that?"

"Yeah, but it's a question I forgot to ask him while I was there," she said cheerfully.

"You've already talked to him?"

"Yep, I sure have."

"So, what are you doing here then?" he asked in frustration.

"I had other questions, and I wanted to confirm this place exists," she explained, still with a sunny smile.

He looked around, clearly confused. "Of course it does. It's what my sister and I do."

"You ever been into boxing?"

"Yeah, all the time. I'm not good at that either."

She frowned. "That's interesting," she noted, eyeing him carefully. "You look as if you could pack quite a punch."

"Oh, I can. ... I'm just not the best at directing it, or controlling its speed," he admitted, with a wry look. "I really am the most comfortable here, at the gym. It's where I belong, and it's the one sport in my world that's really mine."

"Right," she murmured. "I like that."

"What?" he asked, looking at her as if he didn't quite understand what she said.

She nodded. "It's just important to find your place."

"Yeah," he muttered, with obvious relief.

She wasn't sure what was going on, but, when a woman called out, Kate turned to see the sister rushing toward them.

"Hey," Tamzen said to the two people speaking to her brother, frowning. "I didn't expect to see you here. You were at my uncle's earlier."

"Yeah, I just had a couple questions," Kate replied easily.

"You don't need to be asking my brother." She looked over at Tambo and asked, "Is everything okay?"

He nodded, but obvious relief filled his expression that Tamzen was here. "I'll go handle shit in the back," he stated and quickly made his escape.

Kate turned to Tamzen and asked, "Is he okay?"

"He is," she muttered, looking back to where Tambo had disappeared. "He's just ..." She added reluctantly, "He might have taken a blow or two too many, a couple different times. It seems to be something that's catching up to him."

Kate nodded. "We do understand that a lot of football players with head injuries, concussions, can have debilitating effects, particularly over time."

Tamzen sighed. "It does seem to be something that might be happening with him," she conceded, looking in the direction where her brother had gone. "And that would be incredibly painful. It's bad enough that my father, *stepfather*," she corrected, "is in a home. The last thing I want is to see my brother there too."

"Obviously," Kate murmured. "I get it. Family is important."

"It's very important," she declared, looking around the gym. "Sometimes the stress of it gets to you."

"It's a good thing you aren't involved in any fighting or boxing," Kate suggested, eyeing her carefully, "so you won't have to worry about the same issues."

Tamzen shrugged. "I'm not sure I would care if I did. Everybody always talks about it being a man's world out there, but I'm not sure it really is."

"What do you mean?" Kate asked.

"I think women should have just as much self-defense

practice as men. It's a crazy world if you're defenseless."

"That's very true," Kate agreed. "So, are you quite adept at looking after yourself?"

"I am," she declared, "but that doesn't mean I can handle myself against multiple men. There's still that physical factor. I could cause a lot of damage, but that doesn't mean I would be the ultimate winner."

"Right," Kate replied, thinking about that. "I guess that goes for a lot of us."

"You must have a certain amount of training, don't you, to be a detective?"

"I do," Kate said, "but it's not all that intensive." Rodney went to open his mouth, so she shot him a hard look, and he stayed silent, as if not understanding but willing to go along with it.

Tamzen pointed at the entrance. "Look. I've got to head out and take care of other stuff. If you have something else that you need to ask, please come to me and don't talk to my brother," she stated. "As you can see, some of that stuff upsets him, and I don't want that."

"Understood," Kate noted and stepped out of the way.

Tamzen shot her a look and then quickly stepped outside.

Kate turned to Rodney and muttered, "I'm not sure that was very helpful."

"Not at all," he stated, shaking his head. "She doesn't appear to appreciate our interference," he added, with half a smile. "Which just makes her like everybody else on the block."

Kate took one more look around, then looked back at him. "Do you want me to drop you off at home?"

"No, I'll just call a cab from here."

She rolled her eyes at that. "Probably not the smartest thing to do."

"Maybe not, but I'm not too worried about it. You're closer to home here than you would be after taking me home, and I can get there on my own."

"Yes, but … don't forget Simon's warning."

"Yeah, but I'm not a businessman." Then he shuddered. "Maybe I'll just take the bus."

With a laugh, she walked back to her vehicle, then turned back to him, frowning.

"I'm fine."

"Yeah, sure you are," she muttered.

He just waved, and, pulling out his phone, he proceeded to check the bus schedule, she imagined, as he walked out to the street.

Hating this, but not sure what else she was supposed to do, she got into her vehicle, and watched for a few minutes. He seemed to find the bus stop that he wanted pretty quickly, and she knew it was a pretty quick hop over to the other side, as he wasn't very far off from there either.

Not liking it, but knowing this shouldn't be an issue, she proceeded to contact Simon. "I'm on my way home," she said.

"Good enough," he murmured. "I've been working from home for a while."

"I should be there in, … I don't know, maybe twenty." Even at that she wasn't sure she would take that long. As she turned on the engine and proceeded to drive toward Simon's, a nudge came in the back of her mind.

Go back and get Rodney.

Swearing, she quickly turned around and headed back over to where she had just seen him. But there was no sign of him. Either the bus had just come or it was something else entirely. She had no idea what was bugging her. She pulled off to the side, picked up her phone, and called him. When she got no answer, she swore and contacted Lilliana.

Reese was right there as well, so she asked to be put on Speaker.

"Look. I don't have any reason for this," Kate began, "but we need to find Rodney. I just feel as if he's in trouble."

"Where did you last see him?"

"Minutes ago. I left him just across from the bus stop, but, as I tried to drive away, I just couldn't," she explained, "and I have no idea why I feel like this, but something is wrong."

Lilliana said, "Easy, easy now. When you say something is wrong, what do you mean?"

"He's not answering his phone, and it feels as if something is wrong."

Just then a call came through, and it was Rodney. "Oh God," she muttered. "I'm an idiot, just ignore me. He's calling me back right now." She quickly ended her call and answered his. "You had me terrified there for a minute," she cried out. "I thought something had happened to you."

An odd silence came on the other end, and then he whispered, "Yeah, it did."

Kate heard a laugh, then a woman's voice barreled through. "If you want to see him alive again, you'll have to come and do a match-up."

Kate frowned at the voice and asked, "Tamzen, is that you?"

An angry laugh came first. "Yes," she snarled, her tone turning ugly. "You've been a pain in my ass for a couple days now."

"I'm happy to meet up and fight for him," Kate stated coolly, even as she looked around, trying to figure out where they could have gone.

"I don't think so. I think we'll just see how he can do on his own."

"Why?" Kate asked, deciding to poke the bear. "If you've been beating up all these innocent people, who have no training or conditioning at all, they were no challenge for you, right? Are you sure you're ready for a little bit of competition?"

There was silence on the other end. "You think that you are competition for me?" Tamzen asked, outraged.

"I know that somebody who's not fit isn't," she stated, with a playfulness in her tone. "So, yeah, I guess I'm a better choice than he is."

Tamzen murmured, "You could be right."

"You'll just have to tell me where you are."

At that, she laughed. "No. If you're any good at your job, you'll find him all on your own." And, with that, the phone went dead.

Swearing, Kate called back Lilliana and Reese and had Colby added to the call, then filled them in on what happened. "I don't know how she got a hold of Rodney, but she has him now."

"And this is connected to these beating-victims' cases?" Colby asked, dazed.

"Yes, we've had a couple developments today."

"Apparently," he muttered. "And?"

"I guess the motivation can be worked out later," Lilliana interjected, "but we better get to Rodney, preferably before he shows up dead on the docks."

"Yeah, I would prefer that too. Thank you very much,"

Kate snapped. "As for motivation, ... part of it is the fact that her uncle and her brother have both sustained some brain damage, and I'm certain it came from fighting. Being female is a problem, so she can't have the gym in her name, or at least her face on the marketing. Plus, she has zero respect in the fighting world because nobody thinks she could possibly be any good. That would do it for me. Yet I think it's more than that. I think, for her, the ownership of the club is a really big deal," she muttered.

"Christ," Colby muttered, "but that has nothing to do with anybody."

Kate repeated, "We have to find Rodney, and we have to find him fast."

"And then you'll have to fight for him," Lilliana pointed out.

"I know," Kate spat, her tone hard. "Believe me that I don't have a problem with that. I'm looking forward to kicking somebody's ass today," she snapped. "But you know that Rodney is not in the best shape that he could be in, not after getting attacked a time or two recently."

"Right," Colby agreed, "but, by that standard, none of us are. We go to the gym on a regular basis, but that's a whole different story when it comes to this street-fighting element."

Kate noted, "Reese, I need a rundown on any other businesses that this woman may have owned and check out the driving routes from her house to the boxing business and from her brother's residence, the areas that covers, and cross-reference it against the driving routes her uncle's delivery service has. See if a building fits the bill. Desolate, closed off, multiple exits."

"There is the obvious one," Lilliana pointed out, "the

warehouse that Simon owns now."

"True, but I don't know that Tamzen would take the chance of going back there right now," Kate suggested. "That warehouse is pretty damn hot. And we do know that other bodies were dropped at various places."

Colby groaned. "And we never once suspected that a woman was involved."

"It occurred to me today," Kate noted. "I just hadn't gotten very far in terms of getting any proof."

"You must have done something to trigger her," Colby said.

"I don't know if I did it or if it was just the fact that we showed up at her gym. Whatever the reason, this is the situation we're in, and we need to move fast."

As Colby started to work on a plan, Kate said, "I'll get off the phone and call Simon."

Lilliana asked, "Why Simon?"

"Because Simon saw it coming and told me to watch out for Rodney, who would wind up in the ring."

"Christ," Colby muttered. "Do what you have to do and keep us all in the loop. We don't want to be looking for you as well." He disconnected the call.

Kate phoned Simon. "Cancel dinner. Rodney's been snatched." She heard his sucked in breath and added, "It was the damn girl you saw in the van, Tamzen. I don't know if you've had any visions, anything that can help, but now is the time to share if you have. We're cross-referencing every available building within Oscar's delivery route and looking to find any other businesses she's been involved with."

"It could just as easily be the same warehouse."

"I know, but I think that's too easy for her," she snapped. "By the way, I'm expected to sort this out and find them, then go in and fight for him."

"What?" he snapped.

"Yeah, you heard me."

"Well, Christ," he muttered, "nothing like pressure."

"I don't give a crap about that part. She might be an ace boxer, but you know I'll go in there not only with a weapon but with my guard up."

"Sure, and she's also expecting you," he snapped.

"Yes, she is," she confirmed. "And I can't help that. I'm not leaving Rodney to be beaten to a pulp, while she works out whatever frustrations she has over being born female."

"Good God. Take a breath, and I'll see if I can come up with something. Meanwhile, I'll head down to my warehouse to confirm nothing's going on there." When she hesitated, he added, "You can't cover every place, so I can at least do this one."

"And if she's there?" she snapped.

"I will call you."

"You may not be able to," she pointed out.

He smiled. "I love you too." With that, he ended the call.

She stared down at the phone in frustration and anger, but he was right. Kate couldn't cover every place, and they needed other places to target. They didn't have long before Rodney would get put to the test.

And it's not that he wasn't in great shape or that he didn't follow through on all the standard training they had to go through, but he wasn't into martial arts, and he certainly wasn't into anything other than the traditional physical workout required by his job. Tamzen's fitness level would be a challenge for most fighters, except maybe not a pro boxer. Still, Kate figured Tamzen certainly had a ton of boxing experience. Until she heard back from Reese with leads, Kate had absolutely no location to go to, except for maybe the uncle. She quickly raced to Oscar's house.

When he opened the door, looking supertired and stressed, he frowned.

"I know you don't want to see me again, but that's too damn bad. Your niece has snatched my partner."

He blinked at her and asked, "What?"

"Your niece, … Tamzen has snatched up, kidnapped," she spat, chewing on her words, "my partner, a goddamn cop. And that is something we have to deal with right now. She has already declared that, if I cared about seeing him alive, I need to fight her for him. On top of that, I have to find him first."

He just blinked at her, as if nothing she was saying was making any sense.

"I know it's not making sense, and your brain is processing this in an incredibly slow manner," she added, "but I need to know where Tamzen could possibly have taken him."

"Nowhere," he bellowed helplessly. "It doesn't make any sense."

"Maybe not, but she has him, so where could she go?" She was going crazy, and her mind was racing out of control. Yet another inkling of an idea just occurred to her.

"I don't know," he yelled, raising his hands. "It's suicide if she's done that."

"No, not suicide, but it sure as hell will get her both an ass kicking as well as a prison sentence if she's behind these other murders."

He paled at that. "Dear God, no," he cried out. "Our family has been through enough already."

"I met your nephew."

He winced and nodded. "He's showing definite cognitive decline," he admitted. "The boxing, too many head blows, too many concussions." He shook his head. "It's so sad. Why?"

"I don't care about the why. I don't care about the how," she snapped, glaring at him, and totally ready to grab him by the throat and shake him. "I need to know where she might have taken my partner."

"I can't believe she would have done it."

"Then let's find out where she would have gone, and you can prove me wrong, but, just to give you some perspective, I talked to her on the damn phone."

He blinked. "She has a vehicle," he shared reluctantly.

"What kind?"

He frowned at her. "A van, like mine."

"Like yours?"

"Yeah, she had it painted black too."

She swore at that and quickly phoned Reese. "Tamzen," she began, through gritted teeth, "apparently has a vehicle of her own, like Oscar's. He doesn't have a license plate for it." She looked at him and asked, "Is it the business vehicle for the gym?"

"I don't know," he said, lifting his shoulders haplessly.

She gave Reese the name of the gym. "Run it, and see if they have any other property, anything close by. Is there an old warehouse or something where they might have been doing fights in?" she asked, turning to look at him.

Oscar looked at her and nodded. "Yeah, there is. We used to go there all the time. It was set up with a ring and everything," he said, with a smile on his face—which quickly disappeared as he took a look at her. "She wouldn't be there though. That building is pretty-well done for."

"Sounds perfect." Kate asked, "Where is it?"

"It's downtown, in the commercial sector."

She nodded. "And now you're talking my language. I want an address."

"I don't have an address." He frowned. "It's somewhere around the corner of ... just let me think." When he gave her an intersection, she just glared at him. "I know. I know. It's an area being revitalized, out in the commercial area."

"*Sure*," she said. Right near where Simon's warehouse was. Damn it all to hell.

"I heard it," Reese said on the phone. "I'm working on it right now. Hold tight."

Kate heard Reese punching away on her keyboard, as Kate returned her attention to Oscar. "Where else?"

"I don't know anywhere else. ... I can't believe that she would even go there."

"Why?"

"Because she doesn't like fighting," Oscar said in confusion. "She's told me time and time again that she doesn't want any more fighting."

"Are you sure about that? Or has she told you time and time again that *if women were allowed to fight,* it would be a different story?"

The color drained from his face as he stared at her.

Kate nodded. "I couldn't understand what was going on, unless this was about somebody either handicapped, or in really bad shape or something, but the fact that the killer is a woman? ... That makes it a whole lot clearer."

"Makes what clearer?" Oscar asked, still in total denial.

"We have multiple beating victims," she snapped at him. "Beaten to death and dumped into the water. Maybe a couple of them drowned rather than being beaten to death. Most had massive head trauma," she shared, "but we couldn't understand why. Like what was the purpose of fighting these people when they clearly weren't in any shape to fight? These were all just businessmen, heading off on trips around the world for their companies."

He stared at her, speechless.

Kate nodded. "It's all falling into place for you now, isn't it?"

"I hope not," he whispered, his tone revealing his agony. "I really hope not. She idolized her stepfather. The minute she found out about all the fighting, that was the only thing on her mind. It was something she could do, and she could do it better than anybody. We kept telling her that there was a market for women's fighting, but it wasn't quite the same as for men. Times have changed now, but she's past it in a way."

"Past it in a way, why?" Kate asked.

"Well, ... she's that much older. The fighting is geared for the younger people."

"But did she accept that?"

"Yes, she did. She took ..." He gasped.

"Out with it, Oscar."

"She took a really severe beating because she challenged somebody publicly and humiliated him. So he took her out in the back alleyway and beat the crap out of her. Honestly, almost all the guys were on his side because she'd been such a shit to him. The fact that he did it in the alleyway meant that he already knew what he was doing was 100 percent wrong, but he couldn't stop himself, apparently," Oscar said.

"Right, he couldn't stop himself?" She scoffed at that, adding an eye roll. "And how was she afterward?"

"Fine," he automatically replied, but then he winced. "At least somewhat fine. Fine, … but not fine."

"Make up your damn mind."

"It's not that easy," he roared. "This is my family."

"Yeah, and what about all the men who are dead because of Tamzen?" Kate snapped, glaring at him. "What about their families?"

"She wouldn't kill anybody," he muttered, with a head-shake. "No way. She went back and forth over the fighting after that. Sometimes she would think it was beneficial and a great sport. Then other times she would be all kinds of against it all. Probably depending on how she felt that day," he added, looking at Kate oddly.

"Sure," she snapped. "I get that. One day it's good. One day it's bad. And how much of that is about Tamzen's medical condition?"

"That's the problem," Oscar shared. "Not just her brother is having the decline. Tamzen was in a severe coma for a long time after that beating. When she came out, it was all about setting up her own gym and doing all this stuff. But the damage was already there, was already done, but it's like she's forgotten. Even now sometimes, she forgets things. One time she even asked me about where Oliver was, and he's been out of it for a decade now."

"What's her relationship like with Tambo?" Kate asked.

"They need each other," Oscar stated. "Without that kinship, I don't know where either of them will be."

"Prison for one of them," Kate declared, her mind suddenly clicking with possible answers. "Do you think that, if she gave Tambo a good-enough reason, would he have helped her kill these men, dispose of these men?"

"Absolutely," Oscar muttered. "I don't know what that

good reason would be, but he would absolutely help her. If she told her brother that some guy jumped her and tried to attack her, Tambo would have suggested dumping him in a heartbeat." Then he stopped and swore.

"What? Come on, Oscar. Tell me."

"Tambo has dumped somebody in the river before." Oscar held his face in his hands. "Oh my God," he muttered.

"Where was that?"

"It wasn't all that far from here, just down at the harbor. He used to go there to swim, and somebody gave him a hard time one day. Tambo lost it. Anyway he jumped the guy, then dumped him in the river and walked away."

"What happened then?"

"He lived. Otherwise … Tambo probably would have been in trouble."

She faced him straight on. "Do you know for a fact this guy lived?"

He frowned at her and shrugged. "No, but that's what they told me."

"And would that have been the truth?"

He paled visibly. "I hope so. … They're both subject to uncomfortable rages every once in a while. But it's been much better with the medication."

She nodded. "Has Tamzen felt more empowered lately? Has she felt more stable?"

"*Empowered*, that's a good word for it," he said, with a smile. "She's been taking classes to help build up her confidence again, and she's, … as you can tell, she's really, really balanced now."

"*Balanced?*" Kate snapped. "How about a teakettle ready to blow? A cork ready to pop? Choose whatever analogy you want, but I don't think *stable* or *balanced* is the right word."

"Do you really think she's done something to hurt these people?" he asked, with a quiver in his tone.

"*Hurt*? How about murdered? Yes, I do," Kate snapped, "and I know for a fact that she called me to boast how she has my partner." When Oscar just slumped against the door and stared at her, she asked, "And what about you? Did you ever have anything to do with this street fighting?"

"Early on, but it wasn't my thing," he said. "I told you that already. I didn't like getting the crap beaten out of me. I didn't like dealing with any of that."

"Okay, so how did they all get back into it? I thought you mentioned they were Oliver's stepkids?"

"They were technically his stepkids, but he was with them for a long time, so … that relationship was meaningful. I also think my brother had even offered to put up the money for the gym. However, after his divorce, he was in rough shape, physically, monetarily, mentally. I don't know what happened with that offer to start the gym. Tamzen never really told me about that."

"So maybe she feels as if she owes him."

"I don't know about that. I do know that they were close," he replied.

"Close?" she asked, looking at him.

"Yeah, close," he repeated. "It's not unusual. Not all stepfathers and stepdaughters have bad relationships."

"That's true," she acknowledged. "My colleagues are looking into details on that one boxing location," she muttered, looking down at her phone, knowing they would be taping it on the other end. "I'll head there now."

"I'll come with you," he offered.

"That's fine, but you'll go in your own vehicle," she stated, facing him. "I'll meet you down there, but you have to stay out of whatever is going on."

"I could talk to her though," he suggested, pleading with Kate. "Tamzen will listen to me."

"No, she won't," Kate argued, staring at him. "I think the talking point has well and truly passed."

"I can't believe she would have done anything to hurt these men. ... It's not possible. How would she have even found them?"

"That's one of the questions we'll have to answer. She could easily have used your deliveries to find out-of-shape businessmen to take her anger out on. You lied to me, Oscar. You told me that you were the only one who ran the delivery business."

"That's because I didn't have any insurance on the vehicle for another driver," he muttered in frustration. "I can't take the chance of losing my job or my van." She snorted and stared at him. "It will kill my job now, won't it?" he cried out, looking at her in horror.

"I have no idea," she admitted, "but I know of a gym that needs to be managed because I don't see either Tamzen nor your nephew being able to do it. Are you sure their biological father is dead, or did he just escape from family life?"

"He's dead and gone," Oscar confirmed, "for many a year. He was also in the fighting world. There's a long history of it in our families."

"Right," she muttered. "Maybe it's time for the family to come up with a new line of work."

He looked at her and hung his head. "After those two go the way of my brother, ... no one in my family is left," he muttered helplessly. "They are all the family I have."

"I'm sorry to hear that," she said, "because, right about now, things are not looking very good for them." And with that she turned and raced to her vehicle. "Reese, you've got directions for me?"

"Texting you now."

With that, Kate tore off, heading for her destination.

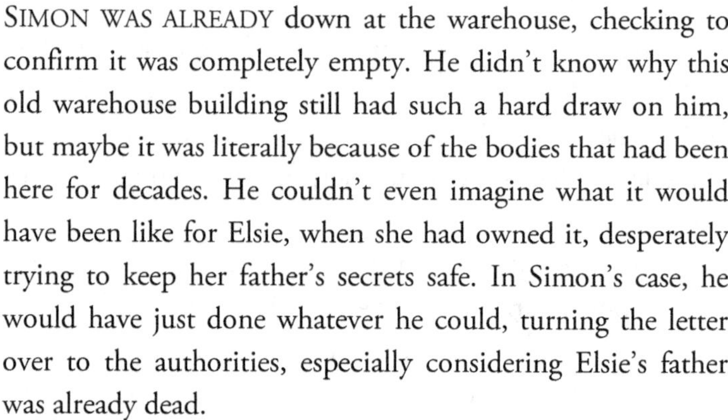

SIMON WAS ALREADY down at the warehouse, checking to confirm it was completely empty. He didn't know why this old warehouse building still had such a hard draw on him, but maybe it was literally because of the bodies that had been here for decades. He couldn't even imagine what it would have been like for Elsie, when she had owned it, desperately trying to keep her father's secrets safe. In Simon's case, he would have just done whatever he could, turning the letter over to the authorities, especially considering Elsie's father was already dead.

But she cared more about keeping the family name un-blemished, keeping her father's secrets, than anything else, and, for that, Simon found it hard to forgive her. She wasn't dead and gone, but she wasn't far from it. He still hadn't received a copy of her father's confession letter, and Simon needed it. He knew Kate could force their hand on it, but the chance of the letter disappearing without anybody ever producing the actual provable copy was something Simon didn't want to risk. Those victims' families needed closure, even after all these years, especially after all these years. They needed to know that something had been done to find their family members.

Simon thought about the world as it was when the old man had run roughshod over everyone. Callously dropping them six feet under, or shooting them and leaving them in the back of a utility room in some basement. How many times had he opened that hidden door to drop in yet another body, only to close it off again? Simon just couldn't imagine it.

That the burial spot was down by the furnaces but hidden away would have kept the bodies dry and hard, more or less safe, even from people who had to work down there. It still just sucked. But now, the fact that Rodney was in this very situation that had shown up in Simon's dreams was something else Simon didn't want to contemplate. He also didn't want to think about the fact that he'd also seen himself in one of those related dreams.

He wasn't sure that he would be any better off against a boxer than Rodney was, but, maybe against a female boxer, Simon and Rodney would be okay. Then he swore at that because that bias was just what put Tamzen into this murderous mind-set to begin with. The simple fact was, she wasn't born male, thus wasn't thought of as strong—or not as strong as those males in the world.

Simon certainly didn't want to get caught up in the whole stigma about which sex was better, male or female, because that wasn't the world he lived in. As far as he was concerned, there was room for everybody, but apparently Tamzen didn't see it from that same perspective.

Realizing that the warehouse was empty, he felt a sense of relief but then panic. He sent Kate a message. **The warehouse is empty. Where are you?** When he got no answer, he phoned Lilliana. "Where's Kate?" he asked.

She hesitated.

"I know shit's going down right now," Simon snapped, "but I just checked the warehouse, and nothing's here, so this isn't the location."

"Do you have anything else?" she asked.

Almost immediately his mind was filled with dripping water, and, in the background, he heard horrific shouting. *Fight, fight, fight.* He cried out as the pain slammed into his head.

"Are you okay? Simon, … what's going on?" Lilliana cried out.

"Nothing good," he muttered. "In my head, … I just got slammed hard."

"Are you being attacked?"

"No, no, it's not me."

"Shit," she muttered. "It's Rodney, isn't it?"

"Yes. Rodney needs help, and he needs it now."

"You got any idea where?"

"I don't know, but my feet are moving," he said.

She asked, "You're walking?"

"Yes, I'm walking toward them."

"Where are you?" she yelled.

He quickly gave her the street and the cross-street, looking around and added, "I think it's just around the corner."

"Everything down there is just around the corner," Lilliana snapped. "Is a wharf close by?"

"We're not far from water, no matter which way I go," he noted. "This is one of the old districts. I've got the harbor all around."

"Right," she muttered. "Okay, we're on the way."

"Yeah, but you need an address. Shit." He was dropped to his knees as another vision of a blow rattled his brain.

"What's happening?" she yelled.

"Rodney's taking a beating," Simon muttered, trying hard to stay conscious and to separate himself from Rodney's vision. "And they're focusing on his head. ... I've got to get there." He ended the call and started to run, not having a clue where he was going. He stopped in front of a building and was just about to enter, when something slammed into the back of his head, and he dropped to the ground.

CHAPTER 17

KATE PARKED RIGHT in front of yet another warehouse, jumping out of the vehicle and running to the door. She stopped, her mind racing, trying to think of all the things she needed to consider before she bolted in headfirst. Just as she was about to go in, her phone buzzed. She pulled it out and whispered, "Hello."

It was Lilliana. "Kate, Simon just called me. He was trying to go in a certain direction but couldn't tell me any more than the street signs he could see, and then he just bolted off in that direction."

"Shit." Kate swore up a storm, as much as she could while whispering. "Now I'll worry about him too."

"We've got backup coming. Where are you?"

"I'm at the warehouse Oscar told me about. The door isn't locked."

"You wait for backup."

"Yeah, and tell Rodney I waited for backup when he comes out of a coma with brain damage?"

"Not every head injury victim ends up with brain damage," she added.

"No, but that's what these guys are focusing on. They want other people to pay, like they have."

"Shit. Kate, don't do anything rash. I'm on my way, and we've got two black-and-whites coming."

"Yeah, I won't do anything stupid." With that, she ended the call.

Now it wasn't just Rodney. It was also Simon, but hopefully he was around and staying out of trouble. Yet, knowing him, he would be right smack in the middle of it. She slipped inside the front door and stopped, acutely aware of the complete and utter silence. She headed toward the back of this massive building. As she finally got to the far side, still moving silently, she heard voices.

"And now you can get started," a man murmured.

But then another voice came, and almost immediately a chant began. "Fight, fight, fight."

She swore, realizing what she would be up against. Two of them in the ring was not part of her plans. It was one thing to fight a single person, and a female at that, but it was another thing entirely to try and take on two women, much less two men.

As she approached the area where the chanting was going on, she heard a woman laughing, then the sound of a blow landing. Tamzen called out, "Bring him over here. That pretty face will have to figure out what life is really all about."

Kate shook her head because she knew instinctively who the pretty face was. As she stepped forward, she saw Simon unconscious on the floor. And Tamzen's brother was hauling him up into a ring. It was a big deserted ring that had definitely seen better days, and somewhere along the line they had converted it or had kept it for their own use.

But the two of them were working together, and that was more than she really wanted to think about.

Rodney was off to the side, apparently unconscious. At least he didn't appear to be responsive. But they were about to wake Simon up and have all kinds of fun with him.

Swearing at that, Kate stepped forward. "I thought you were supposed to be fighting me," she stated, walking coolly toward the ring. At that, both of them turned and stared at her. Kate nodded. "For your first challenge, finding you, I got that beat pretty damn fast. Now, the next challenge is taking you on. But that doesn't even seem to be a challenge at all," she declared in a mocking voice, deliberately trying to get Tamzen to leave Simon alone and to focus all that ire on Kate. She didn't have a clue whether Simon was even in a position or had the skill level to take on either of these two, but it wasn't what she wanted anyway. She was more than ready to take a couple flying kicks at this piece of shit in front of her.

She turned to looked at Tambo. "You've been helping your sister murder people too, *huh?*"

He frowned at Kate, then looked over at his sister and scratched his head.

"Yeah, your sweet sister has been lying to you," Kate revealed, with a mock smile. "All those men who you were helping her ditch, move around, get rid of? … They weren't attacking her because she's what? … Beautiful, capable, or anything else? No. *She* was attacking *them*," she announced, looking at Tambo's face to see if there was any understanding.

He frowned and shook his head several times.

Tamzen looked over at her and laughed. "Do you really think anything you say will make a difference? My brother loves me," she declared. "He knows who I am, inside and out."

"You mean, he knows you're a serial killer?" Kate asked, with a smirk. "Not that we're counting or anything."

"Those men were just useless," she declared. "They were more practice than anything."

"Yeah, I can see that. You were really picking on people who absolutely couldn't defend themselves, so it's not as if they were a challenge at all, right? You didn't want a fair fight. You didn't even give them a chance at a fair fight."

Tamzen stiffened and glared at her.

Kate nodded, as she sauntered forward. "Spare me the details, but don't lie to me now. We are here after all. Nobody else will hear you. It's pretty easy to understand, to clarify what's going on, because these men you specifically chose weren't fighters. None of them were. You are, your brother is, your uncle was, your stepfather definitely was, but something is going on here that you haven't explained to Tambo."

He frowned at his sister and waited.

Kate snorted. "So, Tambo, you didn't even think to question how many times Tamzen seems to run into trouble?"

He pointed at Tamzen. "She's beautiful."

"She is beautiful," Kate noted, "but there are not that many stupid men out there. Okay, there are a lot of stupid men," she corrected, "but not that many are going after your sister unprovoked, looking to give her beating. She's the one doing that. She's the one locking them up, not even giving them a chance at a fair fight," she explained, now facing Tamzen. "Do you even untie their arms, or is that how you classify a fair fight?"

She glared at her. "Of course I do."

"No, you don't. We've found plenty of rope marks on your victims."

"I had to tie them up at some point in time," she muttered, with a shrug.

"And I suppose it depends on what kind of temper you're in as to whether one was just a punching bag or anything approaching a fair fight."

Tamzen glared at her. "You really think you'll just come in here and ruin things? I'll beat these two up, and you won't stop me because Tambo here will take you on, without missing a beat."

Her brother smiled, then he looked over at Kate and nodded. "Except I don't hit women," he pointed out to his sister.

She glared at him and yelled, "You will this time."

He shook his head. "No, I won't."

Kate laughed. "See? It won't be that way at all."

"That's fine," Tamzen smirked, her tone silky. "He won't have a problem beating these two then." She turned and looked at Tambo. "Right? They're not women, so surely you can do that."

He frowned at her again, as if he didn't quite understand what was going on.

"And yet why would you, Tambo?" Kate asked, trying to get him to see some clarity here. "This man," Kate said, as she pointed to Simon, "did he hurt you?"

Tambo shook his head.

"Then why would you beat him up? It's not like he even knows your sister. He hasn't had anything to do with her and hasn't hurt her at all."

Tambo turned to Tamzen, clearly confused.

"We have to beat him up," Tamzen stated, "but we could just kill him. That would suit me to a tee."

Tambo frowned. "That's not fair."

"No, of course it's not fair," she agreed, with a chuckle.

"And I really don't care right now. Obviously"—she pointed to Kate—"we have a situation."

"You do have a situation," Kate confirmed, focusing on Tambo. "And the fact is, Tamzen's the one who's been bringing in these completely innocent victims, simply in order to hurt them, to kill them. They didn't get a fair fight or even a chance to defend themselves."

"Sure, they did," Tamzen said angrily. "I untied them."

"Yeah, after they were unconscious," Kate replied in a mocking tone. "It's not as if you could take on anybody for real. If they're not bound, drugged, or nearly unconscious, you can't fight. That was part of the problem in the first place, right? You're just not good as a fighter. You couldn't make the cut." Tamzen flashed red, and Kate poured it on. "You used the fact that you were female as an excuse, but there are lots of avenues for women fighters right now," Kate noted. "You could have fought in a women's division or something, but you didn't, and why? Because you weren't good enough, and you knew it," Kate mocked.

Tamzen stepped forward, her fists clenched.

Kate nodded. "Yeah, I see who you are. This isn't about you getting revenge. This is about you hating the life that you have, hating the fact that you're not good enough," she snapped. "Hating the fact that Oscar didn't want to fight, didn't like being beaten up, and nobody could change his mind about it. Hating that Tambo is injured, and even now his future is uncertain." Kate continued. "Not to mention Oliver, your ever-loving stepfather. But look at all this, … at everything you've been doing. It isn't making anyone better, is it?"

Tamzen's fists snapped opened and shut, as she struggled with her own rage.

"And you've been hurt yourself. That's what this is all really about, right? Getting revenge, making sure somebody pays, somehow, somewhere. It doesn't matter if they're the ones who needed to pay for each of your brain injuries. It doesn't even matter to you if you pick somebody who you know has done something wrong. As long as somebody pays, as long as you get to beat somebody to a pulp, that's all that matters because you were completely helpless last time. Just like your brother was helpless to stop the fight coming for him, as was your birth father, and now your stepfather, who's already lost that fight," Kate pointed out. "That victim mind-set inside you, that inability to grab power and to get control of your life," Kate added, "is really debilitating, isn't it?"

"You don't have a clue what you're talking about," Tamzen roared, her rage twisting her face in a fury.

But her brother looked at Tamzen and said, "She kind of does have a clue."

"No, she doesn't," Tamzen snapped, "and it doesn't matter. I'll tear her apart."

"In the ring. ... That'll be good," he said, with a bright smile. He then looked over at Kate. "That'll be fair."

Kate shook her head. "You know that Tamzen won't fight fair. She can't win a fair fight. She's worked so hard at making sure the deck is always stacked in her favor that she doesn't even know what a fair fight is anymore."

He looked at his sister. "Fair fight, right?"

"Yes," Tamzen snapped, "fair fight."

"Good." Tambo rubbed his hands together. "That'll be fun."

Kate asked him, "Will you touch these men while I'm busy having a fair fight with her?"

"No, of course not," he agreed cheerfully. He looked down at the men. "I wouldn't hurt them anyway."

"You might not, but Tamzen wants to kill them," Kate pointed out, watching the confusion, disbelief, and hurt crossing his face. Kate nodded. "Yeah, and you've been helping her to kill the men. You were helping her deal with their bodies."

He shook his head. "But that's different," he said, clearly confused. "She was just defending herself, and we know that it doesn't matter what she says, and they'll just get off."

That was the missing piece. She turned to Tamzen. "That's it. That's really what this is all about, isn't it? The man who hurt you so badly was never convicted, was he?"

"I never tried," she said, tossing her head back.

"But you knew he was guilty. You knew he deserved to be punished for it. Why didn't you go to the police?"

"I couldn't," she said. "I would have had to endure all the staring, the questions, the jokes. Nobody would come to the gym anymore, and they all would have mocked me."

"So, it's about saving face, yet knowing it was an unfair fight to begin with."

Her brother looked at her. "But it's okay because we got ours back."

Kate winced at that. "Did you?" Kate asked him. "Did you make sure that he couldn't hurt anybody else ever again?"

He nodded, a big smile on his face. "Yeah, we sure did." His fist smacked into the palm of his other hand. "He ain't doing that to nobody anymore. Never."

Kate nodded and looked over at Tamzen. "So, when did you decide that wasn't enough?" she asked. "When did you decide that killing somebody who beat you wasn't enough?

This man you couldn't take to court because, in your addled mind, you felt you couldn't stop him legally," she pointed out. "When did you decide that it wasn't enough to kill your attacker and that you needed to kill more innocent people?"

Tamzen just stared at her and didn't say a word.

Tambo suddenly walked over and hit a button on a tape player, and the room was filled with the chants of *Fight, fight, fight.* He motioned to the ring. "You get to fight her now," he declared, happiness on his face. "May the best woman win."

Tamzen was standing in the ring right now, and all thoughts of Simon and Rodney were forgotten.

Kate took off her jacket, dropped it on the ground, then bent over to step in between the ropes. Tamzen lunged immediately, not even giving Kate a chance to straighten up. She took a tumble but was back on her feet in seconds, and this time she knew this was a fight she had to win. She caught a glance of Simon on the far side, staring at her in horror, and knew that Rodney was there waiting as well, hoping she would kick this woman's ass before something even worse happened to them.

As Tamzen came toward her with her fists up, Kate immediately went to work, and she pounded her hard and fast, using every bit of skill she had learned. She didn't fight as a boxer. No, that would just help Tamzen. Kate fought with her own martial arts skills, hoping Tamzen had none. It didn't take long before Kate had Tamzen on the ground, bleeding from a busted nose, gasping with broken ribs, and dealing with what Kate hoped was one broken ankle.

As Kate stepped back, her chest heaving, she glared at Tamzen. "Guess what, bitch? You lose."

Then a blow hit her from behind. She went down and

realized that Tambo wouldn't let it be a fair fight at all. Such fury filled his expression.

Kate rolled over and managed to get to her feet, waiting for him to attack again. She stared at him and nodded. "Yeah, it's not about a fair fight with you guys, is it? I guessed as much, but it's got nothing to do with that."

"That wasn't fair," he roared. "She wouldn't have lost if it was fair."

"She lost," Kate snapped, as she eyed him warily.

"No," he roared, "that's not her. She's a winner. She's beaten up every one of those guys. I'm so proud of her for defending herself."

"Well, … guess what, asshole?" Kate cried out. "She hasn't been defending herself. She's been killing innocent men, putting them into this fake boxing ring, all for her own warped satisfaction and fake glory."

He shook his head. "No, no, no." Then he came toward her with his own fists up, and now she was up against somebody way over her size, and she was already tired.

She shook her head. "If you want to do this," she warned him, "I won't hold back."

He gave her an evil smile. "I'll make you pay."

"Yeah, well, fly at it," she taunted him.

The first blow was like a sledgehammer to her ribs. She went down, but, as she'd been taught, she didn't stay down. You never stayed down, and you never showed your belly to the enemy.

She was on her feet in a flash, her body already twisting in the air as her right boot cracked with a punishing kick to his right temple. Then she bounced back, still dancing on her feet, waiting, only to watch the behemoth slowly, in almost a cartoonish slow-motion move, collapse to the ground.

She looked over at Simon, his eyes wide as he stared at Tambo.

He asked her, "Is it wrong that I want to stand here and count to ten, just to confirm he's truly out?"

Kate glanced over at Tamzen.

She was crying on the floor of the ring. She sobbed as she slowly scrambled to her brother. Turning to look at Kate, she shook her head, wild-eyed. "What did you do? What did you do?"

"What did I do?" Kate asked, with a mock smile. "That's called defending myself, something you appear to have a very twisted view of."

And, with that, Kate walked over to Simon, happily realizing that Rodney was awake now, even though one eye was swollen shut, but the other was open wide, staring at her. She quickly untied both men, knowing that Tamzen wouldn't get anywhere very fast, not with her injuries. With Rodney and Simon free and clear, Kate stood up and walked over to the behemoth she'd dropped. She checked for a pulse, then shook her head, looking back over at the other two men.

Both sadness and relief were in their expressions.

Kate stared at the sister. "Look what you did," she murmured.

Tamzen sobbed, shrieking, possibly feeling true heartbreak for the first time in her useless life.

Oscar came running, stepped into the ring quickly.

Kate hadn't even realized he'd been standing in the shadows all this time.

Oscar looked over at Kate, tears in his eyes. "I know why you fought, but, Jesus, did you have to kill him?"

"Whether he lives or dies," Kate noted, "you and I both know this would never end well, not with Tamzen free to murder more innocent people."

Oscar dropped beside the two of them and held his niece as she sobbed in his arms. He looked up at Kate. "She's really killed people? You're sure?"

Kate nodded. "Yes, and Tambo was involved as well. I am certain. We have five of her victims at the moment."

He looked down at Tamzen in disbelief. "Really? Did you kill five men?"

She winced and whispered. "Seven. … I've killed seven." And then she really started to cry.

Kate just stared at her. "And what was the criteria for selecting these men? Why did you pick the ones you did?"

"They had families. They had something to lose."

"And how did you find them?"

She shrugged. "I run cabs sometimes," she shared, "and I used it as a cover to find them."

That confirmed what Kate had already considered.

"Sometimes," Tamzen added, "it seemed they were just assholes. I don't know. … I would look at them, and they would sneer at me because I wasn't whatever they thought I should be," she muttered. "I'm just glad that it's over."

"No, you're not," Kate argued. "You would have kept on going, until I stopped you."

"Maybe," she murmured. "But once you go down this pathway, it's really hard to get out. I just got angrier and angrier because it wasn't stopping, because I wasn't feeling any better. The only relief was taking out the next one and planning to take out the one after that."

SIMON STOOD UP carefully, letting the blood work through his arms as he walked over to where Kate was on the floor beside Rodney, who just looked at her through his swollen eye.

Rodney whispered, "Jesus Christ, you couldn't have come a little earlier, *huh*?"

She groaned. "I'm so damn sorry. I tried. I really did."

He closed his eyes and whispered, "At least you made it. I don't think she wanted me to make it through this."

"No, she wouldn't give you that option," Kate noted. "This wasn't about a fair fight—or even revenge for things that have gone wrong in her world. Her brain injuries added to the explosive backlash of somebody emotionally over-charged and not rationally dealing with the inherent unfairness of her life," Kate pointed out. "But it's over now. You, sir, are on your way to the hospital, or you will be very shortly," she said, with a smile.

Rodney grumbled, "The last thing I want to do is go to the hospital."

Simon smiled. "You may not want to," he interjected, "but, from the looks of your face, ... you'll need to. At the very least, you've got stitches in your future."

Rodney groaned. "But who'll look after Kate at work?" he asked Simon, trying to open his swollen eye. "Do you have any idea how much trouble she gets into?" Simon raised one eyebrow, as Rodney attempted a smile, then moaned. "Don't make me laugh," he said. "This shit hurts."

Moments later, the building swarmed with police cars and ambulances. As two paramedics came over to Kate, she pointed at Simon and Rodney.

Simon frowned at her and bellowed, "Oh, hell no. You got hit twice by Tambo. Check her out first."

She glared and shook her head. "You're at least getting checked over."

"Yeah?" he muttered. "And what about you?"

"What about me?" she asked.

He smiled. "I guess you don't have any idea what you look like right now, do you?"

She stopped, her gaze going from Rodney back to Simon, then she shook her head. "Doesn't matter," she muttered. "I've got shit to do."

"I've got shit to do too," Rodney wailed, as they helped him to his feet. "God, that bitch could hit."

"She could," Kate agreed, "but, as the Irish would say, my dander was up, and no fucking way was I letting her take me down."

Rodney grimaced and shook his head. "You are just making me feel worse."

Now she shook her head. "This ain't nothing. Wait until Colby finds out. He's bound to put you in for extra self-defense training."

He groaned at that. "You know that he will."

At that, Colby, who apparently had arrived with Lilliana, walked over to join them. "She's right. If the bad guys keep up this shit, we'll have to get the team to a different level of fitness."

"Maybe not fitness," Kate clarified, "but training."

He looked over at her and nodded. "What the hell was that you used to kick his ass?"

Simon answered that. "She goes to the dojo almost every week," he shared. "I've watched a couple times but not very much. She's pretty wicked."

Colby just stared at her, then at the hulk of a man on the ground. "You know he's dead, right?"

"I'm not surprised," Kate muttered, followed by a heavy sigh. "Does that mean I'm in deep shit again?"

Colby snorted. "I'm pretty sure the witnesses here will say it was self-defense."

"It was self-defense," Kate confirmed, "plus he's way-the-hell bigger than me. He's got to be three hundred pounds and all of it muscle. I hate to say it, but he was pretty pissed because I'd wiped the floor with his sister."

Simon nodded. "Yeah, and I think that part was what finally made him realize how she'd been lying to him all this time."

Kate agreed. "It wasn't so much that he was angry at me, but he was angry at her, and then ... I was just an easy target."

"An easy target?" Lilliana repeated, staring at her. "I don't think so. You do realize they had cameras in here, right? So we'll get to watch it over and over again."

At that, Rodney groaned. "Please no," he muttered. "Getting my ass kicked by a woman half my size was one thing, but having you guys watch it and bug me about it, or making it a teaching point for the station? Just kill me now."

Colby laughed. "But it is something we need to do," he declared, "to confirm Kate's in the clear."

"She's in the clear," Simon vowed, as he sat for the paramedics. "That was definitely self-defense." He looked over at her and added, "For the record, I probably wouldn't have done it quite the same way, but I would have been just as good."

She smiled at him. "I was pretty sure you would be unimpressed with my saving your ass again," she stated. "However, it just balances things out a little bit."

His gaze warmed, and he laughed. "Okay," he conceded. "If it's important for you to make checks and balances out of this, I'm fine with that."

Colby shook his head. "The two of you just need to stop this shit. How about that?"

"We want to," she noted, "but this is another pretty major case we're closing."

Colby beamed. "It absolutely is, and, if we're lucky, we might even get some more staffing because of it."

"Ah, don't hold your breath," Kate said, with an eye roll. "I'm not sure the higher-ups will be that impressed. After all, Andy has been on extended medical leave for how many months now? And we still don't have a replacement for him. The powers that be don't seem interested in letting you fill that opening."

He smiled. "You could be right," he admitted, yet grinning from ear to ear. "They probably won't. On the other hand, we'll be dealing with this for a while."

"She admitted to killing seven men," Simon noted. "She told us that she got her revenge on her attacker, who put her in a long coma, by murdering him. I'm assuming he's one of the seven she is taking responsibility for."

"That's right," Rodney murmured through his puffy lips. "Those three really old skeletons in the boarded-up basement are too old to lay at Tamzen's feet. However, we have four beating victims in other precincts. Those could be some of Tamzen's victims, but we'll have to confirm that. Maybe she'll cooperate and just give us their names."

"Not sure we can count on that. Hell, did Tamzen even know their names?" Kate frowned. "Yet we have three more bodies in the main area of the same warehouse. Were those Tamzen's too? Or were those just the bodies making up the rumors about that warehouse to begin with? Maybe Tamzen and Tambo heard the same rumors and decided to start dumping their bodies there, instead of the harbor. Like

Sonny, who was probably supposed to die there but we found him first. Still, he didn't make it. We'll have to confirm that we have all Tamzen's victims accounted for. I'm not sure all seven of hers are on the books yet."

Rodney nodded. "So we'll have to go look for more, and they're likely to be in the water."

Simon frowned at a beep and pulled out his phone. He looked at it and smiled. "We might get some closure on the bodies in the basement of my warehouse building too."

Colby and Kate turned to him, frowning.

"Elsie, the woman who owned the warehouse before selling it to me, has just passed on, and her nephew promised to send a letter with a whole lot of information Elsie received from her father years ago. She claimed it kept her imprisoned, as she tried to keep the family secrets."

"Good God," Colby muttered. "Yet it would be awesome to have closure on those deaths too. An awful lot of flak is coming at the city for not having found these bodies for decades."

"The whole story will probably come out in some big memoir," Kate muttered, followed by another eye roll. "In the meantime, if we can resolve that as well, it should make everybody happier." She looked over at Simon. "But you still have to figure out what you'll do with that warehouse—or the land, once you demo the building."

"Yeah, that won't be an overnight decision though," he noted, standing up after getting the all clear from the paramedic. "Great. I'm fine. They told me that I can leave."

Rodney was being led to the ambulance. He stopped to look back at Simon and wailed, "That's not fair."

"I'll come visit you," Kate promised.

"If you do, you better bring some decent food with

you," he muttered. Still groaning, he was loaded into the ambulance and taken away.

When Kate turned to Simon, a paramedic stood behind her, his hands on his hips. "You're next," he announced. She raised an eyebrow and almost instinctively took a fighting stance.

The paramedic sighed. "He warned me that you would be difficult."

She turned and glared at both Colby and Lilliana. Her boss's arms were crossed over his chest. Lilliana had her arms crossed over her chest as well, her foot tapping the floor, as she guarded the only exit.

Simon stood nearby, a big grin on his face. "Sweetheart, you're not getting out of this one."

"You better feed me when I get out of here then," she added, "because, damn, I'm starved."

At that, they all laughed.

"That was the trick, was it? Food as a bribe to act nice for the EMTs?" Simon asked, as he waited patiently for the medic to check her over. Her knuckles were taped, and her leg was killing her, but it was fine. She'd just pulled a muscle. That would be something that she felt for a bit, as was the shot to her back she'd taken from Tambo.

With the paramedic done, he nodded and stated, "Okay, you're cleared to go home."

She groaned, looked over at Simon, and asked, "Did you drive down?"

"My vehicle is at the warehouse, but I can drive yours, if you want."

"Good," she muttered. "I'm really not sure I'm up for driving home."

"I can arrange for mine to get picked up, so I'll take you

home." Simon looked at Colby, "Is she free to go?"

He snorted. "Yeah, she's free to go." He looked over at Lilliana.

Lilliana nodded. "I've got this," she murmured. "At least Kate left me a little something to do. I'll help Simon get you to the car."

Kate snorted. "Feel free to jump in any time," she muttered, as she slowly made her way to the door.

"Actually I'm pretty happy not to be you right now. You'll be one very stiff bitch in the morning," Lilliana warned.

"I know," Kate muttered. "I'll need a hot tub or an ice bath or something." She frowned at Simon and muttered, "You don't even have a hot tub," she muttered. "What's up with that?"

He snorted. "Sorry, I didn't realize we would be kidnapped, thrown into a boxing ring, and have the stuffing kicked out of both of us in the same night," he stated. "Pardon me while I go correct that error."

She laughed. "No worries. I'll make do with a hot bath and pain meds."

"I don't think so," he argued. "Food first. That was the bribe, right? The last thing I want is for you to wake up in the middle of the night, full of pain, plus realize that I didn't feed you. After all, that was a pretty scary demonstration of your talents in that ring."

CHAPTER 18

WHEN KATE WOKE up the next morning, she went to roll over and groaned.

At her side, Simon smiled. "I would have bet good money that you couldn't get out of bed at all," he admitted.

She frowned at him. "Just moving will hurt like a bitch, won't it?"

He laughed. "It so will, no doubt."

"I'm glad you think it's funny," she muttered.

"I don't think it's funny. I think it's great," he declared, with a huge grin. "I absolutely loved being rescued. So thank you, sweetheart."

She smiled, yet shook her head. "You're welcome, but damn it. I'm so sorry about Rodney. I should have gotten there sooner."

"You got there just fine," he declared. "Rodney is a big boy, and part of his job was to see this crap through. But I wouldn't be at all surprised if he doesn't decide he needs a little more training himself."

"Regardless of what Rodney does, I'm pretty sure the bosses will insist on it," she stated. "Colby was right. We've had a few too many of these assaults lately."

"Mostly because of you," he pointed out.

"I know," she said, trying to roll over. "And they'll hold that against me too," she muttered. "Christ, I don't want to get up."

"That's good," he said, with a smirk. "I got no problem with that." He rolled over and gently tucked her up closer. "You do know we could just stay in bed for the day."

"Wouldn't that be nice," she murmured. "And you know, if we had that hot tub …"

He smiled as he nuzzled her gently. "If you had a couple days off and needed to recover, we could go out on the *Running Mate*."

Her eyes opened wide, and she smiled. "That sounds absolutely fantastic."

His hands slid up her hips, across her lean ribs, until she winced and groaned. He lifted his head. "That bad?"

"I took multiple blows to the ribs," she whispered. "I'm sure I'm black and blue." She groaned. "But there'll also be paperwork, lots more than usual."

"That's fine," he murmured, as he kissed her behind her ear and slid his tongue along the edge of her lobe.

She shivered as she murmured, "The only way we're doing this is if I don't have to move."

He chuckled. "I got you this time," he murmured, still smiling. "Believe me that I can hear your pain."

"I don't want to be in pain though," she added, as she twisted, ignoring the sharp jabs of her beaten body. She slowly looped her arms around his neck and suggested, "Why don't you make me feel something different?"

"Oh, I've got you there too," he murmured, as he lowered his head and kissed her gently, as if she were the injured person she was.

But suddenly that wasn't what she wanted. She wanted and needed something more. She wrapped her arms tightly around him, raising the temperature of both of them as she kissed him back, her tongue plunging deep against his, warring softly, even as she wrapped her thighs around his hips.

"Jesus," he muttered. "I thought you wanted to go slow."

"Actually," she replied playfully, "I changed my mind."

"Okay, thanks for the heads-up," he murmured.

She giggled, then laughed, even as she twisted beneath him, pulling him down tighter and tighter against her. When he finally slid inside, she gasped and he paused. "I'm fine," she murmured. "I need this. I need to know I'm alive. I need to know that you're alive and that life will go on. I need to know that even though all these sick, damaged people are out there, we will still win this war. Sometimes I have days when I'm so afraid that it's just too much, too many, and they'll get ahead of us," she admitted.

He leaned over, kissed her with all the tenderness she'd ever imagined was possible in a kiss.

When he lifted his head, he added, "You feel too deeply and too hard and too long, but it's okay. You will survive this. We will survive it together. You're doing an amazing job."

She blinked up at him and smiled. "You're talking too much."

With a shout of laughter, he plunged deep and took her soaring over the edge. By the time he cried out with his own completion, she was already heading off on a second surge.

When he lay down beside her, she groaned and whispered, "Now I really won't get up easily."

"I'm sorry."

"Don't be," she declared, with a big smile. "These are at least aches and pains of victory. It'll be a whole different story for *her*."

"I know," he agreed, "but we'll probably have to call the hospital this morning to see how everybody is."

She nodded. "We also promised food for Rodney."

He chuckled as he held her close. "Is everybody in your office constantly food-starved?"

She shrugged. "Maybe, but given that we work hard at what tends to be a thankless job so many times, I can see it might look that way. Yet that's how we all feed our feelings."

"I get it," he said, massaging her back. "You have given me a completely different appreciation for the life that you've chosen."

"I know, and the reason why I went into it still hasn't been solved."

"And that's okay too," he said, nuzzling her. "Not everything in life has to have answers today. I know you want answers on Timmy as well as all these cases of yours, but they won't always be available."

She nodded. "I just hope that at some point I find out what really happened to my brother, and, if I don't, I guess I get to spend the rest of my life coming to terms with it." As she lay here, she added, "I'm hungry."

He snorted. "So, food first. Do you want to go out and eat, then we can pick up an order to-go for Rodney?"

"Sure, but I need a shower first." As she got up and slowly moved toward the bathroom, she caught sight of herself in the mirror and stopped short, then turned to him. "Good God, look at me."

"I know. I'm struggling to look at you," he murmured. "It hurts me to see you all blue and purple, so damaged."

She glared at him and shook her head. "Any word but that, please. I might be injured. I might be bruised, but I am *not* damaged." And, with that rant over, she asked, "Will you join me in the shower?"

"Sure, if only to confirm you don't have to bend and twist to wash your hair."

She smiled and happily let him. As they came back out, wrapped in towels, her phone rang. She picked it up. "Colby," she greeted him warily, "anything bad going on?"

"Not necessarily bad for any of you," he stated, "but Tamzen committed suicide last night."

"Fuck ..."

"I guess she ended up getting hold of some drugs. I don't know where the hell she got them," he said, cussing. "And, for all I know, that bloody uncle gave them to her. Anyway, she took the whole lot of them, and that will be an entirely different investigation, but thankfully that's the hospital's headache."

"Jesus Christ, how is Rodney?"

"Kicking and screaming, wanting out, wanting to go home, wanting food," he stated, with a laugh.

"I did promise him food," she admitted apologetically.

"He'll be there for most of today, so I highly suggest you get over there before he tries to break out."

"Will do," she agreed. When Colby remained silent, she asked, "Is everything else okay?"

"Yeah, everything is okay," he replied. "I just wanted to say, *Good job*, and, you know, give you the update." And, with that, he ended the call.

She frowned at her phone and shook her head. "It's really a hard thing for those of us who aren't used to it," she began, a sly grin on her face. "Colby just said *Good job* to me."

"But that's normal, right?" Simon asked.

"Not for us. I think it was as hard for him to say it as it

was for me to hear it."

"And you're all nuts," Simon declared, smiling over at her.

"Maybe so," she admitted, "but apparently Rodney is kicking and screaming to get out, so we need to go grab that guy some food."

And that's what they did. Rather than going to a restaurant and then getting his food, they picked up food for him, delivered it, and visited him for a bit. Then, on their way back, they picked up a different order for them and took it down to the *Running Mate*. As she stepped on board, she stopped, sniffed the cold salty air, and smiled. "It's like coming home here."

"Nothing wrong with having a home away from home—even if it's only a few blocks away. Now let's go inside. It's pouring rain and ugly out here. Inside we go, … where it's cozy and warm." He reached out a hand.

Kate placed hers in his, and together they slipped inside to the cozy nest that they'd created—a shelter against the ugliness of the world they both lived in and lived out of. A place just for them …

This concludes Book 11 of Kate Morgan: Simon Says…
Fight.

Read about Kate Morgan: Simon Says… Believe, Book 12

Simon Says... Believe: Kate Morgan (Book #12)

Detective Kate Morgan wishes all holidays were filled with celebration and joy, but her latest crime scene tells a different story. The leftover festive spirits of Christmas and the new year are overshadowed by the grim reality of another murder. No amount of ribbon wrapped around the body or notations on a greeting card to *Believe* can change that.

As she delves into the first murder of this year, Kate unexpectedly uncovers a second case—another victim and another instance of holiday cheer turned sour. Are these cases linked, or is Vancouver experiencing an unusually grim extended holiday season?

Simon stands by Kate, offering his unwavering support in her investigations, just as she stands by him and his architectural rehab projects and his peculiar psychic visions. However, when these visions and unsettling rumors begin to threaten his real estate business, Simon realizes more is at play …

But what exactly is happening, and is Kate involved in all this?

Find Book 12 here!

To find out more visit Dale Mayer's website.

https://geni.us/DMSSSBelieve

Sneak Peek from
Simon Says... Believe

Last Week of January

FOUR DAYS LATER Kate was drowning in paperwork. She heard a noise and looked up to see Rodney come in. His face was still puffy and bruised from the fight in the ring, but he was smiling, cracked lips and all. She got up, walked over, and gave him a gentle hug.

He just held her and whispered, "Thank you."

She nodded. "So, was that thanks for saving your sorry ass or thanks for saving you from hospital food?"

He laughed. "Both. I don't know where in hell Simon got that breakfast, but, man, it was something else."

"It was, wasn't it?" she agreed.

"Is that how you eat all the time?" he asked, rolling his eyes. "I could really get used to that."

"If you order from the same places he does, you could have it whenever you want," she pointed out.

"I don't know that I could afford even a fraction of it."

She stopped to consider that, frowning. "I don't even think about it anymore. I have no idea what any of it costs. He orders it, and I eat it," she said, with a shrug. "It's a deal that seems to work for me."

He burst out laughing. "Of course it does," he muttered, shaking his head. "It would work for anybody. It's a damn-good thing you've got him to keep you on the straight and narrow. But then again, you also saved his sorry ass."

"In all fairness," she pointed out, "it was my turn."

"How about no more turns?" he grumbled.

"Yeah, I did mention that to him, and he was down for stopping whatever this score-keeping was," she admitted, with a smile.

"And I understand that things have been calm these past days."

"Yeah," she replied, "as calm as it ever is. Couple shootings, couple dead bodies on the streets. We're waiting for autopsies, but it seems to be drug overdoses. You know, … the usual."

"Right, … the usual," he repeated. "And it's still the season to be jolly—if the middle of January and beyond counts."

"It does in my book," she stated agreeably, "if anything jolly is to be had."

He looked at her and shrugged. "I don't know, maybe."

Just then Reese walked in, and the frown on her face said everything.

"*Uh-oh*," Kate muttered, frowning back at her. "What's up?"

"We've got"—she hesitated and then relented—"I don't want to say it's a church killing or that it's a religious killing, as the holidays are well and truly over. … Or maybe we're gearing up already for Valentine's Day with this guy. … I don't know. What we do have seems to be a holiday season murder."

Kate frowned. "We all know that murders are the worst at holiday time. What have you got?"

"I've got a man, found in his apartment, no idea what's going on. He's dead, cause unknown."

"So, why is this one any different?"

She looked over at Kate. "Because he's been wrapped in a red bow, around his … manhood," she added delicately.

"What?" Kate asked, staring at her.

Reese held out the crime-scene photos. "Yeah, it'll be another strange one." She handed out files for each of the team—Kate, Rodney, Lilliana—being reduced in number at this time.

Rodney looked over her shoulder at the photo and whistled. "Good God. What is this about? Did someone not like their Christmas gift or something?"

Lilliana frowned as she opened her file copy.

"He was killed in bed?" Kate walked slowly over to her desk, carrying the new file, staring at that image in her folder. "His lips are already turning blue. Yet the crime scene photos show no drugs, prescription or otherwise. Not even a box of rat poison. This looks pretty deliberate."

"It does," Reese agreed.

"Please tell me there are no others."

"Nope, no others," Reese noted, "just the one victim, so hopefully it's an isolated incident."

Kate looked at the next photo and pointed. "What's with this note here?"

"The guy lives alone, but a poinsettia was in his bedroom, with a card. On the card was the word *Believe*."

"And?" Kate asked, turning to Reese.

"One of the techs declared that it'll be another one of those woo-woo cases, so he named it the *Believe It or Not* case."

"That makes no sense," Kate muttered.

"No, it probably doesn't, but all I can tell you is that's what he put it down as."

Kate didn't like it. She frowned. "Generally we identify the cases by the name of the deceased."

"Yeah, generally we do," Reese agreed, with a smirk.

Just then Simon texted her. **How about spending next weekend on the *Running Mate?***

She sent back a quick reply. **I'm doubting it at this point.**

No, none of that. You have to BELIEVE.

She stared at his text, stared down at her case folder, and whispered, "Crap. Maybe that's what this one will be called after all." She held up her phone to show the text message that Simon had just sent.

Lilliana looked at it, turned to Reese, then back to Kate, and shook her head. "No. ... Hell no. Not another woo-woo case already. We're still buried in paperwork from the last one."

"Yeah, you're not kidding," Kate confirmed, as she stared at her phone.

Simon called and asked, "Is there a reason why I just used the word *believe*?"

"You tell me," she muttered, with a sigh. "I just got a case where the victim is wrapped up in a red bow, near a card in a poinsettia plant with just the word *Believe* on it."

"Crap. ... I picked up new blankets and cushions for the boat. Plus it's restocked with supplies and wine. So I thought maybe we could grab next weekend to belatedly set the right tone for the New Year."

"Let's just put it this way," she noted. "If I get free, that would be the real miracle."

"In that case, I'll end on the same note I started with. Just *believe*."

And, with that, he disconnected.

Find Book 12 here!

To find out more visit Dale Mayer's website.

https://geni.us/DMSSSBelieve

Author's Note

Thank you for reading Simon Says... Fight: Kate Morgan, Book 11! If you enjoyed the book, please take a moment and leave a short review.

Dear reader,

I love to hear from readers, and you can contact me at my website: www.dalemayer.com or at my Facebook author page. To be informed of new releases and special offers, sign up for my newsletter or follow me on BookBub. And if you are interested in joining Dale Mayer's Reader Group, here is the Facebook sign up page.
http://geni.us/DaleMayerFBGroup

Cheers,
Dale Mayer

About the Author

Dale Mayer is a *USA Today* best-selling author, best known for her SEALs military romances, her Psychic Visions series, and her Lovely Lethal Garden cozy series. Her contemporary romances are raw and full of passion and emotion (Broken But … Mending, Hathaway House series). Her thrillers will keep you guessing (Kate Morgan, By Death series), and her romantic comedies will keep you giggling (*It's a Dog's Life*, a stand-alone novella; and the Broken Protocols series, starring Charming Marvin, the cat).

Dale honors the stories that come to her—and some of them are crazy, break all the rules and cross multiple genres!

To go with her fiction, she also writes nonfiction in many different fields, with books available on résumé writing, companion gardening, and the US mortgage system. All her books are available in print and ebook format.

Connect with Dale Mayer Online

Dale's Website – www.dalemayer.com

Twitter – @DaleMayer

Facebook Page – geni.us/DaleMayerFBFanPage

Facebook Group – geni.us/DaleMayerFBGroup

BookBub – geni.us/DaleMayerBookbub

Instagram – geni.us/DaleMayerInstagram

Goodreads – geni.us/DaleMayerGoodreads

Newsletter – geni.us/DaleNews